VLADIMIR PETROV:
An American Life

VLADIMIR PETROV:
An American Life

John R. Green Jr.

Vladimir Petrov:
An American Life

© John R. Green Jr. 2018

Published by
Lighthouse Christian Publishing
SAN 257-4330
5531 Dufferin Drive
Savage, Minnesota, 55378
United States of America

www.lighthousechristianpublishing.com

Chapter 1
Russian Raiders

A bullet barely missed the back of Vladimir Petrov's head as he rode with the twenty-four other Russian soldiers in his group away from the Polish village of Sokolka. They had just raided the peasant village in a surprise attack, stealing a little gold, food, and everything else of value that they found, which was not much. The angry villagers lived under the threat of such raids. They prepared as best they could, but this one had caught them off-guard due to the skill of the raiders. After the Russian soldiers mounted their horses and turned away, the villagers quickly produced guns from hidden places, ready to fire.

Vlad was a corporal, and his official orders as part of Czar Nicholas I's Army in this year of 1854 were to patrol a section of the border and protect the nearby Russian villages from Polish raids. Russia and Poland were not formally at war, but they were not at peace, either. The Russian Army barely paid and supplied the soldiers in Vlad's group, so his commander ordered the men to raid Polish villages to supplement their needs. They had seized some food and valuables from each village. As they raided more villages, they began accumulating a small bit of wealth, but Vlad had thought to himself a number of times how it was not enough to justify the risk.

The more villages they raided, the more the Poles had learned new ways to fight them. Vlad had already lost two of his fellow soldiers, and three more had been wounded and forced to return to their homes in the interior of Russia. They were officially listed as killed or wounded during Polish attacks in Russia, but the truth was that the deaths and injuries occurred on Polish soil. These wounded men were disabled, and returned home to possible starvation and death. They returned home to try to work, as best they could, on farms that barely provided enough food to feed those who were healthy enough to work long hours every day. With winter always present or looming just weeks ahead, it was a bitter struggle. Vlad fought hard and smart to avoid ending up like those men. When he was ordered to cover villagers so the rest of his group could escape, he made certain that the villagers understood that he would shoot them if they made any move.

As a trusted corporal, Vlad often covered villagers while the others mounted their horses, and he was often the last to mount and ride off. By then, the villagers were primed and ready to move towards their hidden weapons. No matter what Vlad did, the villagers could usually get off at least a couple of hasty shots at him, but most of the time he was well out of effective range. Occasionally, Vlad would fire a couple of shots to cover his mounting and escape to keep the villagers down and prevent them from moving quickly to their hidden guns. This time, a new soldier was supposed to cover their escape, but he did not wait for the others to get clear before mounting his own horse and riding off. Since Vlad was near the rear, this left him exposed.

Vlad did not like stealing, but aside from being ordered to participate, he justified to himself that raiding Polish villages kept the Poles on the defensive and prevented them from raiding Russian ones. The Russian raids protected their borders by keeping the inevitable skirmishes on Polish soil. Also, Vlad had to eat. He found that he could fill his belly with food and accumulate gold to buy necessities when needed in the future. It was easier to store gold than larger items of the same value. When he received other valuables, he traded them for bits of gold. Gold could be concealed and transported easily. Given its value per ounce, gold was ideal.

Vlad fashioned hiding places in his boots and belt for the gold, and he even sewed compartments in his suspenders and hidden seams in his clothes, which he changed from time to time as his clothes wore out. He dreamed that, one day, he could use the gold to pay his way west to America. He knew it was an improbable dream, but that dream kept him going. He wanted freedom and to live in a warm climate where he could have a farm and raise a family. If he survived five years in the Russian Army, he might have enough gold to go west around Poland, pay for transport, and even buy a small piece of land once he got to America. He knew that gold was the universal money. He had no real idea if he could make it to America, but he knew that he had to try. There was nothing left for him in his native Russia.

In all of his twenty years, he had never had enough money or valuables to guarantee his next week's meals or lodging. His mother Anya bled to death during his birth. His father drank vodka, and any other type of alcohol he could find, day and night. He was not a mean drunk, though. He cared a great deal about Vlad, who was an only child, but he was simply not cut out to be both a father and a mother. Vlad's father made arrangements for Vlad to stay with a neighbor while he worked. The neighbor was a former teacher before she married her husband. She taught Vlad and her own two children, who were about the same age as Vlad, to read and write Russian. Vlad's father had a locket from Anya engraved with the English words, "Love is patient and kind." He taught these words to Vlad, and it was the only English that Vlad knew. Vlad was remarkably intelligent, but without money or family status, he could not expect to go far in Russia.

Vlad's father was an only child like Vlad, since his mother had died young and his father was too heartbroken to remarry. He was tall with high cheek bones, steely eyes, and muscular shoulders and arms. Vlad's father had a difficult life, like his parents before him. Vlad's grandparents were all dead, each having died before the age of 55. His father worked 12-hour days, six days per week since he was 13 years old. They lived in a small stone cottage with three rooms, which Vlad's father's parents had built on a piece of land that they overworked each year trying to grow food to help feed themselves. The roof leaked when it rained, requiring constant patching with straw and mud.

Although alcoholism would have killed Vlad's father before long, he died when a smelter exploded due to lack of maintenance and overuse from the owners pushing production just a bit further. The working conditions in the ironworks would have, by comparison, made Charles Dickens believe that social reform had been achieved in England. There was no workers' compensation or insurance. Such things were not even dreamed of by the Russian peasants. Vlad had worked helping his father at the shop, and he was outside chopping wood for the fire when the smelter exploded. He saw his father's torn body, bloody and lifeless, the first mutilated body he had ever seen. He was sixteen.

Vlad thought that he looked like his father and feared he would have a similar fate. He joined the Russian Army out of necessity more than anything else. It was surprisingly hard to get accepted, and he learned quickly not to complain. Although it did not pay much, it provided him with a horse to ride. The Army trained him to ride and to fight, which were two valuable skills in the mid-nineteenth century. He had become an expert rider, and learned great respect for his horse.

Vlad had a shrewd commander, and he learned by watching and listening to his every word. For his part, Vlad worked hard and did not talk a lot, or carry on like some of the other young men. He earned his commander's respect for his quiet hard work, and, over time, the commander trusted Vlad with more and more responsibility.   Finally, his commander made him a corporal.   With that promotion, Vlad was frequently responsible for covering the group's mounting and withdrawal from a village after a raid. This "rear guard" position was one of the most respected positions, because the men knew that they were entrusting their lives to the man who did this job. The man whom Vlad had replaced as corporal had been captured and killed without mercy while protecting the group's withdrawal from a Polish village.

Vlad's life depended on his horse. He sacrificed for his horse, making sure that the animal received food and water before he did. Since he had helped his dad in the ironworks, he knew a little bit about blacksmithing and repairing horseshoes. He was able to care for his horse and the other horses, too, and that also helped him earn respect from most of the other soldiers.

While Vlad tried to save enough gold to get to America someday, he had a more pressing and practical concern. It was mid-October, and he needed new winter clothes and another blanket. It would be very cold in just a few weeks. Vlad thought that if the Poles did not kill him, the cold would. During this latest raid, he was able to grab a woolen rug, which could be altered and used as a large greatcoat. He had thrown it across his horse just in front of the saddle during the raid. He would spend time at night around the campfire roughly tailoring it into a winter coat. For the next several months, it would be more valuable than gold and would never be far from him.

As he and his men hurried back across the Russian border and to the marginal safety of their camp, he felt his stomach ache for something, anything, to eat. It had been eight hours since he last ate or drank anything. Although he had a headache from dehydration, it was the hunger that hurt him more. He reached down into the bag of items he had stolen from one of the Poles, pulling out a crushed raw potato. It did not taste bad. In fact, with the biting cold on his body, he hardly tasted it at all. The sharp wind and stomach pains were soothed by the substance that his mouth labored to chew and swallow.

In a vain attempt to prevent Vlad from taking the potato and other vegetables, a Polish farmer had almost taken Vlad's head off with a shovel. The farmer took his swing just as Vlad jumped on his horse with a bag full of semi-rotted vegetables piled up for the hogs. Vlad pointed his pistol at the farmer and began squeezing the trigger, but he stopped, surprised that the gun had not already gone off. The farmer's eyes grew large, and he backed away. Vlad was so angry that he almost squeezed the trigger again to kill the farmer, who was quite old. Vlad did not shoot only because of something inside of him, and he then quickly reasoned that ammunition and gunpowder were expensive. They were better saved for threats from the other villagers as the group of soldiers rode off.

As Vlad and the other Russian men rode into their camp, he hopped off his horse, and gave him plenty of the vegetables that had not gone bad. Vlad made sure his horse had enough water, too. Once again, Vlad attended to his horse's needs before his own, even though he was desperately hungry.

The horse was a fairly spirited stallion, but had become accepting of Vlad. The horse was light brown with white patches on its nose and body. He had four numbers branded on his rear end. When read upside down, the numbers roughly resembled letters which spelled a Russian four-letter word. Vlad thought that it was the Czar's way of letting him know what the tyrant really thought of him. Vlad felt the same about the Czar and all those in the aristocracy. Vlad thought that they held no value for the lives of peasants and that people like him lived only for their benefit. He was accurate in his thinking.

After Vlad had attended to his horse and secured him for the night, he turned and walked to a nearby stream. A nearby spring fed the stream with groundwater that came out clean and chilly, but above freezing. The men drank, washed, and urinated in the stream. Although they had sense enough to drink upstream of where they washed and relieved themselves, they had no knowledge of bacteria, nor could they even understand that their intestinal illnesses might be caused by drinking downstream from others. Vlad always drank many yards upstream from the others. He drank the rushing water where it went over rocks by the cupped-hands' full. On this occasion, the cold water soothed his painful stomach and renewed him. He was beyond dehydrated, with a throbbing headache, light-headedness, and loss of balance. The stream's cold water was both a necessity and a luxury. If only the food he would eat that night would be as soothing, but at least it would contain some nutrients, fat, and salt.

He turned over the remaining food he had collected to the cook to add to what the others had given him. The man was not really a cook. It was just his turn to cook, and the food proved that fact. The cook meted out small rations of bland, tasteless food. Good tasting and filling food was an unaffordable luxury. Vlad ate and went to bed, tired and sore from riding miles upon miles to a village to raid desperate peasants and then ride miles upon miles back to camp. As the October Russian night turned colder, he and his tent mate, Alexander, laid back to back to share warmth. Vlad thought that Alexander smelled like a mixture of human body odor and horse manure.

Vlad's exhaustion overcame his sense of smell, and he passed into the unconscious world of dreams; one of the few common denominators and equalizers of people. Rich or poor, dreams could lift a person's spirits or cause him to wake up worried and unrefreshed. Tonight, Vlad was trying to ride away from angry Poles on a horse that would not move. He had to keep getting off and pushing his horse while Poles, armed with crude farm tools, kept getting closer and closer until they were within reach, and he woke up in fear as one swung a pick at him. Vlad's dream bothered him, because he believed it was reality while it played, but it also seemed unreal. It denied him proper rest. The stark cold and the increasing hunger, which never completely went away, also interfered with his rest. When he awoke, it took him a few moments to realize that he had been dreaming.

The sun was just beginning to rise. Its milky sunlight, tempered by clouds, revealed the frozen silver landscape from early snowfall overnight. The snow and ice, hardened like an iron horseshoe, locked the life of summer beneath. The growing sunlight revealed the disorderly camp with tents pitched randomly and non-essential equipment strewn around. A shirt washed in the creek the night before had frozen hard and flat over a rope that supported a tent. Bones from previous meals, broken wine and liquor bottles, and even chicken feathers littered the campsite.

For breakfast, the cook was preparing two chickens that had been captured the day before. Vlad's mouth watered at the thought of roasted chicken, and he wished he could eat an entire one instead of the few mouthfuls of skin, meat, and bones that he would receive. The men ate just about every part, leaving nothing to waste.

After they saddled their horses, they departed for another day of patrolling the border, which meant finding a new Polish village to ravage. Vlad had a sense of honor, although he was not fully conscious of it. The same could not be said of some of his companions. Vlad had never raped anyone. He had killed two men, but his life was in mortal danger both times. Twice, Vlad had stopped two of his fellow Russian soldiers from raping villagers. They despised him for it, but he used the excuse that time did not permit it, because they needed to make their escape before Polish soldiers came to the villagers' rescue. Vlad's commander strongly chastised the soldiers who tried to rape the villagers because he had three daughters and a wife back home.

That day's target was Soce. It was sixteen miles or so inside of the Polish border. They reached it just after noon, circling around and coming in from the West, as they thought that the Poles would not be expecting an attack from that direction. They hit a store in town, which had food and supplies, and loaded a wagon they had brought. Then, they divided into four small groups to raid small farms nearby. The farm that Vlad's group raided was large. The main house was made of stone with painted wood doors and trim. The other buildings, including the barn and detached kitchen, were freshly painted. Even the outhouses looked comfortable. Vlad thought this farmer was rich. His greed and eagerness to get delicious food, perhaps even steak, briefly overcame his fear.

At the farm, Vlad ran into trouble while searching for food in a barn. While other men were pilfering the house for valuables, his sense of hunger overcame his sense of greed. He wanted food, good food, but any edible food would do. What he found was three farm hands hiding. They lunged at him, out of fear, self-defense, and self-preservation, rather than any sense of defense of home and honor. They pummeled him with punches. Vlad was tall and muscular from his days hauling iron ore and wood for his father. He repelled the first assault by bowing low and pushing the three men back. He quickly grabbed his pistol, fired, and cut the odds to 2 to 1. He then took the butt of the pistol and buried it into the collar bone of a second man lunging for him. The force of the blow caused Vlad to lose his grip on the pistol, and it fell to the ground. The third man had grabbed a hoe and swung it at Vlad, but Vlad lunged forward, taking the brunt of the hit in his left arm from the wooden handle. The handle broke, but badly bruised Vlad. He then punched and kicked at the third man.

Both men fought without honor. They fought to win and to live, so to fight fairly did not cross either man's mind. They swung wildly at each other. They would have spit or bitten had those things been to their advantage. Finally, Vlad was able to go low and pick up the man, hauling him upward and throwing him towards the wall. The man hit the wall and was impaled on a large protruding spike. He screamed loudly. As the blood flowed, the man yelled more loudly in Polish, "Help me!" Vlad grabbed his pistol, cocked it, and took a defensive stand. The screaming man died quickly, but his screams stuck in Vlad's mind.

The remaining injured farm hand, with his left collar bone clutched in his right hand, looked at Vlad from the ground. Vlad pointed the pistol at the man. The man offered no resistance, and he appeared to be no threat. The man was apparently immobile from pain, but Vlad signaled for him to slide over to a far corner.

With pistol cocked, Vlad looked around the barn to make sure no one else was there. He searched for food and found a few eggs and some vegetables for the animals, which he put into his coat. He protected the eggs as if they were the Czar's crown jewels. He then heard a shuffling noise from behind. As he turned with his pistol, the injured man charged with a pitch fork. Vlad fired towards the man and hit him in the stomach. The ball-shaped bullet traveled through the man's stomach and punctured his aorta. The man kept charging, full of rage, but with decreased ability to deliver a skewering blow. Vlad was able to side-step out of the way, with the fork just missing him. He then took the pistol butt and hit the man several times in the back of the head. The man was incapacitated from the head wounds before the blood could run out of the aorta to kill him.

Vlad looked at the blood and brains on the butt of his pistol, and he wiped them off on the hard dirt floor of the barn. He bent over and dry heaved once, then quickly looked back for his to see if anyone else was coming after him. He was sickened again by the sight of three dead men, whose eyes made them look alive, but frozen in time. Their expressions were of empty horror. Their wounds were ghastly. Vlad knew that he had taken three lives and had almost lost his own. He suddenly threw up in gut-wrenching waves that made him think he would die. He thought that he would not stop vomiting. Once he did stop, he gathered the vegetables, for which three men had died, and looked for anything else. The eggs he had in his coat were broken. He then went into the loft and found flour hidden there in a crate. He brought a large bag down and out past the dead men, then quickly left the barn and headed towards his horse, shaking violently. His mind was in a state of near shock and trauma from fear, adrenaline, and guilt.

Vlad quickly realized that he needed to find his men and rejoin the larger group. He headed towards the house to gather his men. As he entered it, he heard the screams of women. The women had been hiding in the house, but the men had just found them. Vlad drew his pistol and threatened, "I'll kill the first one of you who touches the women. We have no time for this. If we don't rejoin the group quickly, they will leave us, and we'll be trapped and outnumbered by the Polish Army or the villagers. If they capture us, they'll torture us in punishment and retaliation before killing us."

While it was true that they needed to get moving, Vlad had just killed three workers or family members of these women. True, the men had tried to kill him, but they were defending their farm and their lives. Vlad was sick with fear from having almost been killed, and he could not stomach the added atrocity of his men harming these women. He wanted to leave as quickly as possible to get to safety.

Vlad further convinced the men not to rape the women by telling them that the women could possibly show them where valuables were hidden. Vlad then told one of the men, who spoke broken Polish, to tell the women that if they showed them where the valuables were, they would not be harmed. The man did as Vlad said, adding a lot of threats. One of the women got up and led them to a room with a rug. She drew back the rug and pointed to a floor board. One of the men took out his knife and pried up the board. He reached down and pulled up a satchel. Vlad took the satchel and poured its contents onto the floor. There were a number of gold coins, and Vlad told the men to divide up the gold equally, and to do it fast. The men divided the gold as the thieves that they were, with Vlad taking his share. Vlad was sick to his stomach, but knew that someone would get the gold, and he might just as well get his share. With the gold in hand, he wanted to get out of there.

As the men began again to make comments about raping the women, Vlad emphasized, "We must rejoin the larger group. Polish border scouts and Army patrols will have been alerted by now by someone who saw us travel towards the village. We've been here far too long, and every minute is dangerous. If you want to keep your lives, much less the gold, we'd better go, now!"

His arguments worked, and the men began to leave. One of the women looked at him with tears flowing down her face. She was terrified and full of hate at the same time. Her expression seared itself into Vlad's mind. As he turned and began walking, she threw a cup at him. It hit him squarely in the back and bounced off. Vlad turned, pointed his gun towards her, and gave her a cold look of warning.

Vlad knew they needed to leave the farm, but that the men would resent him for stopping the rapes, so he thought they should see the dead bodies to hopefully make them a bit afraid of him. Vlad said, "There's more flour in the barn's loft. Go and get it quickly while I keep lookout." When the men did, they saw the three dead bodies. Any of the men who had wanted to jump Vlad and go back after the women quickly forgot about that idea when they saw what he had done single handedly. Vlad may not have been proud of it, but the men feared him, if not respected him, when they saw the carnage. They gathered more flour and some other goods that Vlad had overlooked. They then hurried out and one asked, "What happened in there?" Vlad said, "Three men charged me, and I killed them. Now let's go!" He told them more about the encounter as they rode. He did not have to exaggerate.

That day, they had hit the jackpot. They rejoined the others, who had similar success raiding other homes and farms. Everyone was weighed down as they carried back their loot. In one of the houses, some of the men had found jugs of home-made liquor. Half of the men were drunk by the time they reached camp. That night, they all ate until they could eat no more. All passed out drunk, except for Vlad, who only drank enough to ease his sore muscles. He went off by himself and looked at the gold he had gotten that day: several gold coins, which he hid in his boots.

That night, he dozed, but true sleep eluded him. He could not stop thinking of the men he had killed and the women who were left behind to discover the grisly dead inside the barn. He wondered if they were husbands, sons, brothers, or unrelated workers. Over and over again, his vivid imagination ran through the women discovering the dead men and the look upon the men's faces just after life had left them.

During the next few weeks, they raided a few more Polish villages, collecting more gold and food. The villages they were now raiding were more prosperous than before. Vlad was accumulating a sizable amount of gold, and he was very concerned about protecting it from theft. Given the opportunity, any of the other men would take it from him as quickly as they had from the Poles. He sewed the gold coins into the lining of his vest, which he wore almost constantly. In addition to keeping the gold close to his body for safe-keeping, the gold actually protected him. It provided a suit of armor of sorts. It might or might not stop a bullet, and it might simply weigh him down, but when an angry farmer fired a volley of shot from a muzzle-loaded gun eighty yards away, it might just save his life.

Unfortunately for Vlad and his fellow soldiers, the Polish village of Soce was politically well connected. Word of the raid was exaggerated by the time it reached the regional government, and then the Polish central government at Warsaw. The central government also received reports of the raids on its other border villages. The government was tired of its sovereignty being taken bit by bit with the goods stolen in every raid, so it sent a full division to that part of its border.

Chapter 2
Attack on Witowo, Poland

In early November of 1854, the men rode towards Witowo, Poland. However, a detachment of Polish soldiers had been recently stationed there to kill the Russian raiders. Disguised as peasants, the Polish soldiers kept constant watch with scouts stationed on high ground at the approaches to the town. They had set signals from the outlying scouts to men in the steeple of the church in the town's center to alert their commander of any oncoming Russians. When Vlad's group approached the town from the east, the scouts signaled the watchmen positioned in the steeple, who notified the Polish commander. He sent reinforcements to a place along stone walls covering the Russians' approach from the east. All directions were covered with men behind the short stone walls around the town. The Polish soldiers were on foot, and they crouched down to give themselves the element of surprise.

The Russians swung around and approached the village from the south. As they neared the village, they clumped together out of natural apprehension towards approaching a strange town. Vlad was in the back left. His horse had wanted to stop for water at a stream, and Vlad had no choice but to oblige the ornery beast. "Hurry up!" he said to the horse, jerking at the reins almost as soon as the horse began drinking. Vlad soon took off and had almost caught up to the men to regain his place near the front.

The road on which the men approached the village narrowed as it neared an opening in the stone walls. When they got within 30 yards, half of the Polish men stationed there rose up and fired, yelling as they did. They were terribly excited and scared, which affected their aim. As the bullets flew, the experienced Russians reacted instinctively, shouting, and drawing and firing their weapons, but they, too, were inaccurate. The return fire kept the Poles scared, so that the ones who had not yet fired aimed poorly, too. However, with the number of men shooting from the wall at such a short distance, the Polish firing squad line had served its purpose. Six of the Russians died on the spot, and six more were wounded and fell off of their horses. The other thirteen men, including Vlad, quickly turned and rode away, firing over their shoulders as they went. Some of them still riding had been hit, and two were hit severely.

The Polish militia continued firing, reloading, and firing again. They only lost one of their own men to a bullet, which was fired by a wounded man as he laid on the ground. The Poles shot and then stabbed the wounded and dead Russians repeatedly. As a pistol was fired at his head, one young Russian begged, "Please don't kill--" The bullet interrupted his plea, and he fell over gushing warm, bright red blood onto the icy ground.

Vlad was hit in the chest on the left side, but the lack of rifling in the Polish gun, the distance, the gold coins, and the clothes he was wearing blocked and cushioned the blow. Vlad suffered severe bruising and a flesh wound with the bullet lodging under the skin and next to a rib. While the wound was seemingly minor, infection was the major killer of wounded men. As he hurried away, the important thing to Vlad was that his horse was not harmed, which would have meant certain death for him miles from his camp. Had the Polish soldiers been on horseback or shot his horse from beneath him, Vlad's life would have soon ended in a torrent of blood draining into the cold Polish dirt.

Vlad and the twelve other men rode hard back to the Russian frontier bloodied and beaten, but alive. Vlad heard the screams of the Russian wounded as the Poles stabbed, tortured, and shot them repeatedly. He could hear his tent-mate Alexander begging for his life and screaming in terror and pain. The Poles sent a clear message to the fleeing Russians through the dead and dying men. Vlad and his compatriots got that message. There would be no more raids on Polish towns by them.

Vlad and the other survivors crossed the border and rode a safe distance into mother Russia, stopping only long enough to tend to their horses and their wounds. They drank heartily from a cold fast-moving stream, as they looked over their shoulders for Poles who might be following. Vlad told the men, "Make sure your horses drink enough so we can ride straight to headquarters. Make sure you get enough, too, but hurry!"

They quickly headed for that sector's army command station. After reporting what had occurred, they were reprimanded and almost jailed for what had happened. Their commander had been killed, so he could not be punished for failing to anticipate an ambush. The two severely wounded men died.

Vlad had to wait a long time to have his wound treated by a young woman nurse, who was the assistant to the corps' doctor. Although this was before the time of knowledge of the cause of infection, he wanted to take full advantage of the bath house at corps headquarters while he waited. The water was heated by a fire, but the soap was quite hard on his skin. It felt wonderful to bathe, except for the sharp horrendous pain he felt when he washed his wound with soapy water. The bath soothed the other parts of his body.

After the bath, Vlad dressed in his dirty clothes and continued waiting for the nurse. When she finally entered the room, she commanded, "Strip." While he was amazingly modest about it, she ordered, "Now or you won't be treated." She wanted him to hurry so she could get this business concluded and get on with the rest of her many duties. He took off the vest carefully, so as not to alert her to the presence of the gold inside it. It genuinely hurt to take it off, so he amplified the pain to take it off slowly so that the coins did not make noise. The cloth protected them from making the noise he feared.

The nurse had no anesthesia. She dug into his flesh quickly and without concern for his pain. Vlad screamed and orderlies had to hold him down. She maneuvered around, digging out the bullet, which moved between his skin and ribs as she tried to fish it out. As soon as the nurse finished, she quickly left the room without saying anything. Vlad was left nearly unconscious with his excruciating pain and a fair amount of bleeding, mostly under the skin with excess blood finding its way out through the wound. She left a dirty rag for him to press against it.

As the orderlies were leaving, one of them took pity on him, stopped, and dressed the wound. He said, "It's not much of a bandage, but at least it's clean." The orderly could have just as easily used a soiled dressing or left Vlad to his own devices. Vlad then grabbed his vest and clothes and hobbled over to a cot, falling on top of his vest and clothes, but pulling a sheet over himself. He passed out from sheer pain and exhaustion.

The room was warm from a nice stove. The bed sheets were surprisingly clean and crisp, with a soft pillow and warm blanket, which he tucked his feet and legs under. It was the first time he had been warm and comfortable in what seemed like years. Vlad slept for fifteen hours, until another orderly discovered him asleep in the room and made him leave because the doctor was coming and did not want to see his facility cluttered with sick or injured people. He certainly did not want to see a young corporal, who meant nothing to him, and who could do nothing to get the doctor reassigned out of this rat trap to a better army camp. The orderly screamed, "Get out. You should be in the enlisted barracks with the other varmints in your group!"

Vlad walked slowly over to the barracks where the other men from his group were billeted. His wound hurt with every fast or uneven step. A comrade told him, "We've been given orders to fall out in fifteen minutes." "Alright," Vlad said, as he struggled to get dressed. He worried about facing the wrath of superiors, who were more concerned with having been bothered than with sympathizing with the loss of his other comrades, or with sharing his sense of amazement that he and the few others had survived and returned to Russia. They would just as soon wish that the men had been killed than have to deal with reassigning them.

After much yelling and threats by a variety of officers, Vlad and the other survivors were not reassigned to another unit. The last officer said, "You are going to go back to the frontier, and you are going to do your duty of protecting Russia." They were assigned new replacement soldiers, including several additional ones to increase the unit's strength, and a recently promoted commander. Then, they were all sent back to the same area. Scarcely forty hours had passed since the ambush at Witowo before they were once again facing the Polish border. Rather than looking for targets of opportunity, they felt like hunted animals from their new-found fear of the Poles. As far as the Russian Army was concerned, they were the chaff that protected the kernel of Russia.

They hardly slept as they wondered when the Poles would ambush them, how many there would be, and whether they would get out alive. However, the Poles never attacked. They were too concerned with another Russian attack, and with protecting the other villages with what they thought were their own scarce resources. As with many examples in history, mutual assured destruction kept the peace, through some psychological phenomena that few people understood; fear motivated and drove actions in many circumstances more than any other emotion.

With the fear that a camp fire would bring the Poles to them in the middle of the night, Vlad understood that it would be a race between whether the elements or the Poles would kill him as winter advanced. Vlad still had his gold, which was actually a great deal more than he thought. Although it served as a crude bullet shield, it could not keep him warm or safe from angry Poles.

Chapter 3
Attack on Russian Villages

Five of the twenty new replacements outright deserted within the first week. They would not make it fifteen miles before the Poles killed the ones who went west, and the Russian Army captured and shot the deserters who headed in other directions. During this time, relations between the Russian and Polish governments began to improve. The Russians even signed a peace and mutual trade treaty with the Poles. A written order reached Vlad's group just as they were preparing to attack a small Polish village further to the south from the ones they had attacked previously. They wanted food and supplies more than gold. The order simply read, "Under penalty of death, you are ordered in the name of Czar Nicholas I to cease attacking Polish villages and not enter Poland for any reason." It was signed by the general in charge of the Russian border defenses along the Russian-Polish frontier.

As Vlad and the others considered their predicament, they knew that the only way they could survive the winter was to live off of Russian farms and villages. They began "confiscating" certain goods from Russian farms, but the poor peasant farmers stood steadfastly. They were armed surprisingly well and refused to give the armed soldiers the few scraps they had with which to survive the oncoming winter. Being barred from attacking Polish villages, and with no other apparent choice, the men started outright raiding Russian villages for survival. The harvest that year had been poor. Vlad thought of using his gold to buy food, but he knew he needed to save it for the dead of winter. Also, if the new replacements or his commander knew he had gold, they might take it from him. More likely, someone would kill him as he slept and take it. Vlad believed that he had to raid Russian villages for food, or else starve to death.

To raid fellow Russians and get away with it without being reported to higher authorities meant either killing all witnesses, disguising themselves as Poles, or hitting far away villages and riding away very quickly. Vlad did not have the stomach for butchering innocent men, women, and children, especially not his fellow Russians. After all, he had grown up in a Russian village not too different from the ones they would raid. But hunger in his stomach and cold throughout his body were powerful motivators.

He discussed his concerns about killing Russians with his commander and the other men. Vlad said, "We must avoid killing fellow Russians whenever possible. If we do, we will surely be caught and executed. Theft is one thing, but killing is another." Vlad's commander agreed, but added, "We will threaten or beat the ones who need it, though." They all realized that if they killed Russians, they, too, would be killed if captured. One soldier reasoned, "If we are caught raiding Russian villages, we will be killed, anyway." The commander said, "Perhaps, but we mustn't kill any Russian unless we have to. To prevent capture, we will need to disguise ourselves as

Poles. If our government believes that the Poles are responsible, it will disregard the treaty and we can begin raiding Polish villages again. And, if we have to kill a Russian, everybody may just believe it was the Poles who did it."

In early December, Vlad was hunkered down in a pit he had dug to stay warm. He and his new tent mate, who was no more than seventeen, practically buried their tent in the hole with dirt covering the sides, trying to protect themselves from the stinging wind. It seemed that nothing stood between them and the cold Arctic. The digging helped, but they had to patrol the border as ordered and frequently move camp to avoid being identified as raiders.

As the days went by, members of the squad became sick. Three of the men were close to death from pneumonia. All of the rest were sick with fevers, and all had some form of frostbite. Vlad had trouble even keeping his horse alive. The men had built a make-shift stable, which protected the horses better than the men. They also built fires to protect the horses and warm themselves. A soldier complained, "The fires will lead an enemy right to us!" Vlad replied, "We have no choice. Both we and the animals will die without the warmth from fire."

Their duty was to protect the Russian border, but they knew that they could not patrol as wandering nomads in the snow. They did send out day patrols, but more to protect themselves than out of any sense of duty. Duty, honor, and morale had all left with the last colors of the autumn leaves.

Finally, the cold became too much. Even headquarters recognized that its patrol soldiers were becoming ineffective, especially with mounting raids from raiders whom it thought were Polish. It ordered the various units to billet themselves in villages along the border. Vlad's group force-billeted themselves in a small village that was a prosperous agricultural trading center. Vlad's commander selected the village, telling the men, "There should be warehouses of food for us to eat until spring." The men were cautiously optimistic, but that was a false rumor. They stayed indoors, but there was little food for them.

As Christmas approached, Vlad did not think of Christmases past. There were no memories of a small, warm cottage with a loving family eating a hearty meal. Such memories may have filled British and American homes, but the long struggle of the Russian people left them without such memories. Centuries of brutal poverty and the long Russian winters made the average Russian different from his British and American counterpart. The average Russian saw death so often that his quality of life was much lower.

As Vlad rode on patrol, he decided that he needed to go somewhere, anywhere where it was warm. He again thought of America, but he had no idea how he could get there. Plus, stories about it were as likely to be as false -

or at least as exaggerated - as his own government's promise of plenty of hearty food and a warm place to stay if he joined the Army. He even had to beg to get into the Army. He knew that beggars could not expect anything. However, he did not expect to be near-death for months out of the year.

Vlad figured that if he went west, towards the ports that could take him to America, either the Russians would kill him for deserting, or the Poles for raiding their villages. "That settles it", he thought. He would eventually die in the Army.

He continued on his mission of patrolling the border, but really of protecting his group and scouting out some dying village to raid. One day, Vlad spotted a small Russian village that looked extremely wealthy. He thought the village was Novovolynsk. Unbeknownst to him, it was really Volodymyr-Volynsky. He and the other men on patrol carefully marked their way as they returned to their host village, over twenty miles away. They reported their find to the commander, who ordered that the group raid it the following day.

Vlad was exhausted. However, he took care of his horse before attending to his own needs, which were many. The next morning, he awoke after twelve hours of sleep, which could be described as deep unconsciousness. The men rode in the direction of the village. They were so anxious to get to the village and relied so heavily upon the markers that no one bothered to confirm where they were on any map. From moving so frequently, they were often confused about their precise location as they rode through the countryside on patrol. They rode towards the village with thoughts of ample food and gold.

When they neared the village, they studied it from concealed positions on a knoll and planned their moves. Something just did not seem right to Vlad. The fact that this village looked prosperous, more prosperous than the dozens of other villages they had raided, suddenly bothered Vlad. Vlad's stomach was roiling. He quickly became nauseated, and his worry was more than just the stark fear of being killed by a villager. The other men were consumed by greed at the sight. They circled around behind a small knoll and rode hard into the town, attacking it without much difficulty and securing large quantities of food and gold. Vlad even found some jewels in one home. Then, they made their escape without incident.

There was only one problem, though. They had raided the hometown of one of the advisors of Czar Nicholas. By any account, they should be dead men. Thankfully, they had not killed anyone or raided the home of anyone dear to the advisor. These seemingly small mitigating factors just might save their lives, but their lives would no longer be lives worth living, even by Russian standards of the day.

By now, Vlad had a small fortune stored up for himself, but his heart was heavier. He became increasingly clever in hiding his gold, and he traded the jewels for more gold. He would melt the gold and use it to fill portions of his clothes and a necklace that had a flat shield across his vest. Although the metal was a poor insulator, it did help to create small pockets of trapped air in his clothes that insulated him. He learned to sit near the fire and heat the gold, which would radiate heat when he went to bed. He constantly had to work hard to hide the gold from the others.

Chapter 4
Capture

As Vlad rode back to the camp from the Volodymyr-Volynsky raid, he felt an overwhelming sense of exhaustion and anxiety about the future. He had no idea where his meals would come from after the food from this village or the next ran out. Sooner or later, the Russian villagers would either fight back or hide their food and gold more carefully. The cold from the savage winter and the prospects for poor future raids almost caused him to lose his will to go on.

As he continued to ride, he wondered how he had gotten into this predicament. After his squad arrived at camp, he just went through the motions, taking care of his horse as best he could before seeing to his own needs. He went to the house in which he was billeted to try to rest and get warm, but succeeded in neither, as the cold went through him. After a while, he got up and went over to a fire in another room. He sat so close to it that his clothes began to roast, and he could smell the sweet stench. It was the first time he had been warm in days, but his side facing away from the fire was cold and uncomfortable. He mumbled to himself, "I hate the cold and this place."

As Vlad sat half roasting, yet still cold from the day, he retreated into his imagination. Other men in such circumstances may have been almost suicidal, but he was not. Strangely, he was depressed, but determined.

Ending his miserable life was not an option for him. Something drove him onward, even without his being aware of it.

The wool from his uniform had finally come to terms with his white Russian skin after having pierced through his underclothes at the worst times and in the worst places. Providing neither warmth nor cool comfort, it left him cold in the winter, and was oppressively hot in the summer. Although it had pricked and chaffed him when new, the sweat, dirt and filth that had penetrated between the fibers made them less caustic. Likewise, his skin had become rough, almost like a scab.

When he finally got a little comfortable, he daydreamed of Elena, his first and only girlfriend, and of the long walks they took together during the brief summer after they had met. Those walks sometimes ended with them embracing. Her death the following winter quickly made her memory too painful to bear. He truly loved her.

Elena was like an infection. She had not returned his affections at first, and always seemed a bit cautious with her commitment to him. However, there were times of almost abandonment, when she had to hold him. Her firm body underneath incredibly soft skin drove him wild. Despite her young age, her dark eyes were steeped in mystery. She walked with her head high, like a sophisticated woman in the Czar's court. Elena dressed beyond her years with a hint of cleavage and snug dresses that revealed her hourglass figure. Her dark brown hair perfectly cradled the nape of her neck. She would tell Vlad about her love for him and profess other promises, which she would inevitably seek to retract after her passion had cooled. This made him all the more obsessed with having her.

Elena's actions towards Vlad were intentional, and yet her true ability to capture him was primal and subconscious. She had him, and he would never forget her. He could not forget her. Now that she was gone, he could not have her. She was gone and yet always with him. He had told her he would love her forever, and he knew he would. He had to live with that the best he could.

Even those strong bittersweet memories vanished instantly when a blast of the January wind pierced the holes in the walls of the uninsulated house during a 30-knot gust. After repositioning himself, he just stared into the fire, feeling sorry for himself and thinking that things could not get any worse. He was a man who had lost his family and his love, and he was beginning to lose his sense of who he was. He was drifting on a sea of endless ice. The fact that Russian farmland was beneath him made no difference. It might just as well have been a slab of ice on the Arctic.

After backing a foot or two away from the heat and lying down on a primitive feather-stuffed mattress with his cold side facing the fire, he fell asleep. He slept for only twenty minutes, but during that time, Elena was in his dreams. She took him along a path down by a creek. She allowed him to get close to her, acting innocent about what she was doing; probably denying it to herself. He could not resist the way that she kissed him. He did not want to resist her. He wanted her to want him, and yet he knew that she would think of ways to discourage him. He was not everything she wanted. She thought that someone else better was out there for her. Although a dream, it precisely reflected their relationship years ago.

When he awoke and immediately realized his true circumstances, his head ached while his stomach felt the pang of loss and anxiety. He was even more empty and hollow. He had been emotionally close to her again, but he also had relived the pain of rejection and permanent loss upon waking. At least when she was alive, he had the hope that tomorrow would bring them together, and that she would confess her undying love for him. Now, she was dead, and there was no promise of them tomorrow or ever. There was just his love for her, and the torment of the memories of her half love for him. Wanting and needing her as he did, yet being unable to hold her, he just could not bear those dreams. He had plenty of them in the four years since her death. Even in dreams, when she seemed so alive, something continued to gnaw at him, which made him feel like it was not real. No matter how deep and real the dream seemed, he had a nagging sense that something was not right.

Now awake, he was deeply dehydrated and yet had to urinate. He took care of both and went to bed in the other room of the house. His roommate had been in the room expelling gas that could have made a horse run for fresh air. Vlad opened a door to the outside for a few seconds. The Russian winter cleared the air, but took out the relative warmth along with the stagnant air. He laid down and eventually fell asleep.

After two days of staying close to camp, Vlad finally got a long night's restful sleep. However, he awoke mid-morning to the sounds of yelling and horses. The village was surrounded by a company of well-fed and dressed elite Russian soldiers. They were heavily armed, and their leader was berating Vlad's commander, "You will tell me the truth about your raid on Volodymy-Volynsky! You will not lie to me or I will have you dragged through the streets and shot!"

The commander denied it, "The raiders must have been Poles who hit the village while we were patrolling in another area. We are given far too much area to protect for what few men we have." But the evidence was all around. All of the men were ordered, under penalty of death, to disarm, pack up, mount up, and move out. They rode, under close watch of the other soldiers, until they reached a major fort. There they were relegated to the servants' barracks and told that if they left the compound area, they would be shot. Vlad thought that they would be executed, anyway. However, the barracks were at least windproof. There was a fire, fresh water from melted snow and a half-frozen well. They were provided a modest amount of stale bread and other bland but edible food.

Vlad did not fully appreciate the political dynamics involved in his men having raided Volodymyr-Volynsky rather than Novovolnsk, because he figured getting caught raiding either one likely meant death. His life would be spared, though, because of the need for soldiers in Siberia and in Russian America, known later as Alaska. Also, the certain nobleman over whom the town was protected was, at the moment, out of favor with Czar Nicholas I. The Czar suspected him of stealing. A noble stealing from peasants was of no concern to a Czar, but this particular nobleman had stolen from the wrong people. Through a business deal, he had defrauded a family of rich merchants who had befriended the Czar through gifts of gold to fund the Russian treasury. They wanted a noble title, which would lead them to greater riches and power.

Chapter 5
Military Trial

The men were confined to the barracks for a number of days. One of the men told the group, "I've been hearing from some of the guards that we will be sent east to Siberia to work." Vlad asked, "Will we still be in the Army or sent as prisoners?" Another man said, "What difference does it make?"

With news of being sent to the east, Vlad's concern about being shot subsided. Vlad thought he would live for now, but was being sent east to die eventually. This was a life sentence of sorts, because being so far east meant he'd probably never return home, much less go to Western Europe or America. Although his future was even bleaker than before, he enjoyed the moment. Once the fear of being shot passed, the following days happened to be the best that Vlad had spent in the Army. He had fresh water and a permanent shelter, and with warm, more filling rations of food, he even put on a couple of pounds.

His gold was safe in his clothes, belt, and boots. His clothes and boots smelled and looked so filthy that no one would have taken them from him or searched them. His horse was even being cared for, but it was army property, and it was being taken from him permanently to help pull the wagons along with the other horses that had been used by Vlad's group.

The trial, really an inquest, was as fair as they came during that time. With the outcome predetermined, regardless of whether some undeniable piece of exonerating evidence came to light, it would last less than twenty minutes, and everyone but Vlad's commander was tried as a group. Vlad's commander was sent to Moscow to face trial by higher officers, with grave consequences. The trial was designed to make sure that nothing incriminating or important had been overlooked in deciding what to do with the men. Due process, guarantees on the reliability of evidence, and a trial by an impartial jury of one's peers was a luxury to which not even the merchant or noble classes were entitled.

The outcome of Vlad's trial had been pre-determined by the Czar himself, having personally ordered that the unit be sent to Siberia for hard labor, with the possibility of sending them on farther to Alaska to populate a garrison there. The Czar, impressed with reports of the cunning and effort of their bold crimes, figured them worthy of hard physical labor before they succumbed to the cold, disease, enemies, wild animals, or starvation. Vlad was just glad that he had not received a fair trial followed by execution, though the local noble had requested that the unit be shot. Regarding the commander, the Czar thought that an example had to be set to prevent similar acts, and he ordered that, after trial, the commander would face a public execution in Moscow.

Vlad had no legal counsel. Rather, he did his best to defend himself with statements that the cold and hunger caused them to do it, and, generally, to ask for mercy. While some of the men who had spoken before him tried to say that they thought it was a Polish village, their lies were obvious, and the court meted out a harsher punishment of flogging before transporting them. Vlad did not mind asking for mercy. Pride was an expensive and foolish luxury in his current circumstance. Even though Vlad did not cry or get on his knees to beg, it would not have mattered, and no one would have remembered such desperate acts even ten minutes later. Vlad was humble, honest, and largely quiet, which saved him from a thorough whipping.

Vlad did mention his life growing up. However, all the judges heard was that Vlad had worked in an ironworks shop and had done some blacksmithing. This actually helped him, because it meant that he was earmarked for more skilled labor, and would receive better food. It also meant that he would not be considered as expendable and exposed to the most serious risks as he traveled. His skills could be useful in case a horse broke a shoe or something made of iron needed repair.

Vlad and the others would be taken to Moscow and then south to go around the Ural mountain range to Kirovograd, which was a transportation center for wagon trains heading deep into Siberia. Vlad saw a map of Russia hanging on the wall of an Army officer in the compound, and the width of the country was beyond his comprehension. The route they would take, along with others joining their wagon train, would hop from town to town as they headed east. As they headed east, the towns would become fewer and farther between until they finally reached the town of Susuman. From there, if they were to be sent to Alaska, they would travel on to the port city of Magadan. From Magadan, ships departed for places all over the northern Pacific, including Alaska.

The Czar encouraged Russian settlement into Alaska in hopes of solidifying Russia's claim to it against a growing American and Canadian presence in the region. When Vlad studied their route, he thought that if he could only get to Alaska, he would have a chance of breaking free, making it to an American or Canadian outpost, and, then, on to America. He knew it was a long shot, but his alternative was spending the rest of his life, which would likely be a fairly short one, in Eastern Siberia.

Vlad immediately requested to be sent to Alaska to work, but the leader of the troops guarding him only laughed and hit him with the back of his gloved hand. He told Vlad that he was going to die in Siberia or en route like the rest of them. Even the leader knew he probably had only a one way ticket given the number of soldiers who died on the trip.

Vlad was held for another two days until the wagons, numbering over one hundred, were ready. He spent his last couple of days in the confines of the barracks with his other comrades, resting and eating as much as he could before he left, as he truly had no idea what he would eat as he traveled. He figured they would take supplies, which meant incredibly hard bread and salted meat or pork, but that there would be shortages of even those unpleasant items.

Chapter 6
Journey to Siberia

Sure enough, Vlad was given only a pittance of food during the entire journey. The weight he had gained in captivity - largely through inactivity - was quickly lost. The rutted roads were hard to travel when frozen, but they would be more difficult when they turned to mud during the spring rains. They traveled from one hopeless village to another. Half-starved people looked at them with glassy eyes and weather-worn faces. Forty-year olds were elderly, and twenty-year olds were middle-aged. Their children were underfed, but well-loved. Love of family kept them all going. Vlad could see the love in the children's faces, and he envied them for a moment. They had nothing and everything at the same time. Vlad yearned for a family and a normal life on a simple farm. The harshness of winter would yield to the hope of spring when food sprouted and bellies were filled, first with berries, and then with other foods as they ripened.

The farmers who Vlad saw worked themselves to exhaustion all summer to store enough food to make it through another long, Russian winter. The endlessness of work and hunger were tempered by the softness of a wife's touch and a hug from a four-year old who thought her daddy was greater than any czar.

Vlad pressed on, trying to stay warm and comfortable. The bitter cold and poor food kept them from forming an effective fighting force to break free and head south. Vlad was encouraged, however, when a guard told him with certainty that his entire group was needed for work, and some of them, including the guards, would be sent from Russia across the Bering Sea of the Pacific Ocean to Alaska. The guard told Vlad that they were receiving better treatment than in years past, but Vlad wondered how on earth anyone survived any harsher treatment. Similar trips usually killed a number of the men, which was acceptable to the Czar because the criminals were problems for the state. His hunger pangs allowed him only partial rest, and malnutrition weakened him. The calories he ate did little more than keep him alive. He did not have the energy to fight or escape, and even if he had wanted to, he simply could not separate from the others without the certainty of quick assistance in the form of food, shelter, and warmth. From the look of the peasants, he could not expect them to share what little they had.

Moreover, the captain of the guards told Vlad and the others, "There is a large price on each of your heads, dead or alive. Should you escape, the villagers all want to capture you, because they've been told that they will be paid a huge reward, which means a good life for them. They will surely kill you to prevent your further escape, because they've been told they will be punished if they capture an escapee and allow him to escape. They also know that any person caught harboring an escapee will be killed, his possessions taken from him, and his family left to starve homeless. You escape – you die!"

Given all these factors, Vlad told himself that he must wait until he arrived at his final destination - hopefully Alaska - before trying any escape. He knew that if he escaped now, the peasants would fight each other for the chance to kill him and collect the reward.

The remainder of the trip was horrid and seemed like it would never end. All the men suffered, and Vlad lost 25 pounds. He tried to stay comfortable and was always obedient towards his captors. He wanted to earn their trust so that they would go easier on him, so he worked hard and did the best that he could at whatever task was given to him. For the time-being, survival was his only priority.

Chapter 7
Siberia

As he traveled deep into Siberia, he realized the hopelessness of his situation. It was a vast wilderness. He wondered why the government did not simply shoot them, but the dead became martyrs and could not work or colonize remote places. Prisoners gave their loved ones hope of return. They also served as hostages, because if the ones left behind revolted, their imprisoned loved ones might be killed or harmed. That did not matter to Vlad, because he had no close family left in Russia. He had uncles, aunts, and cousins, but most of them had looked upon him as a liability – another mouth to feed – when his father had passed away. Since he had left to join the Army, they had nothing to do with him. They never sent him any letters or gifts. To the officials, though, he was still a source of free labor.

Vlad looked upon the harsh land and re-evaluated his circumstances. He knew he would die here unless he got away. However, if he escaped, where would he go? He would be a dead man if he headed west, because the peasants in the towns through which they had passed would kill him for the reward. The lands to the south were unknown. If he did make it to the south and out of Russia, he would be in the Mongol or Chinese lands where he would definitely be unwelcome and unable to speak the language. To the north, there was only ice and cold, and to the east, there was a vast ocean. The guards repeatedly told them this as the towns became fewer and the threat of capture by peasants diminished. They were so confident, they even showed the men maps to prove it, which gave Vlad another opportunity to study the geography.

By the time they finally arrived in Susuman, it was spring. Vlad stood in line to receive an assignment to quarters, which were really a number of shacks. While in line, an Army officer came through seeking volunteers to go to Alaska to work. The men were told that they would never return to Russia, but they could work in a land of plentiful fish and moderate temperatures. Vlad's hope returned.

Vlad again thought through the matter. Although Alaska belonged to Russia, it was at least on the same continent as America. America might even take over Alaska as it expanded westward. After all, it had already made California a state, and it was on the Pacific coast. He again thought that if he could just get on the same continent, he might have a chance to go there eventually by escaping or earning his release. It was a grand dream, but it was his only chance to be free.

When Vlad volunteered, the officer looked him over and told him where to go stand. Several other men volunteered, too, but a large number did not. They held on to the dream of being released to return to their wives and children in Western Russia. It was a hopeless dream, but it was the only thing that kept them going.

When all the volunteers were assembled, the officer needed five more men, so he ordered five of the strongest remaining men to go. They screamed and cried in protest because they had wives and young children in Western Russia. The officer pulled out his gun, pointed it at the head of one of them, and pulled the trigger. The gun misfired from lack of care in the cool damp weather, and the intended victim shook as he begged for mercy and quickly ran to join the volunteers. The other men hurried over as well while the officer worked on his gun. He finally holstered it in frustration and told the men, "The next time, it will work, and I will shoot two of you!"

The men spent the night in shacks separated from the others. The next day, they were taken by wagons eastward towards Magadan, a port city on the Sea of Okhotsk. It took a few weeks to get to Magadan. From there, they boarded a ship for Alaska. At sea, Vlad volunteered to help so that he could get out of the hold. He helped replace rotten or broken wood and iron, he helped with the sails, and he did anything else that he was told to do. He took precious moments to breathe the fresh salt air and look out over the cold ocean. At first, the ocean excited him, but after awhile, the scenery rarely changed. The ocean was a bland shade of dark blue with occasional white foam from the ship's wake. He saw land when the ship passed between two of the Kuril Islands and headed north by Cape Lopatka. The large rocks and cliffs with little greenery made the islands look cold and uninviting. The monotony of seagulls flying and squawking overhead in search of a meal returned whenever they neared land.

After weeks on the sea, the ship docked at Petropavlovsk-Kamchatsky to resupply. The crew and guards were allowed to go to shore in shifts, but not the prisoners. Still, Vlad found it exciting to see the small remote port town, even if it was from a distance. He could see smoke from the chimneys of the homes and buildings, and people working along the docks. A hint of freedom teased him, a town from which Vlad could catch a ship to America or dozens of other countries. However, he knew he couldn't get free. Even if he reached shore, he would be quickly recaptured in the small port.

After a couple of days, the ship sailed northeast with the tide, tracking near the coast of Russia until it reached the Aleutian Islands. The seas were usually rough and the water very cold, even though it was now summer. The ship sailed for many more days until it reached the town now known as Skagway. Had Vlad been sent to one of the island settlements, escape would have been all but impossible; however, Skagway was located on the mainland, but there were still numerous obstacles preventing a successful escape.

Upon arrival, Vlad and the others from his group were assimilated into a larger existing camp. There were over seven hundred men there, and they were led by about one hundred Army soldiers. The commander was a colonel. He had a major, two captains, five lieutenants, and a number of sergeants. They had a lot of leaders because the laborers were basically the privates in the strict, regimented scheme devised by a minister of the Czar. They cut timber and made lumber to expand the town. The plan was that they would build the town and other Russians - especially merchants and opportunists - would come and assist them in extracting the bountiful natural riches and taking as much as they could profitably transport back to Russia. Given that most of occupied Russia was in Europe, it was a most ambitious plan.

Chapter 8
Alaska

In a dozen years, Czar Alexander II would realize that Alaska was too far away to be of any real use or profit. It was also hard to control such a remote colony. He would sell it to the United States in a deal that the Soviet leaders would later regret, although it may have prevented World War III a hundred years later by keeping the opposing forces miles apart from one another across the rough and icy Bering Sea, rather than within pistol shot of each other across a strip of land and a string of fences.

The fact that Alaska was still in Russian hands meant the difference between Vlad's possible freedom, however remote, and an early death in the Siberian cold. His opportunity to go to Alaska, even under harsh conditions, sparked the birth of a practical plan to fulfill his dreams of freedom. He was no expert on geography, but he had seen and memorized additional maps while performing cleaning work in the cabins on board the ship. He knew that he had to cross hundreds of miles of mountains, freezing cold rivers, and forest to reach the interior settlements of Canada, and he knew that the sea cut deep inland in places, up wide bays and rivers.

For the first time in his entire rotten, frost-bitten life, he had real hope, and with hope, a glimmer of happiness. He again dreamed of America and of a better life. It was not much, but it was immensely more than he had ever known, including the few, fleeting moments with his late girlfriend, Elena. Her memory now seemed as distant as the fleeting warmth of a Russian summer. His new reality was the world of Alaska.

When he now thought back on his earlier life, being so far in miles and time from much of it, he felt as if he had not actually lived it, but simply watched it. His life had recently changed so much that it seemed for a few moments as if his past had happened to someone else. When he thought of a happy memory from years ago, the details of his many hardships since then would come rushing into his mind. There were so many hardships and losses that even memories of happy times were painful because of the thoughts of having lived through the intervening calamities.

Anxiety and dread at the thought of those calamities debilitated him. They were monuments that overshadowed the good times. He determined and said to himself, "If I live to be a hundred or die soon after landing, my life begins when I step foot on Alaskan soil. I will either be free or die on this continent."

As Vlad contemplated his new found mental freedom, he realized that, physically, he was just as chained as if he were in a Russian gulag. His guards would no more allow him to walk away than they would a good dairy cow. He was an asset, and the fact that he was human was of little consequence or concern to them. They could shoot him on the spot and no one would care. They would not shoot him without reason, of course, no more than they would a dairy cow. He represented profit to them, and as long as he did, his life was worth something. If he had been disabled through injury or illness to the point that recovery was unlikely, he would be treated as any other farm animal would be in such circumstances, except that his owners would not cannibalize him. If he or anyone else tried to escape, however, they may lead the other men into believing that they could too. That would give the commander reason to set an example, and he would order the guards to kill the escapee as a warning to the others.

Vlad knew that if he had any hope of escaping to freedom, he first needed to gain his commander's trust. That meant being patient and not taking the first opportunity to escape. He had to wait until he gained the commander's trust, for surely he and his lieutenants would test him. Vlad told himself that this would not take long, but he had a nagging feeling of doubt that it could take years. He also needed to escape in spring, when he had a long warm growing season ahead and food readily available during the trip. He could not make it across endless snow carrying all the food he would need. Unfortunately, the current summer would end in a matter of weeks. He had to stay for the fall and winter, but he reasoned that his staying would give him the time he needed to plan properly.

Because of his military experience and prior rank of corporal, Vlad was assigned to supervise one group of about eight laborers. He tried to treat the workers fairly, because he did not need enemies. He followed orders to the letter, but did not act with marked cruelty. He had witnessed such cruelty, which is the hallmark of some people who are in the position of being both a superior and a subordinate. He had seen them kiss-up to their superiors and stomp down their subordinates, including him.

Vlad knew that resentment was a lasting emotion. If the men under him resented him, then his life would be in greater danger. He would do small things to show he did not agree with the unpopular orders he was required to give, sneaking in water and rest breaks, and doing some of the work himself when a man was too weary to finish what must be done. Even so, there were some among the men, both inside and outside of his group, who despised Vlad. They would despise anyone in his position.

Vlad saw other supervisors stomp the men under their command, and then grovel to their superiors. Vlad was shocked at how their superiors reacted, even the Colonel. Surely they must see through such transparent boot-licking. Vlad acted out of the dutiful respect owed towards a superior, and he did not go out of his way to make enemies with them. However, he did not stoop to the level of his fellow supervisors. He kept silent, except when he had something he thought his superiors would find useful.

Vlad observed that the most incompetent supervisors did the most boot-licking, and they were the most popular with their superiors. They drew the lightest duties, were given frequent praise for work done by others, and ate and drank the very finest. On the other hand, Vlad would have to work twice as hard and sometimes suffer life-threatening criticism for the substantial contributions he made. He was given tremendously difficult projects, but met them with success. However, he made mistakes, as anyone would, and his superiors, having listened to the jealous slanders of the boot-lickers, would concentrate on the mistakes. The situation was intolerable for Vlad.

While Vlad was severely criticized for minute mistakes in bringing substantial results, his superiors began to recognize that they needed him. He was the only one who consistently told them the right thing to do. Plus, Vlad was a natural leader, and the men under his command followed him. His knowledge and instinctive gifts were invaluable in gaining him what little power he had.

Over time, Vlad's superiors began to trust him, and he was allowed to roam with some freedom to do the most work for them. They gave him increasingly difficult projects, including cutting some of the most difficult trees on cliffs and hard to reach hillsides. Vlad lost two men that year to accidents, but he succeeded overall.

Other groups also lost men, and the guards lost several of their men to influenza, which they caught from each other in the close confines of their quarters. The loss of guards left the camp even more vulnerable, and the Colonel had to devise a system of rewards and punishments to keep the men in line. Because of Vlad's leadership experience, the Colonel gave him three groups of eight men to supervise, with threats in case Vlad failed to keep his men in line or one escaped, and rewards for keeping them in line and meeting production goals. Vlad hated it. The rules made him personally responsible for any breaches of discipline, and he could be put to death if anyone under him escaped and was not recaptured. Vlad had a set amount of vodka he could give to the men each week, and he used it at week's end to reward good work. The Colonel turned prisoner against prisoner by giving other men with similar positions the same threats and rewards.

Some supervisors even resorted to whipping the men under them. These supervisors had been beaten previously by the guards. In turn, they beat their subordinates more savagely than the guards had ever beaten them. Vlad wondered how someone who had been beaten and suffered alongside another person could turn and treat the other person even worse. The Colonel was a genius at manipulating and feeding the greed and fear naturally present in each man.

Chapter 9
A Deadly Warning

One day, in March 1856, one of the men in another group slipped away from his supervisor. He tried to make it to a camp of Canadians which the men had heard were further south, just over the Alaskan-Canadian border. Unfortunately, he was unfamiliar with the geography of the area and ended up trapped at the end of a point of land. The ocean was on one side and a bay was on the other. The water was too cold and wide to think of swimming across, even if he had known how to swim. There were no boats and no one around. He turned back to try to go around the water and ran into the search party.

The search party beat him severely and took him back to camp. He was brought before the Colonel, who had him stripped and tied to a pole about 100 yards from camp, then ordered that the man's skin be cut ten times with a knife and left overnight. He was cut so that he would bleed, but not die from the cuts. Not long after dark, the men of the camp heard him scream in terror. The screaming intensified, then suddenly stopped.

In the morning, the man was dead and half-eaten by a large, brown bear. He had been ripped from the pole, and his body was in a contorted, disjointed position. The man's thigh bones were exposed where the bear had feasted on those muscles, along with other parts of him. The Colonel ordered the men to assemble near the body, and most of them dry heaved in disgust. When they had all assembled, the Colonel told them that if anyone else tried to escape, they would meet an even worse fate.

For Vlad, the Colonel's threat did not have the desired effect. Although it frightened him, it also angered him to his core, deepening his resolve to escape, and to do so as soon as he had properly planned and spring arrived. He knew he needed to know basic geography, or else he would be trapped by ice-cold bays or the huge mountains off in the distance to the north. He needed to find a pass through the mountains that would take him to a trading path or trail.

Chapter 10
The Plan

A month later, in April of 1856, Vlad was ordered to go east to cut some lumber along a ridge wall. He had been along that mountain before on a partly cloudy day, and he knew from being on top of that mountain that the other side lead to a gentle valley, with streams and a river. Now, when he climbed to the top, the visibility was clear with no clouds. He could see flat land leading away from the Russians, and he thought he might have a chance to run. He just needed to get to Canadians or Americans. From there, he would need to go quickly into the interior of Canada or the United States, blend in, and go where the Russians would not follow. It seemed simple, provided he could just break free. If he could travel 50-100 miles with certainty and speed, he could afford to make some mistakes requiring him to back-track after that.

Vlad thought that he would be followed for only a few days, and then his pursuers would give up and turn back, lest they get lost. He decided to leave in early May, 1856, when he was told that the days would become longer and warmer. The foliage would grow full during the weeks after that, and there would be plenty of water from the melted snow in crystal clear streams. He thought that he could find food on the way. However, he needed to carry some food with him for the first 100 miles or so.

His plan was to convince his supervisors to allow him to go scout for super-tall straight trees for shipbuilding and skid trails and a water course by which to drag them with horses to water and then float them back to camp. Very tall straight trees were ideal for ship's masts and were worth a fortune in Europe. The Colonel had used a great deal of the best trees in the immediate area for building the camp, and ships from many different countries would frequently call needing supplies, including very tall straight masks. It was a way for the Colonel to make immediate money or barter for scarce supplies, and he readily agreed to Vlad's plan.

Vlad used all of his abilities to get his superiors to provide dry, durable food. He tried to trade his useful men for men in other groups who would not know how to follow him, either through lack of geographical knowledge or sheer incompetence. The other supervisors were glad to trade because Vlad's trained men would make their production go up, and they would be glad to see Vlad fail. Vlad traded two of his most competent assistants to one of the boot-lickers in exchange for that man's two most incompetent workers. Vlad knew from observing them that the two incompetent men disliked one another, caused conflict, and vocally disagreed with any plan that the other suggested, and he hoped that they would quarrel with each other about what to do as soon as they discovered his disappearance, giving him time to escape.

Vlad kept a few of his own men who were not the brightest, strongest or fastest. He made certain that he traded away anyone who had a sense of direction or who could beat him in a fight. He had a hand-picked team designed to fail. If Vlad did not or could not go through with his escape plan, he would probably die in a logging accident from these incompetent men or be beaten and starved by his superiors for his failure to complete any job after that. It was all or nothing.

Instead of preparing the troop for locating and marking the route to huge trees, Vlad spent his time planning his route. Because of the distance, he was entrusted with maps, but he could only review them in the presence of an assistant to the commander. He viewed maps leading farther south than he was going, and he saw that he needed to head northeast before turning southeast to get around mountain and water obstacles. He also found a series of mountains and valleys that he would need to cross, and counted them. He had become excellent at geography from his training and practical experience in the Russian Army, and also from reviewing maps over the past year or so.

He mentally mapped a way through the wilderness to a small, Canadian trading post to the southeast. It was on the edge of the map. He figured if there was one, there would be others in case he could not find his way to that small location. He also figured he would cross a path at some point that would lead him to an outpost village.

Vlad knew that after he took his first step, a number of variables beyond his control could change his plans. Therefore, it was important for him not to be too concerned with a specific route, but to know first and foremost of the major obstacles that could trap him. He was most concerned with an escape corridor or general route, as he would not be able to measure miles or even note geographical features beyond major ones like the Pacific Ocean - which he never planned to see during his escape - or a major mountain range.

Vlad studied the maps for hours and learned a great deal. He had to be careful, covering his work with plans for harvesting and returning the logs. From the crude maps available, he learned that the rivers generally ran from the northeast to the southwest. They formed large bays near the ocean, one of which had trapped the last escapee. Vlad knew that he would need to head in one direction first, such as southeast, then cut to the northeast. If the commander suspected that Vlad was heading northeast, he could cut him off, trap him, and kill him.

Vlad knew that he needed to travel light and fast until he had lost his pursuers. Then, he thought he could concentrate on getting his precise bearings and reaching a friendly settlement in a matter of days. Still, he knew that he had to plan for the contingency of having to wander for weeks or months until he found such a settlement. He had to be prepared to live off the land long after the food that he brought had been eaten. He needed protection not only from Russians, but from wild animals. He needed a gun, along with plenty of powder and shot. There was every sort of danger present, and he would have to expect the unexpected in order to survive if things did not go according to plan. He realized that few complex plans ever did go smoothly, so he was in for a hard time. Still, he planned with a joyous heart full of optimism. It was a chance to be free, and it was worth taking the calculated risk.

Vlad ordered his men to assemble the goods and worked them hard. He wanted them all tired, so he assigned and reassigned them to both meaningless and necessary tasks. The meaningless tasks were full of physical labor. He had them carry little food, so that they could not follow him for long. He packed the extra food on his horse and left other food behind. To cover up the fact that he had left some food behind, he placed extra stores of vodka and stones in the food supply boxes reserved for three-plus days out of camp. He did not want the food to be missed right away. He had the men carry as much as they could shoulder and packed lighter boxes on wagons hauled by horses. He figured that the men would be both tired and disoriented after carrying heavy loads over a long distance on foot.

As the party left and headed northeast, he led the parade confidently, saluting his superiors as he passed them. He yelled praises for the Czar, and everyone echoed even louder praises for the Czar. After he cleared the camp, he began giving mildly contradictory and duplicitous orders to his assistants, rekindling their competitive nature and creating further enmity between them. He then refereed the disputes between them, finding the one whose case was stronger wrong and rewarding the other. Then, he would privately tell the loser, "The base commander has high hopes for him. You watch, he will be promoted very soon and outrank us all." That made the two men further hate each other.

Vlad gave them overlapping supervision over about two-thirds of the men. The contradictory orders which followed caused the men to distrust the assistants and become disoriented. The orders frustrated the men towards the assistants. Vlad would step in, mediate the dispute, and always reward the men. During the first late afternoon when they camped, Vlad sent the assistants ahead for scouting. As soon as they left, Vlad cracked open some of the stores of vodka that he had stolen from a supply cabin and hidden a week earlier. The men got drunk and loved him for it.

Chapter 11
Escape

During the following day, the men awoke late to the loud, angry orders of the assistants, who had returned from scouting after dawn. As their heads throbbed, their resentment grew. The assistants were exhausted, but reported to Vlad details of the geography ahead. Vlad ordered them, "Pack up and get the men ready to move out." He headed up the rear, keeping out of sight and mind of the hung-over men. Finally, the men arrived at their destination. They set up camp, and began to eat supper. Vlad then secretly packed what he would need and stowed it away in the bushes, ready to move when he was. The men built a large warm fire, and went to bed. Vlad made them keep watch, rotating the men, four by four, every two hours, so that they got little sleep.

The following day, he worked the men hard – all of them. They were exhausted after 12 hours of work. He gave them little food, so that their strength would be drained. During the day, he scattered most of their food supply, leaving them just two days' worth. That would presumably give them the choice, when the time came, between making it back to the Russian village with just enough to eat or coming after him and running out of food. Then, he cracked open the rest of the vodka, giving it to the assistants first.

Vlad waited until the men were sauced, and then he absconded with his belongings, his stash of food, and the finest horse, which he had kept from being worked hard. The moon was full and bright, and he rode hard. The horse could hardly take it, as they rode all night. The next morning, the men awoke slowly, only to find no Vlad and little food. They were hung-over, tired, and hungry. They ate more than their proportionate share of the remaining food. The assistants argued about what to do. They even resorted to a fist-fight.

Finally, the men realized what Vlad had done. One assistant thought they should track him. The other thought they should return to camp to get help. They agreed to split the group, and one-half set off with one assistant to follow Vlad. They followed his horse's tracks, leaving markers as they went for the other group to follow with reinforcements. The other half went with the other assistant back to the Russian camp to report what had happened and to get more men, leadership, and supplies for the tracking party. Though the two assistants quarreled, they ended up doing exactly what they should have done to have the best chance at capturing Vlad. Vlad's plan so far had partially failed, because in spite of their incompetence, the two men made the correct decisions at a critically early stage.

Vlad stopped several times, but only briefly. He pushed the horse without rest until around noon. The horse rebelled, and Vlad had to stop for longer. The horse was lame from many missteps in the darkness. It was finally bitten by a large rattlesnake, which made it deathly ill. Vlad realized that he would have to go the rest of the way on foot. He packed up what he could, ate all he could tolerate, threw his belongings over his shoulder, including his gold, and set off on foot. He was tempted to kill the horse, but thought it more humane to leave the animal alone, near a stream, in case it healed. If not, then Vlad thought that a grizzly bear would make quick work of it. He simply could not kill the animal.

Vlad thought he was twenty miles away from his men, but he was only eight. He almost ran, not pacing himself at all. After about an hour, he was exhausted. He stopped by a stream and drank until he was nearly sick. He was excited, scared and had tremendous joy, all at the same time. He had a taste of freedom, and it felt like a weight had been lifted off of him. He had known excitement and fear before, but this time they were on his terms, and his attitude carried him another ten miles before dark.

As he ran and walked through the wilderness, he had the mid-May sunshine to warm him. He crossed streams full of salmon and had plenty of fresh water from the melting snow and ice at higher elevations. It was crystal clear mountain water, which tasted a bit fresher and cleaner than any water he had ever tasted. It may have been the cold temperature, but it could have been that this was the first water he had drunk as a truly free man. Full of hope and bright expectation, the crushing pain from sore muscles, the threat of being recaptured, and the lack of certainty of his precise heading were secondary. He was free.

The long Alaskan days allowed him to cover a lot of ground. However, he could not keep traveling 21 hours per day, every day. He had to stop and sleep. When he did, he had to make sure that he was not leaving a trail to where he was sleeping, so he walked through ice-cold streams, over jagged rocks, and in different directions to throw off any trail, devoting about an hour to this each day before collapsing into a deep, exhausted sleep.

He built a fire only once when it was very cloudy. When he did, he cooked salmon and ate the fatty fish to the point where he felt he could not eat another bite. The salmon provided protein and fat. It gave him energy and allowed him to save his dried food for times when food might be scarce, such as when at high altitudes crossing high mountain passes as he ran for his life and freedom.

Chapter 12
Ambush

When he had been gone for three days, he found a secluded valley protected by three cliff walls. There was a stream nearby and plenty of fish in it, and it looked comfortable and safe. He had not seen or heard any evidence of anyone following him, so he decided to rest there. He gathered fish and even made a fire in the protected valley. He cooked the fish and ate until his stomach was full of delicious fresh salmon.

As he laid down to rest, three men on horseback rode towards him, armed with knives and swords. Vlad had only rocks nearby and a small piece of metal. He took one rock about the size of his fist, and threw it forcefully, aiming it just below the chin of the first horseman. The man instinctively ducked, but the rock found his skull, and crushed it, killing him instantly. The other two men were horrified at the sound of the rock crushing the other's skull, along with the brains and blood that had scattered about them. The man's head was spurting blood and dumped what looked to be gallons upon the ground.

Vlad grabbed another rock and took off towards the base of a cliff. He began to climb. As the other two men regained their thoughts, they went after Vlad. Vlad took the rock and threatened to throw it at the men. The men cursed him in Russian and drew their knives. Vlad climbed about twenty feet off the ground, aimed, and threw the stone at the approaching men. He missed both them and their horses. They dismounted and began to climb after him.

As he climbed, he didn't know whether he would run out of hand-holds. He just climbed, looking for a route up as best he could. He was absolutely terrified of heights, but what choice did he have? He had about 100 feet to go to reach the top, and then he did not know where that would lead him.

As the men climbed after him, Vlad's heart pounded at what seemed to be close to 200 beats per minute. He breathed deeply and quickly. As he reached for one hand-hold, he pulled out loose rock and almost fell, but was saved by his tremendous arm and leg strength and his secure grip with the other hand. He took the loose stone and carefully aimed it at one of the men below him, who was climbing quickly. Vlad did not throw it, but merely hovered his hand above the other man and dropped the heavy rock. Unfortunately, it hit an outcropping of rock just above the man's head and deflected outward, just missing the man. However, the shock of the impact frightened both men. They were slower to climb and watched Vlad more carefully.

Vlad was able to out-climb the men. The upper slope of the cliff was not as bad as he had feared, and the rough rock provided many foot and handholds. He found more loose rock and ceremoniously dropped it down upon the men.   Each bombardier's load missed its mark, but served the same purpose of allowing Vlad's escape.

As he neared the top, he wondered what he would do. Eventually, the men would return to their horses. They would find a way to track him down, and he could not outrun them. When he reached the top, he saw that it led away over hills. However, he immediately ran to the other side and began climbing down a less-steep incline. The men could have beaten him to the top by going that way, but they tore after him in such a hurry that they did not bother to check.

Vlad made it down to the bottom and snuck around to see the men approaching the top of the cliff. He quietly collected most of his gear and gun, and he went over to one of their horses. He mounted the horse, and rode over to another horse. The third horse that belonged to the dead man was standing nearby. Vlad could not get to that horse without alerting the two men. He grabbed the reins of the second horse and rode off. He had two horses, plus his gear and an additional two saddle bags. However, he had forgotten his gold in another pack. He quickly rode back and gathered his bag. The men saw him and yelled after him. Vlad took off again and made it away.

He rode as hard and as fast as he could towards the southeast. He must have covered five miles before the horses bitterly complained, so he stopped and watered them, allowing them to rest. It was getting dark, so he gathered food for the horses and took the provisions and saddles off of them. As he looked through the saddlebags, he found more gunpowder and shot, both bird shot and heavy grain balls. He carefully rewrapped and stored these provisions because they likely would mean the difference between life and death. He then bedded down for the night.

Chapter 13
Night of Decision

That night, he was bothered by every sound. He listened fearfully for the sounds of approaching men. He saw the face, brains, and blood of the man he had killed. He tried to sleep, but his nerves were shot. His stomach ached with the guilt of a killer. He dry-heaved several times at the thought of what he had done. By a law other than Russian law, he may have been justified, but his conscience still tore his insides apart.

He again thought of his childhood home and of the late Elena. He was now separated by her not only by years, but by miles. At least when he was in Russia, he had the commonality of home to bridge the years and make her seem closer. Being far away from the place where her memories were made seemed to lengthen the years. It was as if the years since they were last together had doubled. It was not just a matter of time, though. It was a completely different life for him now. The change in circumstances and the number of life-altering events since she had died had made the world a different place for him. His common everyday experiences had changed drastically.

Vlad knew that grief was eating him, and he had too much else threatening his life. There was no going back to her, or to anything else related to his earlier life. They were all gone, and the reminders of them were as far away from him as he was from safety. He knew that the continued thought of her would forever chain him to a mediocre life, if he even survived the next few hours, days, and months. Right then and there, he decided that he would always love her, but he simply must move on. He had cried and grieved inwardly for years. As with her death, only death remained for him with the Russians. He had just severed all possibility of returning to his countrymen or to Russia. He reaffirmed to himself that he either would begin a new life or die trying. He had nothing to lose by going forward, and everything to lose if he turned back or was captured. He was a dead man among the Russians.

At first light very early in the morning, Vlad watered and fed the horses, taking time for a long drink of water. He had sweated through his clothes and was shivering from the cold. He urinated for a long time. He could smell it, and it smelled like fear. He packed his belongings on the horse he had ridden the day before, and he mounted the other horse. He rode for four hours without stopping, following animal trails through the woods and fields, and following stream beds to disguise his trail.

He stopped to rest for a bit, and again searched through the saddlebags of the men from whom he had taken the horses. He found food and maps. The maps were of little use, since he had no idea where he was. He made quick use of the food, saving some for later. He feared that the two men would be after him on the remaining horse. However, they returned to their camp with their dead comrade.

When he again thought of the man he had killed, he reasoned that the man and the two others were going to kill him. They would have killed him and thrown him over a horse to carry back to camp and put on display. He was still very troubled by having killed one of them, and by the faces of the other men he had killed during the past few years. He knew that those faces would stay with him until the day he died. He would never forget the look of surprised horror on their faces as life left each of them. However, he also felt a great deal of concern at how he had barely escaped the same fate. Had the three men not charged him, but instead taken enough time to plan a proper attack against him, he would be the one dead.

Vlad snapped back to the reality of the moment. He knew he had to persevere. His love of freedom and his desire for it made him determined to succeed. Years later, people would call this type of determination the American spirit. Actually, it was the inherent love of freedom in each person. It was the basic desire not to be confined or crushed under the thumb of a dictator. When Americans pondered why their government was often deadlocked between counter-opposing political parties and nothing seemed to get done, the resulting freedom from those very checks and balances and lack of governmental action was the intended result. So many times the Czar, and other countries' leaders with absolute power, would make rash decisions out of selfishness or even thinking that the result would be good for their people. However, they often failed to think through the problems created by their decisions.

Vlad hungered for basic human freedom. He preferred a vast and empty Alaskan wilderness to the confines of a Russian work camp. As he traveled, he was paranoid that he was being followed and that he would be overwhelmed any moment from behind by the men from the Russian camp. His fear made him travel harder and longer than he otherwise would have. His main limitation was the horses; he stopped when they needed to stop. He would alternate between them, riding one in the morning and the other in the afternoon. After traveling hard for three more days, he decided that he may be safe, as he thought he had covered well over one hundred miles through the wilderness. He had taken precautions to try to cover his tracks, but there was only so much of that he could do and still cover large distances. He hoped he had enough breaks in his tracks, and he had turned and taken different animal trails through the woods often enough that he thought it would be difficult for anyone to follow him.

That night, Vlad was a bit cold during the northern spring night. He was very tempted to build a roaring, warm fire to warm both himself and the horses. He used the horses as an excuse to satisfy his own needs. He wanted some cooked salmon and a comfortable place to sleep, and he longed for the security of the fire. However, just as he began to gather wood, something inside of him told him not to build it, but to go on for a few more days, just to make sure he was far away from any pursuers. Knowing that capture meant death, especially after his last encounter, he decided to try to make the horses comfortable without fire by putting them close together to share body heat. He reasoned that the cost of freedom was for him to shiver a bit and to bear the taste of raw salmon for a little longer. It had an oily fish taste, and he did not bother to scale it first, but simply spit out the scales as he ate. He had a basic hunger that reached into his core, but the oily fish satisfied it. He fell asleep quickly, about a half an hour after dark.

Chapter 14
Near Miss

Vlad awoke very early the next morning, packed hastily, and took off. He soon came upon a clearing that had been burned by a forest fire during the past year, probably started by lightning. He saw a fairly steep, but manageable, foothill that had been cleared by the fire. He thought he would ride to the top of it to lookout for any men following him and to try to see if there were any settlements nearby. He also just wanted to try to get his bearings on where he was going. Although he used the sun to navigate, he felt claustrophobic, and he felt that he had no control of his circumstances, because he literally could not see the forest for all the trees surrounding him.

In reality, Vlad had even less control of his circumstances than he feared. He was in a truly vast wilderness, about which he knew nothing, riding on an unknown course towards an uncertain destination. He could miss a village by a hundred yards and never know it. If he headed northeast, he could travel for a thousand miles and never see another human. At least the sun could help with general direction. Also, while he tried not to travel at night, he knew that the moon rose in the east before midnight and in the west after it. Even so, only God knew where he was heading.

Vlad reached the top of the foothill in about a half an hour. When he got to the top, it offered a spectacular view of the beautiful Alaskan wilderness. The vast natural beauty was practically untouched by European man. In the distance in front of him, he could see herds of elk, rolling hills, small mountains covered in trees, and taller mountains capped with snow. He could see a giant snow-covered mountain about sixty miles to the north. The springtime warmth and long hours of sunlight were painting the landscape a tender green along the valleys, while the tops of hills and the sides of the smaller mountains were just showing a hint of light green. It was gorgeous. He saw God's majesty and might in the beauty that stretched in front of him, and as his initial anxiety at having to cross such vast wilderness was replaced with hope, he began to feel calm and relaxed.

As Vlad looked back in the general direction from which he had come, he saw a remnant of dark smoke reaching straight upwards. A sharp needle of thought hit him. Panic squeezed his chest and raced to his head. The smoke was from a camp fire. He lost his breath when terror seized his body as he realized that he was being followed closely, probably by a dozen men. He thought, "They camped less than 400 yards from me last night. Had I gorged myself on cooked salmon over a warm campfire as I wanted to, I'd be dead by now!" In fact, the men would have draped his lifeless body across a horse and taken him back to the Colonel, who would have displayed him as a warning to others.

Although Vlad did not know how many men there were following him, there were eight. These were not the incompetent men that Vlad had brought with him; but rather, they were the ones dispatched by the Colonel. On horseback, they had quickly followed the trail that the men had marked, returning to the camp and the trail marked by those originally searching for Vlad. They were led by the Major, an experienced soldier and hunter. He had successfully tracked numerous game animals during his life. Even so, the logistics of waking, feeding, and moving even eight men gave Vlad the opportunity to move out before they did, which saved his life. The eight men were now just beginning to saddle their horses to go in pursuit of Vlad's trail, which was easier to follow than Vlad thought. They were on it.

Vlad tore off immediately down the opposite side of the hill, riding hard for five minutes before the realization hit him that he was traveling in a specific direction. He rode on anyway, just to put distance between himself and his pursuers. He then thought he should travel in a more easterly direction, riding just to the north of the rising sun. He thought that if he did that, he could throw the pursuers off, as they probably guessed that he was heading towards a large Canadian fur traders' village about two hundred miles south, southeast of the Russian camp.

When he next stopped to gather himself, his mind was still racing. Severe anxiety and panic continued to control him. He was in the middle of a seemingly endless wilderness. He did not know where any village was specifically located. He thought he had a dozen or two pursuers just yards behind him, and he knew genuine fear. To give up was to die, but to continue could mean drifting into a slower, but just as certain, death. Given the approaching summer, he thought if he headed too far north or northeast, he could be trapped by snow during the fall months and either freeze or starve to death. If he headed westerly, he could run into the pursuers or the sea. If he headed due south, he could run into the sea and be trapped on a peninsula.

His thoughts were facts mixed with fear, which meant that they were not truly rational. He decided that he needed to alter his plan of traveling southeast by traveling east for several days. Only then would turn southeast and travel until he ran into a settlement, whether that be in Canada or the United States several hundred miles away.

He rode hard again, pushing himself and his horses for three hours, and then he stopped to rest briefly because the horses demanded it. He watered the horses and himself, letting the horses graze in a clearing while he took out some fish and ate it. He was growing tired of raw salmon, but it was fatty and gave him energy. He sucked the fatty oils and tried his best to stomach the fishy taste, then mounted the other horse and rode again. This time, he was even more careful to observe what kind of tracks he was leaving.

He rode through a creek bed until he found a rocky place where he could exit without leaving a trail. He did so carefully. After entering the woods, he rode for about a hundred yards and stopped. He went back with branches of leaves and covered his tracks both by brushing them out and gathering leaves to fill in the deeper prints. The sun and breeze would dry the damp leaves that he had had placed over the trail, making them look natural. He then kept riding deeper into the woods.

The men following him had been able to track him. He had followed animal trails, which were easier for his horses to walk upon. When they lost the trail, they would send scouts out to circle in slightly different directions. One would quickly find the trail and report back to the others.

When the men got to his campsite that morning, they were amazed at how close they had been to him. Had Vlad's horses loudly neighed with the wind just right, they might have heard that sound and known of his presence close by. Had he simply stopped and camped earlier, or had they stopped later, they would have caught him. They had been quite tired the night before from riding hard to catch up with him. When they reached the clearing that morning, Vlad was already two miles ahead and pulling away. They rode up the clearing carefully, expecting to find him lying in wait at the top. Their slow approach to the top gave Vlad more time to gain distance from them. He traveled as quickly as the prudent use of his horses allowed. Their care was a priority, but he still pushed them as much as reasonably possible to make speed to save his own life.

When the group reached the top, they saw the hoof prints of the horses much farther apart, signaling a full gallop. They knew something had startled Vlad. They looked back and could see a remnant of smoke still rising from their campsite, and they immediately knew that Vlad had discovered them, although it appeared that he had only recently done so. In fact, Vlad could have discovered them sooner, but he had been extra cautious climbing with the horses, making certain that their footfalls were on solid ground.

The Major figured that Vlad would change course, but he thought that Vlad would try to circle around and then head south. Since he was dealing with one man, he did not believe that dividing his forces would create a problem. However, he did not fully respect Vlad's army training and experiences or his natural skill, and he underestimated how each of his men would act when searching alone instead of in pairs or small groups. The Major sent a group of men in a southerly semi-circle to try to cut off Vlad and ambush him. He ordered the rest of the men to follow him on Vlad's current trail. He thought he would either overtake and attack Vlad or push him into the ambush. It was a simple plan that could have worked on many people.

When the Major came to the creek bed, he followed it. Predictably, he figured that Vlad would exit at a rocky area to avoid leaving footprints, such as those made in soft soil. The Major surveyed the rocky area that Vlad had used to exit the creek bed. He looked carefully around the edges for signs of hoof prints, but saw none. He saw an animal trail and followed it for fifty yards, but saw no trace of any hoof prints. He sent his men out in different directions from the end of the rocky area to look for any sign of Vlad, but they found nothing. Given that he only had three men, they could not make a thorough search. Plus, the three men knew what Vlad had done to one of their comrades with just a rock, and they had no appetite for running into him alone.

The three men did not go as far out as ordered, and instead of looking intently at the ground, they kept an eye out for what might be waiting to drop down on them from above or out from behind a tree. Vlad's reputation in Poland was well known to them from long winter campfire stories told by one of the men who had been in Vlad's unit at the Polish border. He had been sent to Alaska along with Vlad, and he told them of the carnage he had seen in the barn caused by Vlad alone against three farm hands.

The searchers only found their courage when they rejoined the Major. Then, they embellished the details of their search to make it sound much more thorough. They talked bravely of how far they had gone into the woods, each bettering the other, but reported that they saw nothing. Then, the men rode along the creek bed to the next rocky place on which a horse could travel. They made the same half-hearted search. After about five of these so-called searches, they gave up and traveled southeast to rejoin the men laying in ambush. After almost two days, they approached the men lying in wait, who almost fired upon them. They then began the long journey back to camp to report failure, which would not be tolerated well.

After covering the tracks left by his horses, Vlad had found a faint trail that paralleled the main one. Such trails were created by a bull elk or buck mule deer. Vlad was able to use this trail for about a mile.

As Vlad traveled on, he thought he was heading due east. However, thick vegetation had caused him to veer a bit south, and he nearly stumbled into the ambush. Thankfully, the men attempting it had made too much noise, and Vlad heard one of them talking. Even so, Vlad came within 100 yards of them before he heard a low chatter. He quickly returned the way he came for a quarter mile. He wanted to travel down a path familiar to the horses mainly to keep them silent from any surprises that would make them neigh. Vlad then walked a wide two-mile swath around the ambush. He dismounted to slowly lead the horses through the woods. At this point, direction was not as important as avoidance.

Chapter 15
Wild Beauty

Having confronted what he thought were two separate groups of Russians, Vlad believed that the entire camp was after him. He thought that there were two separate groups because they had been behind and in front of him. He figured that it was best to stay off of major animal trails for a while, but that was difficult to do because of the undergrowth and topography. Animals created these trails over time because they were the easiest routes.

Once Vlad had put some distance between himself and the last group of Russians, he stop and marked the path of the sun as it moved across the sky for about thirty minutes. He calculated due east and then headed that way, knowing that the farther east he travelled, the more total land area the Russians would have to search. He doubted that the Russians would want to come too far into the continent. Still, the Pacific coast ran from the northwest to the southeast, and he was concerned that he had not moved as far away from the Pacific Ocean as he had thought. By moving slightly more east than south, he figured that he had at least avoided running into other Russian settlements. While the other settlements may not have been alerted, the sight of a lone Russian from another settlement would have triggered that settlement's commander to hold him until his identity and purpose were fully known. That would have meant certain death for Vlad.

Vlad would not enjoy any comfort for weeks. He was anxious and his nerves were shot. Being hunted would unnerve anyone. At night, Vlad dreamed violent dreams and awoke often. He only got about three good hours of sleep per night. Cracking sounds of limbs in the breeze sounded like men approaching him. His heart raced, and he dry-heaved often from nausea caused by chronic fear.

Moreover, he was beginning to lose weight. He caught cold and even ran a bit of a fever. He needed warmth and nourishment, but the weather was damp and chilly, and he caught only an occasional fish to eat. Because he could not take long to stop and try to capture fish, he began to deplete the dry food that he had stored. At least that lightened his load. He knew that he had to keep moving and fast. He headed in the direction that he believed was east for six days and then, only when he began to get concerned that he might miss civilization completely, he turned slightly south.

As the days passed, he made more maneuvers through streams and over rocky soil. He found a knoll and climbed a tree at the top of it, surveying the vast landscape full of greening trees on the mountains. He saw no signs of other humans, especially no smoke from campfires. After a few more days, he broke down and built a small fire near dusk on a cloudy, misty day. The damp cold weather chilled him to his core. The mist was very thick with heavy low clouds, and the slight breeze was from the southwest, so he figured that no one following him could see the smoke. Since light breezes tend to become variable, he was concerned that someone could smell the smoke should the wind change direction. Still, he needed the warmth. He caught a large salmon in a nearby stream and cooked it. He added a little salt that he scraped off some salted meat, and the cooked salmon was delicious. He had cooked it just to the point of being done, so it was still moist inside. His horses grazed in a nearby meadow. That night, he finally got eight hours sleep, with a full belly and warmth throughout the night.

The next morning, he mounted one of the horses and began to ride in a more southerly direction. Other than knowing his general direction, he was completely lost. By now, he could be in Canada or still in Alaska. He rode for four hours, and then came upon a large bear. The horses sensed the creature first, and he immediately turned around and rode away. The bear was a huge grizzly bear. He had never seen a bear that large, even though he had seen drawings of some bears in Russia. He was able to get away before the horses panicked or the bear thought to cause problems. He cut a wide swath around where he saw the bear and continued onward. He was amazed by the size of the beast. He changed the load in his gun from birdshot to a large lead ball, doubling the powder and seating the ball-shaped bullet tightly against it. He created a super-magnum load. In case he ran into another large bear that took interest in him or the horses, he needed something to stop the bear. Given its size, he hoped the ball would do, but he figured that he would have to hit it in the brain, neck, or spine to stop it cold.

During his journey, he saw elk and caribou, some of which had massive antlers. When he approached them from upwind, they would move away quickly. However, when he stalked them from downwind, he was able to get in close. Vlad wanted some fresh meat and fur to keep him warm. He also thought that antlers and fur would provide him with something to trade, should he ever reach civilization.

As he continued to ride, he saw a group of cow elk grazing in a pasture, and a few younger bulls nearby out in the field. Vlad thought they resembled European deer that he had occasionally seen, but the elk were much larger with broader, meaty shoulders, longer snouts, and darker brown in color. He caught a glimmer or movement in the bushes next to the pasture. It was a massive bull elk. Both of the animal's long antlers branched like leafless trees growing up and back from above its ears. Vlad counted seven points on each side. A century and a half later, hunters would pay tens of thousands of dollars to outfitters and guides to hunt these woods in search of something of its size. Few would ever see, let alone harvest, such a trophy animal.

One of the elk bugled with a sound that terrified Vlad at first. However, he quickly grew to marvel at the sound, which was beautiful and majestic. To a man who limited noise and visibility for fear of who may be stalking him, it was a sound of freedom and power. Certainly, no animal would make such a sound if any predator could get it. Vlad took a moment to look at the majestic animal and the scenery. The pasture - which was probably created by fire and kept low by grazing - and the surrounding hills were indescribably beautiful.

Vlad quietly tied the horses to a tree, grabbed his gun, and went in pursuit. He circled the pasture, trying to keep from getting directly upwind of the massive bull elk, which had bedded in the brush. He knew from trying to approach other elk not to let them smell him. Also, local hunters around where he grew up talked of stalking an animal from downwind. He climbed quietly over rocks and downed trees, taking almost an hour to go just 100 yards. Vlad tried to stay still, but he frequently shivered from the cool damp air. Finally, he was about 35 yards from the massive bull elk and was hidden by the leaves of a bush. He could see the shoulder and antlers of the bull.

He tried to raise his gun, but it felt five times heavier than before. His heart was beating so fast that he could feel his heart moving in his chest, and he thought that the elk could hear it. He finally raised the gun to his shoulder and took aim. The bull caught his movement and stood up, giving Vlad a brief but perfect broadside. Vlad quickly aimed for just behind the shoulder, right at the lungs, which are the boiler room of the huge animal. He fired, and a blinding cloud of smoke blocked his view. He moved around the bush, but really more through it to get out of the smoke. He pressed forward to get a view and began the process of reloading as he went, making certain that he used double the normal amount of powder and seated the ball bullet tightly against it. He could no longer see the animal. He finished reloading and approached the spot where the animal had been, but there was nothing there.

As he stepped on the spot where the animal had been, he thought he had missed. All the younger bulls and cows had bolted. He thought he had nothing for his efforts. He had wasted powder and lead. If anyone was within two miles of him, they would know of his presence from the noise. His hunger and his despair were sharper than ever.

As he examined the spot where the large bull had been standing, he saw blood on the grass and the ground nearby. He also saw what looked to be a spray of blood leading away from the spot. Vlad followed that trail, which was now highly visible. There were just a few gaps in the blood trail until he found the bull elk about 60 yards away, just inside the wood line. His aim had not been true. The heavy trigger had caused him to pull the gun, and he missed the bull elk's heart and lungs. However, the bullet had severed the femoral artery in the rear of the animal. He could not have hit the elk there had he tried, but the shot made for a very effective and humane kill. The massive bull had lost blood at an incredibly rapid rate from the large severed artery as he ran and died while on the run.

As the bull elk bled out quickly, darkness from blood loss overcame it. His last act was to dart slightly to the side into some thick cover of bushes, but he fell almost sideways into them, leaving a large area of pressed down weeds and small bushes. Vlad found him a few minutes after death.

Vlad approached cautiously and prodded the animal to make certain that it was dead. The animal's body was warm and limp. Vlad was briefly hot from the excitement and race to reach the animal, but the ache of chronic damp cold quickly returned. Vlad saw water vapor coming off of the warm elk, so he got down on his knees and laid down against the animal there in the brush to absorb its warmth. He then dug under the animal, placing a carpet of dry leaves underneath to insulate himself from the damp earth. He was sheltered by the animal on three sides, much of it was the soft belly. Vlad stayed away from the blood as best he could, so he would not get wet. He stayed there half an hour bathed in the luxury of warmth. It was a feeling of natural warmth, unlike a fire which always overheated one side of him while the other side was cold. Just like a cold piece of meat is good for removing the heat from a bruised area of the skin, the warmth from the animal's flesh transferred into Vlad's skin, muscles, and bones.

Vlad did not even mind the horrible stench from the musky, gut-shot animal. Enduring the slightly sweet and otherwise sickening smell was a small price to pay for the warmth of the massive animal's body. By even the standards of his day, Vlad's actions were disgusting. However, the instinct and desire to survive caused Vlad to do drastic things. His circumstances necessitated it and constraining forces were removed. While Vlad thought of the stench and filth, he needed the warmth. His dire need made his actions appropriate. Failure to take advantage of this life-saving warmth would have been foolish.

At the point of sleep, a shrill neigh jolted him. Something was near the horses. He grabbed his gun and powder bag and ran as fast as he could towards the horses. He arrived to find a bear circling near one. Vlad quickly raised the rifle from 75 yards and fired. There was a slight delay between the firing of the cap and ignition of the powder. He moved to his left side to see around the thick smoke, and saw that he had missed. In his excitement, he must have pulled the gun during the hang-fire. The bear looked at Vlad as the new subject of his curious interest. Vlad managed to reload quickly while the bear examined him. He realized that he would need to reload with a lot of powder to knock down the bear. Vlad poured too much powder down the barrel, almost three times as much as normal, then pressed the 50 caliber ball bullet down the barrel and rammed it home. He quickly cocked the gun and overloaded the powder pan.

Vlad thought about closing the distance on the bear before firing the second shot, but the bear did that for him, and was beginning to move more quickly, though at a watchful pace. This was the first human that the bear had ever encountered. Vlad raised the rifle at the bear, which was only 20 yards away. Vlad aimed just above the nose of the bear, right between its ears. He pulled the trigger and held the gun on target as it immediately fired. The previous shot had cleared the firing port into the barrel, and the large amount of powder easily ignited. A mass of blood and brains blew out the back of the bear's head. Vlad could not see them because of the smoke, but there was a penumbra of blood, like a red halo, around the bear's head for just a moment. The bear dropped right away.

Not knowing the result, Vlad used the cover provided by the smoke to move back and to the right to dodge the bear should it charge him. He went behind a few trees, reloading as he went. Vlad was good at reloading on the move from his days on the Polish frontier. He hid behind bushes until he could scout for the bear, looking close by and then scanning out. He saw the bear's left rear foot in the air, so he slowly raised his head to see the entire body. Vlad took no chances. He propped the reloaded gun against a nearby tree, aimed at the bear's heart and lung area, and fired again. This time, Vlad stayed put to reload. He then moved further to the right and peered up and over at the bear again. Convinced that the bear was at least incapacitated, Vlad approached it slowly. Only when Vlad saw the massive head wound did he realize that the bear was dead. He then became conscious of the tremendous pain in his shoulder from the recoil caused by the excessive gunpowder used.

Vlad fell down shaking, but keeping his eye out in case the brainless bear somehow came to life. The bear was a huge brown bear, and it would have killed him had he missed or only wounded him. Vlad was in the middle of the wilderness, where man was not necessarily at the top of the food chain. He continued to suffer emotionally and physically. Death could be upon him in a second, either from the Russians or some wild beast, and cold and hunger still constantly clawed at him.

Vlad picked himself up and left the bear there. He went and got the horses, and he rode over to within 20 yards of the elk. He was not sure how to properly skin and gut the elk, but by trial and error, he got good skins and a lot of meat. He kept the antlers attached to a large portion of the skull. The bear's fur would have provided better warmth, but Vlad did not want to be near it. He wrapped the elk meat inside of the skinned elk and fastened everything to the antlers with a small amount of rope from a saddlebag. He started dragging it out by the antlers. Although he needed to take it only 20 yards, he had to cross downed trees and go through bushes. He then had to load it all onto the other horse. He was covered in sweat and was sore all over. When he had finished packing everything, he decided to put a few miles between himself and the location where he had killed the elk and bear. If anyone was trailing him or was nearby, they would have heard 3 or 4 shots to guide them to him and plenty of time to close the distance.

He rode for a few hours, forded a shallow river, and found a good site to set up camp near the water, with some thick brush nearby and a view of the river and the opposite bank. He watered the horses, and they grazed on nutritious grasses that grew along the river bank. He then led them into the shelter of the forest and used downed trees to form a corral for the night.

Clouds moved in as night approached, and it began to rain lightly with a northwesterly breeze. He dug a pit and built a small camp fire at dark. The pit and surrounding brush hid the light, and the darkness hid the smoke, which blew to the southeast. He fixed a make-shift rotisserie and began cooking the elk meat. As it roasted, the fat drippings hit the flame and burst afire. The meat hissed as it cooked. Finally, it was ready, and Vlad took it from the fire.

By other people's standards, the meat was strong and gamey. However, hunger makes food palatable, if not delicious, and it was at least a change from the mostly raw salmon that he had been eating. Most people in the Twenty-First Century have never tasted such meat. If they have, it was usually soaked for days in marinade, covered with bacon, and served along with extra-delicious and filling portions of side dishes in case they could only stomach a bite or two. Vlad had no dressing-covered salad or butter-soaked baked potato, but to him, it was a wonderful as any meal served in an expensive restaurant in Moscow. The meat was as tasty to him as a filet mignon or chateaubriand. More importantly, the meat gave Vlad much needed calories and protein. He had lost 25 pounds over the past few weeks, which had left him emaciated. Vlad consumed about 2 ½ pounds of the meat. Such quantities would cause him some digestive problems later, but for now, the satisfaction was comforting.

Vlad cooked a dozen or two pounds of the meat for later. He then fell into a deep sleep. About 3:00 a.m., he heard the cries of wolves. He jumped, grabbed his gun, threw another log on the fire and ran to check on the horses, which were nervous but alright. He brought them closer to the fire and tied them about 20 feet away. He laid back down, heard more calls and figured that they were about a quarter mile away. Their calls were unnerving, and they were just close enough to where he could not go back to sleep. The weight of the world was back on his shoulders.

At first light, he opened his eyes. He had been in a daze close to sleep. However, a wave of mild anxiety ran through him. He quickly looked around and everything was calm. As the rays of light grew a little stronger, he scouted a bit to see if he had been found. Everything looked fine, but he continued to keep his eyes and ears open. He got some meat and took a bite. It was cold and not as good as when it was sizzling hot. He walked a few yards to a bush and relieved himself at length. He dumped water from the river onto the fire and threw the remaining logs into the river to keep them from smoking later. It was still cloudy, but he did not want to take any chances. He walked over to the horses, and threw some cut weeds and grasses in front of them. The fire sizzled loudly as the water quenched the embers. He put more water where the fire had been to make certain that it would not fire back up and later give a smoky beacon for anyone who might be trying to track him.

Vlad walked back to the river and drank cold clean water until his head hurt. It was delicious and pure, and it quenched his deep thirst. He then checked his gun and made sure that it was ready to fire. He kept it close and felt worried that he had not checked it since he had awoken. He began to pack his gear, which was a noisy task.

All of a sudden, he heard a grunting-type sound and bushes rustling. He raised his gun at the general direction from which the sound was coming. About 20 yards away emerged a grizzly bear, which stood on its hind legs when it came into the clearing. Vlad reached to pull back the hammer and it slipped due to his shaking hand. He tried again and this time it locked. He took aim right at the face. The grizzly and Vlad were looking dead at each other, and the grizzly raised its clawed hands. Vlad aimed a little low because he tended to fire high at times. He pulled the trigger, and the gun fired with a cloud of blinding smoke. The gun kicked extremely hard from the powder charge, the amount of which was dangerously close to that needed to blow apart the barrel. Vlad used the smokescreen to hide as he dove to his right. The bullet hit the bear in the neck just below the chin. It smashed the animal's spine at the brain stem, and the force and shock of the bullet severed an artery. The huge bear fell down paralyzed and incapacitated. Death came quickly to it.

In mortal terror, Vlad scrambled into a bush to hide in case the bear got up. Had Vlad missed the bear's spine or failed to hit its brain stem, he would have had no real chance. Even a heart or lung shot would not have stopped the bear from killing him. Had Vlad missed the bear altogether or only superficially wounded it, the gigantic animal would have been on him quickly, and he would have been breakfast for the bear. The bear would have devoured his thighs first, which contain the most meat. Vlad even may have been alive for the first part of the bear's feast.

When the smoke blew away, he saw the bear lying dead where he had stood. Blood was everywhere and spreading out around the bear's head. Vlad quickly reloaded and shot the bear in the head, so that brains and blood blew out. Finally, realizing that the bear was dead, Vlad dropped to his knees and continued looking at the bear for any movement until Vlad vomited. A rush of nausea mixed with fear hit him hard. He shook uncontrollably. He quickly reloaded his gun and slowly stood up, all the while watching the lifeless body of the bear for any movement and watching the woods for another attacking bear.

Finally, Vlad settled down a little and approached the bear, still with one eye on it and one eye on his surroundings. His gun was ready to fire. Vlad poked the bear with the tip of the gun to make extra certain that it was dead. The bear's lifeless flesh moved little, and Vladimir shot it again out of panic, then quickly reloaded.

Vlad brushed his own thick dark hair off of his forehead. Although not long, it was growing longer, and he usually had it cut before its present length. It was at the stage where its little extra length was annoying to him. He rubbed his eyes and wanted to get out of there as quickly as possible. As part of his strong desire to flee, Vlad did not bother taking any of the animal's meat, although he had enough elk meat. He did quickly chop off the animal's claws. He wanted no trophy or reminder of this event, but he reasoned that he could possibly use the claws as tools or trade with any natives later. He also roughly skinned the bear. From his hard Russian existence, he knew to make use of things, good or bad. It was basic Russian peasant survival, and he had regretted not skinning the first bear. He knew that the fur and skin would be waterproof and warm. It would smell terribly until properly fleshed and dried or until the flesh rotted off on its own, but it was too useful not to take, despite his anxiety and desire to flee.

He quickly packed and rushed to get out of there. He was packed and riding within five minutes of skinning the bear. On top of a horse, he felt he had some degree of protection by the height and the fact that another wild beast would likely strike the horse first and not him. After all, another such bear attack would likely be against a horse first as long as Vlad was on it. He looked around violently as he rode hard. He saw movement in the nearby trees and what looked to be two small bears. The large grizzly had cubs, which frightened Vlad. Like Vlad, the cubs would have to fend for themselves in this hostile place. Vlad gave no thought to the cubs' future. Rather, not knowing bear family dynamics very well, Vlad was afraid that they were part of a large group or herd. He rode for two hours before stopping to allow the winded horses a chance to drink at a stream.

His nausea was finally replaced by slight hunger, which had grown substantially during the last fifteen minutes as the horses rested, drank, and fed. He took a few bites of the elk meat that he had in his coat pocket. After the first bite, he felt even hungrier, and the gamey meat satisfied that hunger. After giving the horses a bit more rest, with his gun cocked and covering all directions with frequent turns that made him dizzy, he crossed the stream and rode along an animal trail for another hour.

As he rode, he began to calm himself. He told himself that the bear must have been quite hungry to have charged him like that. He could have been at a spot that the bear thought was its own. He did not think rationally, and he certainly knew little about bears' habits. It finally occurred to him that the smell of food brought the bear to him, and he would have to be more careful about storing his food. He would need to care for the bear hide, too. He also thought that he would build a larger fire that night, as the bear did not bother him until well after the fire had burned out. He thought he would sleep in a tree, if he was able to sleep at all. It then occurred to him that he had learned as a child that bears could climb trees. He did not know what he should do.

Vlad rode about 30 miles that day. He was able to cover much ground because he crossed a number of fairly level meadows. The woods he went through were open with gigantic trees and little undergrowth. On a hilltop clearing, he could see in the distance beautiful mountains with white capped peaks. He thought of how wild this land seemed in comparison to where he had grown up in his native Russia. There was danger in both places, but here it was a natural danger, except for the Russians trailing him. Here, a wild animal could kill you, but it was part of survival, not out of greed, envy, or spite. "Even so, dead is dead", he thought. He certainly did not want to end up as a meal for some monster of an animal any more than he wanted to be murdered by another man.

Chapter 16
The Travel Onward

At around 7 p.m., Vlad found a creek on the west side of a knoll. He thought he would build a fire by the stream at dark, so that the darkness would hide the smoke and the hill would hide the light. He watered the horses, and found grasses for them to eat along the creek, and made sure that their needs were met, which took well over an hour. Once satisfied that they were alright for the evening, he set out to gather firewood. The days were longer now. Before the sun went down, he climbed the knoll and surveyed the land. He saw nothing threatening. Herds of elk and deer were grazing in different parts of the meadows off in the distance. He then returned to his new camp and built a roaring fire to keep away wild animals and warm the cooling evening breeze. He placed the elk meat in a bag and secured it under a large rock in a nearby ice-cold stream which flowed from the direction of the ice-capped mountains, then placed another large rock over the meat to keep it from washing away.

He kept some of the meat and heated it in the fire, then ate about two pounds of it. This satisfied him, but he wanted something different. He thought that, in another day or so, the meat that he did not consume would be spoiled. Actually, had he not placed it in the stream, the remaining meat would not have lasted the night. It was already beyond the quality that people with an abundance of food would eat.

He remembered a meat preservation method that he had seen in Russia. As a child, he had seen some neighbors smoke meat by laying thinly cut strips near a fire to dry it. He did not remember how to do it, but he tried his best. He quickly cut about four dozen thin strips. He placed – really threw – a boulder from the stream into the fire, then placed the strips of meat on it. The heat from the fire caused the water inside of the fractures in the rock to boil and then hiss as it escaped as steam. As the unnatural hissing sound changed pitch and tone, it put Vlad further on edge.

Vlad took sharper stones and began scraping out the bear hide. He picked up a log that had one end in the fire and used the fire to burn away pieces of bloody meat. He worked hard and fast to make the bear hide usable to him. It would smell horribly for many days and could easily attract the attention of wild animals. However, he needed its protection, and he knew it. It could get him through a hard cold rain or a snow storm while he crossed the mountains.

Before going to sleep, he stacked logs beside a downed tree for a make-shift fortress. Any bear half the size of the one that attacked him would have knocked it down in 2 seconds, but it gave Vlad a small feeling of security. At least it would possibly slow a creature down enough to give Vlad time to fire his gun. He turned the bear hide so that the fur side was against him and used it as a blanket. The fur smelled musky, and it also smelled of feces. The inside stank of scorched raw flesh and iron from blood.

Finally, Vlad's exhaustion overcame his fear, and he was in a deep sleep. As happens when exhaustion overrules fear, fear regains its hold as sleep cures the exhaustion. Vlad woke up several times that night. He carefully made his way to the fire and placed logs upon it. The boulder occasionally screamed as the heated moisture inside it continued to turn to steam and escape through small cracks. He did not realize it, but that heated moisture expanded as it turned to steam, and it could have caused the boulder to explode and injure him.

After adding the wood to the fire, Vlad quickly ran back to the safety of his small fort, his heart pounding all the time. He settled down and slowly went back to sleep. He woke about 3:30 a.m. unable to get back to sleep again, and the sky was beginning to lighten, so he flooded the fire. In all, he had a total of about 4-5 hours of sleep. While he could have used more, it was sufficient for him to function the next day. His body slept long enough to regenerate, but not enough to fully satisfy him.

After killing the fire, he returned to his fort and sat up feeling very groggy. He listened to the sounds of the early dawn, some soothing and some frightening. The ones that frightened him did so only because he was not sure what they were. Vlad watched the pale light in the eastern sky brighten. As the sun rose, he was able to see large shapes, then smaller shapes and finally colors. He watched the horses, which were fine. He looked in every direction, remembering that it was about this time of the day when the bear had attacked. After the sun had risen a bit higher in the sky, he again ventured out of the small fort, and he saw mule deer grazing in a nearby field as peaceful as sheep. He learned by watching prey animals, such as deer. When they were calm and in the open, things were usually fine. When they became alarmed, he knew to become alarmed, too.   When they ran, he learned to grab his gun, protect the horses, take cover, and look for danger.

Vlad retrieved the meat and led the horses to feed upon grasses along the creek. He washed himself a bit. While washing, he saw glimmering, golden chunks in the stream, and he began picking up what turned out to be many gold nuggets. With his gun strapped over his shoulder and with one eye out for bears, Vlad spent a few hours up and down the stream collecting enough nuggets to double his gold collection. This virgin stream had never had a European man walk through it. The gold had washed down from the mountains over the centuries. Years later, streams like this one would be over-mined in a series of gold rushes. Vlad had no idea where he was, so he could not mark a return path in case he survived and wanted to return in later years. After collecting several pounds of gold, he packed and began riding again.

Over the next several days, Vlad repeated his custom of making a secure camp and sleeping 4-5 hours. He rode to the tops of hills to look back to see if he was being followed. He rode along the base of the large mountains until he saw a pass that looked like he could cross. He finally found a pass that he crossed easily despite its high altitude. He had already traveled numerous miles up rivers to where they were shallow enough to cross. These detours added many days to his journey.

After riding about 200 miles from the scene of the bear attack, Vlad finally started to feel a bit safer from the Russians. He felt safe from them in part because he had absolutely no idea where he was. He had ridden up and down so many different streams that it would take an army spread out to find him, given the randomness of his movements. Based on the course of the sun throughout the day, he had tried to move in a southeasterly direction until he reached the mountains.

He was not really lost because he had no idea where was going in the first place, other than south and east, hopefully towards Canadian settlements. The sun kept him from going north toward the cold and ice. He was not concerned about going too far east, because he had learned that English-speaking and French-Canadian settlements were in that direction across the continent. Still, if he traveled towards the southeast, he stood a better chance of more quickly running into an English-speaking town away from the Russians.

He had heard about Indian Tribes as roaming bands of man-killers, but he had incorrectly been told that they were far away and deep in the United States. He had also heard that some of them would trade with white men, so he kept items to trade just in case. However, he believed that he would run into a Canadian settlement long before he encountered such people.

Chapter 17
The Meaning of Freedom

After about two more weeks, the horses were holding up well, as Vlad cared for them as he had his Army horse in Western Russia. He knew when he could push them and when he could not. He understood that they were his lifeline, and he put most of their needs above his, except in situations that meant life or death for him.

While the horses were holding up well, Vlad was tired of riding and sleeping out in the elements. Part of him was becoming more confident that he was no longer being hunted, but part of him was not. These conflicts and the overall ordeal had caused -- and were still causing -- mental and emotional distress. He was able to cope with it for the most part, but he suffered from terrible nightmares every night. When they were not about animals attacking him, he saw the faces of the men he had killed, faces locked in the agony of life being forcibly taken from them. Regardless of the justification, he thought of them with equal horror. Just because he thought he had killed a pursuer in self-defense did not make the fact that he had killed easier.

Vlad rode on with only the desire to press forward. He did not dare to dream too much of life in America or other future happiness. He was so deep in the woods and so far from everything he knew that he simply kept going; day-by-day, he persevered. During that time, he saw large eagles, beautiful sunsets, and rolling hills. His mind was often locked in a dull state, but still his mind's eye recorded what he saw for future recall – should he survive. The scenery was too beautiful to ignore.

Vlad faced repeated failures. A few times, he ran into large lakes or deep rushing rivers. He had to travel for days around the lakes and upstream of rivers to where he could cross them safely. This meant going in a set direction, and with it came the sense that the Russians could easily trap him on the banks.

The lakes and large rivers contained hundreds of thousands of ducks. Vlad witnessed first-hand the splendor and majesty of the unspoiled Pacific Northwest, prior to the market hunters who would decimate the duck flocks a few decades later as the ducks migrated annually south into the United States. He saw mallards, pintail, a few different varieties of teal, and geese. Although he did not know the names of their species, he enjoyed looking at the colors of the individual ducks. Some had iridescent green and blue feathers. One that Vlad saw had a green head ending in a white band around its neck. They were beautiful. Once, Vlad came upon a lake with what he thought were over 10,000 white birds with black wingtips floating on it. They saw Vlad and took off all at once, making an incredibly loud two-pitched sharp sound. They looked like a large cloud as they flew away in under a minute.

Vlad also had to ride up or down mountain ranges for days until he discerned a way around or passes over them. He wasted a lot of time on failed attempts to cross them. Still, his perseverance kept him going. His sporadic travel and turning to go around such obstacles had actually helped to throw the last of the Russians off his trail. What he thought were failures were actually small victories towards his ultimate prize. Even so, it was a grueling ordeal.

After days of riding half-asleep and staying up most of each night scared senseless, Vlad reached a breaking point of mental exhaustion. During the few moments where he felt a little secure, he wondered about the meaning of his life and of the world. He asked himself why he was on this earth and why this earth even existed. He also asked himself what he had done, striking out through a vast unknown wilderness going "southeast" with no real idea where he was heading and with only the hope that someday, somehow he would run into Canadians or Americans. Even if he did survive long enough to encounter such people, he did not know whether they would help him or kill him on the spot.

He second-guessed himself about running from the Russian camp. At least he was alive there. He thought, in time, he could have possibly befriended the camp commander further and maybe even earned his freedom in the years to come. Then, he quickly realized that he would have worked himself to death in that camp. Illness brought on by overwork and starvation would have taken him. He knew that the camp's purpose was two-fold: to provide cheap labor for developing the

Russian outposts into permanent settlements for trade, and to eventually work to death persons who posed problems for the Czar.

Vlad calmed himself with the realization that he had nothing to lose by running. He also realized that he was truly free, although the threat of death and all of the uncertainties he faced diminished any happiness that such freedom brought. He further reasoned that while he had been living free all these weeks, he would not be truly free until he was also safe. He concluded that freedom without safety is not true freedom because the mind is a slave to fear. He knew he must obtain safety to accomplish his complete goal of being free.

Chapter 18
Wild Turkeys

It was late in the afternoon when he stopped near a creek lined with huge trees. There was a large meadow on the other side which paralleled the creek and ran for about one hundred yards long and about fifty yards wide. He watered and feed the horses, then used downed logs for a make-shift pen where three large boulders created a natural pen. He was too tired for a fire, but the sun was bathing a dark fractured bolder with weeds growing out of and around it across the creek in the meadow. He hopped on rocks to cross the creek, then leaned against the boulder and weeds, blending in to his surroundings. Although in the sunshine, he felt the sensation that he was hiding, and he was concealed quite well. He had his weapons at the ready, and he felt as though he was finally wrapped in warm protection. He just sat there and looked at the field as the sun went down. The horses were behind the boulders and some brush, just out of sight.

Vlad sat motionless, resting and slowly eating some dried meat. He saw some huge birds enter and then walk across the meadow from left to right towards the creek and trees near him. They looked like they were eating bugs and the tops of grasses as they walked. He heard purrs and clucks from these strange large birds, which were like dark chickens, but much larger. Then, he saw a bird with a beard, like a brush hanging from his chest, enter from the side. One bird in the flock made a long series of loud cutting yelps. In response, the bird with the beard leaned his head and neck forward and gobbled.

The loud gobble both startled and intrigued Vlad. The gobbling bird then puffed out his feathers and spread his tail into a beautiful fan. As the bird turned, the sun struck it and brought out its iridescent bronze color, with white tips on its fanned tail. Its wings drug the ground as the bird strutted. As it turned, he watched its red, white, and blue head, and the sun reflected a touch of blue or purple off the bird's body. Biologists would later call this type of bird a Merriam's Wild Turkey, and later market hunting would reduce its range primarily down into the continental United States.

The bird actually strutted for what seemed like a minute, and then partially closed its fan. Vlad then heard a bird make another series of cutting yelps. In quick response, this "gobbler" gobbled and strutted again, and the distant bird came charging towards the gobbler. As the traveling bird approached the gobbler, it knelt down and the gobbler clearly bred the bird. Vlad quickly figured out that the kneeling bird was a hen, like a chicken, and the gobbler was a male, like a rooster.

After the brief courtship, the birds separated a little from each other. A short time later, all of the birds began to fly to the branches of the large trees downstream over the creek. They roosted, not unlike chickens, but high off the ground. Vlad remained perfectly still, except to imitate the sounds of the hen. Vlad had practiced making bird sounds as a kid, but he sounded terrible making the yelps of these birds. Since no one had ever hunted these birds, and no predator that they had encountered had imitated their sounds either, they were not suspicious that the yelps were from a predator, much less a human one. However, by their nature, they were cautious and wary birds. Every one of them had experienced a close call with a predator, with most having lost a mother and all of them having lost siblings as young poults.

As Vlad yelped with his mouth, trying to imitate the hen of these strange birds, the dominant gobbler and a smaller one nearby gobbled in response. With both on the roost, they both gobbled loudly. While on the roost in separate trees and high above the ground, the subordinate one was less afraid of the dominant one. In fact, both tried to out-do each other, which fired up the dominant bird even more. This was excellent entertainment to Vlad. It was also a great distraction, which soothed his nerves.

While he sat there, he formed a plan. He would wait until dark, and then, and only then, would he move from his spot. He wanted to remain undetected, as he knew that birds generally could see very well. After dark, he crept over to get some water from the stream, and grab a quick bite of his dried meat. He took a blanket, too, and checked on the horses, then cut a few small bushy trees and put them in front of where he had sat against the rock to conceal himself in the morning from the birds. He planned to try to shoot one of these large birds. It had been a long time since he had roasted chicken or anything like it. Even though these birds were huge and he had no idea how they would taste, he thought of a delicious roasting chicken.

It was a clear, cool night, with a full moon. Because the trees were full of leaves, he could not see the birds roosted just 75 yards downstream along the creek. He did not know that he had fired up the gobbler that mated only a short time before with the hen. That dominant gobbler and a subordinate one were both over four years old and trophy birds by modern hunting standards. The subordinate male would not try to breed, because to even attempt to do so would draw a serious whipping from the dominant bird, which had previously established its dominance.

In a ritual conducted early each spring, the males would fight to determine who was dominant. They used their spurs to thrash each other until one gave ground or, occasionally, was injured or even killed. While a subordinate bird could sometimes sneak in to breed a hen, he did so under possible penalty of injury from the dominant bird.

With his belly full of dried meat and fresh stream water, Vlad settled against the boulder. He wrapped the blanket around himself from his chest down and scattered cut weeds and grasses all over it to conceal himself further. As he lay there, his thoughts drifted to a warm bed and a roaring fire. He was at least warm under the blanket and weeds, and he quickly drifted off and slept soundly for several hours. He desperately needed this sleep. The rest restored his muscles and his mental health. Vlad needed the security of believing that he was hidden in case the soldiers had been tracking him. The safety of the large smooth rock and vegetation were comforting. The hours of deep sleep allowed him to awaken even before the sky began to turn pale.

As the light of dawn made visible the large trees and the contour of the field, Vlad began calling. He tried purrs, since they were the easiest for him to make. He also tried yelps.   It did not take long for him to hear loud gobbles in response to his awful, but loud, yelps. He kept making them and enjoyed hearing the gobbles in response. With each gobble, his heart raced and jumped into his throat. It was a loud and incredible sound, unlike anything else he had heard in nature before, a magnificent call from a most majestic bird. Vlad thought that these birds were splendid, and they were the most fascinating and beautiful birds he had ever encountered. Not even the bald eagles he saw were as wonderful as these birds.   However, he was also hungry, and something that he imagined tasted like chicken would be a great change from dried gamey meat and oily fish.

After the sun rose high enough for him to clearly see the colors of the grass and trees, the birds started to fly down and assemble somewhat. Leading the way was an old hen, coming to see what squawking hen was trying to take away her gobbler. The dominant gobbler followed close in tow, strutting and gobbling as he came. The other gobbler followed, but only put out his tail fan briefly. He stayed several yards behind the dominant gobbler. Whenever the dominant bird would turn his way, the subordinate one would quickly retract his fan and prepare to flee. He knew the sharp piercing pain from the more aggressive bird's 1 ¼ inch spurs.

Vlad waited until the flock was about 15 yards away. He wanted to fire sooner, but the approaching birds were all staring directly at him, or so he thought. He could not move for fear of being seen until he knew that the birds were close enough to the cut bushy trees that their vision of him was blocked. He watched them study everything around him as they came, but he sat motionless, with a hat brim covering his predatory eyes. He had his gun raised and resting on his knee. His drab brown clothes matched the color of the rock on which he rested, and the weeds covering him broke up his outline, helping him to stay concealed.

The hen circled around the downed trees to get a better look. As her face was briefly hidden by leaves and while the other birds' eyes also were obscured by the make-shift blind, the big gobbler came into view in a small gap between the leaves. Vlad moved his gun slightly to center, aimed it, and quickly fired. Just before he moved the gun and fired, one turkey saw him and made a putting sound. The shot reached the bird just as his muscles were starting him on his escape.

The bullet entered the bird low, sawed through the top of a drumstick, and entered the bird's gut. The rest of the flock ran and partially flew away, squawking and flapping as they fled. Vlad got up, ran to the bird, and swung at its head with the butt of his rifle. The flapping bird ducked the swing, and stumbled along on the ground very quickly. Without use of his leg, the bird could not run and propel himself airborne. Vlad did not want to use more powder and shot, but he did not want his bird to get away. He swung again and again with the rifle, until he connected, knocking the bird unconscious. Vlad then grabbed the bird by the neck and dispatched it quickly.

After killing the bird, Vlad knelt quietly, spreading out its wings and tail fan. He admired the beauty of this fascinating creature, and he began to understand that there truly must be an all-powerful God to create such a wonderful bird as this. Vlad always felt a little guilty when he took an animal's life. It humbled him. Animals provided food and sometimes clothing, but it was easy to regret having to kill them to survive.

It took Vlad thirty minutes to clean the bird the best he could, using stream water to wash it. He saved the beautiful fan and numerous feathers, thinking that they might be useful in trade, should he ever find someone friendly enough to trade with him. He liked the meadow, and the horses desperately needed a rest, so he decided that he and the horses would rest for the day there. He built a small fire, keeping smoke to a minimum, and began roasting the bird. He allowed the horses to rest and graze freely close by. He organized and repacked his gear.

When the bird was cooked on the make-shift roaster, Vlad took huge bites of the fleshy bird. It tasted a little wilder and gamier than chicken, but to a hungry man wanting a change from the super-gamey red meat and oily fish he had been eating, it was wonderful. The red meat and fish had saved his life, but the same taste of it over many weeks, along with the smell of the animal skins, made it less and less palatable.

Vlad finished both breasts and a thigh. He packed the rest and took a bath, using rounded stones to clean himself. The water was cold, but as before, Vlad thought that it was important to minimize his smell, so that bears would be less likely to pursue him. Vlad did not know that a bear's sense of smell was so powerful that it could still smell him, washed or not. However, the baths served to keep his odor less than that of the horses and the meat that he carried. If a bear attacked again, it might go after one of the horses or the meat itself. It also rejuvenated him mentally to be clean from a bath.

Vlad moved his provisions just into the wood line to keep them out of view. He had been moving for so long and in such differing routes, he thought he had at least a day's lead on anyone following. Vlad was exhausted. His body was feverish from stress and lack of sleep. He walked over to a different boulder than the one against which he had slept. It was a fractured boulder. As he approached, he heard something rustle in the leaves as it moved away. He thought it was a small animal, such as a mouse.

Vlad sat down, leaning far back onto the boulder. His knees were up in the air as he comfortably reclined. He was largely hidden from view in case someone approached, and he had his gun propped up on his right knee. The stock was pressed into his chest by the weight of his right and left hands, which were interlocked across the top of the stock. With a few minor adjustments, the gun balanced there perfectly. When his hands tired, he slumped down further and pulled the gun back, so that it balanced without him needing to have his hands across it.

In a short time, he fell fast asleep. He slept for about thirty minutes before he heard the rustling sound return. He thought he would lay still and surprise the small animal. Instead, he saw the flash of a snake whipping around the corner of the rock. In a split second, it passed within inches of his right elbow and went under his knees.

In Russian, Vlad yelled, "It's a sn-snake!" Because he was reclined so far back, he had to place his hand on the ground to get up. He placed his left hand beside his left hip, knowing that he would get bitten. In one motion, he leapt up and away from the snake, which moved and coiled up in response to the surprise movement. It rattled at Vlad. Unbitten, Vlad quickly took his gun, placed the muzzle near the snake's head and fired. The bullet tore through the snake, but the muzzle blast alone blew most of the snake's head off. The lifeless snake then twisted in its coil as its central nervous system kept moving its thick body.

Rattlesnake meat is quite delicious, and Vlad had another meal of fresh meat available to him. However, he did not think of that. Rather, he thought of his close encounter with certain death. One of the Russians in his camp had been bitten by a snake and died after three agonizing days. He had seen that snake, which someone else had killed. The rattle, the shape of this snake's head, and its markings convinced Vlad that this was the same type of snake. Vlad thought that one bite from it meant certain death, even though that was not necessarily true.   In fact, had the snake bitten Vlad it may not have injected any venom. Many snakes bites of people who surprise the snakes result in either no venom being delivered or a large dose from a snake too young and scared to regulate the venom stream. That would not have mattered to Vlad, even if he had known it. That snake scared him worse than the Russians. His fear was based upon strong instinct, but also upon years of self-taught, unjustifiable fear of all snakes.

As Vlad realized that he was unharmed and safe from the snake, he thought that he had now fired twice from the same general location. Anyone hearing the first shot would be better drawn to his location by the second one. Safety dictated that he move on. Plus, he was in no mood to stay in this area. He drowned the fire, packed his horses, and headed off upstream northeast for a half mile, then turned due east. He wanted to change his route slightly in case he was being followed. He traveled on for about three hours and then came to a nice brook with a smaller clearing. He still wanted and needed to take the day off as a day of rest for himself and the horses, so he took care of the horses and laid down in the field, away from rocks and downed trees. Tall grass concealed him. He fell asleep for a few hours in the warm summer sun, and awoke to the falling light of evening. Although it was still light, he built a fire, more for protection than warmth, and he ate the rest of the turkey. He checked on the horses and laid back down.

Chapter 19
The Depths of Fear

Vlad spent a sleepless night. The stress of his experiences came back to him. Fear of the snake quickly yielded to fear of being captured. He worried that he had yielded valuable time to possible pursuers. He obsessed that they could be watching him and planning their attack. He could already be trapped, so he panicked, quickly gathering the horses, packing up, and leaving at first light. He put out the fire with gallons of creek water to prevent the smoke from continuing to betray his position. He thought how stupid he had been to build a fire during the daylight hours on two consecutive days, when smoke could be seen for miles. Two smoke trails plus gunshots would give any pursuer a more definitive understanding of his location and heading.

Vlad headed off in a northeasterly direction for a few days before again turning southeast to try to outpace and outmaneuver anyone who saw the smoke from the fires and tried to cut him off along his previous route. As he rode, he sank into a dark mood. He pressed the horses as hard as he dared to put miles between himself and the beautiful meadow and last camp site. He would allow his horses care, but he told himself that he would not let his guard down again unless and until he reached true safety. He would press forward as hard as he could.

On one afternoon, he was so tired of riding that he got down and led the horses on foot. He moved quietly along a game trail next to a creek for a short distance. He continued his practice of moving upstream along the banks of deep or fast-moving rivers or creeks until the water was shallow or slow enough for a safe, uneventful crossing. Frequently, animal trails led to the best place to ford the waterway. As he walked along, it was not uncommon for him to see squirrels and other small game.

On one particular occasion, he was wading in front of the horses to give them a break when he came upon a furry black and white animal. It was bigger than a squirrel, but it looked just as harmless. The animal appeared to puff out its fur, and it raised its tail straight in the air. Vlad did not stop or alter his course. He just keep walking straight for the black and white little fur-ball with the tall tail. Vlad thought sarcastically, "What a little terror you are. I could snap you in two." Just then, the animal sprayed Vlad with the foulest smelling juice. The horses even jumped back and turned to move away, but they were hit by some of the juice, too. It was concentrated and smelled like decaying flesh.

Vlad wiped his face with his sleeve and withdrew at once. The black and white animal moved away and into some bushes. Vlad wanted to shoot it for what it had done, but it was gone. He tried to collect the horses, but they moved away a few feet whenever he approached them. He took 15 minutes to wash off in the creek, even scrubbing with mud. He tried scraping himself with rocks and washed out his clothes thoroughly. Even after he got much of the juice out, the smell remained, as it would for days thereafter. At least he got clean enough so that the horses would accept him. He knew to watch out for big animals like grizzlies and brown bears, but if he had to watch out for the small ones too, he did not think he would like this new world. He thought that he may have made a mistake and that maybe he should have fled west to one of the German-speaking countries, or to France or England back when he was raiding Polish villages. However, as a Russian, he would have never made it far into the Polish frontier.

The next three nights were filled with terror from the weather. Huge thunderstorms, lasting hours each, cleansed him and the horses, but robbed them of precious rest. Vlad spent all of his time caring for the horses and keeping them from running away. He was drenched with cold rain, night after night, with no comfort. Everything with which he could start a fire was wet, except for his gunpowder wrapped in the bearskin along with other supplies, and he had to save the gunpowder for future use. He managed just six hours of sleep total during those three nights, and he was nearing his mental end.

Vlad came upon more mountains, but saw what looked to be a pass. It was very high, but it looked as though he could cross it. He camped for the night near the base, figuring that he could begin early in the morning, go up in altitude, and descend on the other side before the cold of night hit him. He was wrong. As he neared the top, he could see that the pass ended in a valley with tall mountains all along the other side. He would have to return the way he came. He traveled up and down a few more false passes before he finally found a real pass and crossed the mountains.

As Vlad started his descent from what proved to be the final pass, the weather changed from mild and sunny to windy and cloudy. A tremendous storm was approaching. He was so high in elevation that there were piles of unmelted snow nearby. As the storm quickly approached, the temperature plummeted, and he had to find shelter. He went into a small ravine and gathered downed trees for shelter and a wind break for the horses, then unloaded the horses and brought his possessions over to where he would stay. He built a wind break for himself in a stand of dense small trees a little further down the ravine. The wind was so bad that he could not make a fire, so he got the bear hide and put it over himself and his store of gunpowder. He laid down next to the wind break and curled up for a long night. Amazingly, the bear hide kept him warm and dry. Its wind and water-proof qualities had certainly kept the grizzly bear comfortable in this hostile climate.

Although he was warm and dry, the wind howled all night. If he slept at all, it was only for a few minutes at a time. He tried to lose himself in made-up dreams, but the wind frequently brought him back to reality. It was a tough night.

In the morning, he awoke to find that one horse was gone and the other was too sick to move. The missing horse had simply vanished. The sick horse was hot and acted lame. Vlad looked at its frail body and then at his own. They had been through the same experiences, but he had at least rested as he rode on a horse. He felt extremely sorry for the animal. Horses had always taken care of him, carrying him quickly away from all sorts of dangers. He would have never made it this far without the horses, as surely the Russian pursuers would have overtaken him quickly without them. He actually cried as he contemplated what he must do. He thought of leaving the horse, but he knew that a wild animal would tear it to shreds in a painful death. Vlad feared that if he fired his gun, the sound would betray his location, and he was going to need every advantage now that he no longer had any horses.

Vlad found a large stone and knocked the horse unconscious in one blow. He then slit the horse's throat and cried again as the horse bled to death. The horrible experience of killing the horse in this manner made Vlad fall to the ground. He hugged the horse as life left it, shaking and crying hysterically. He was worse than a child with a favorite pet killed in right front of him. Although deeply bothered by the brutality of how he had to kill the beloved horse, Vlad's cries were not only for the horse, but for his own predicament. He cried out of fear of the future and out of the traumatic events of his journey, and also from sheer mental and physical exhaustion. After what he had been through, there was no false bravado. He had endured more than he ever dreamed he would, and he knew that he was near his end. Still, he knew that he needed to press onward until he could not anymore.

Vlad wanted to continue searching for the other horse, but he was too afraid of losing his belongings if he wandered away from them. He could take 20 steps and have trouble seeing them in the brush. Instead of risking their loss, he jettisoned all but the essential items and his turkey fan, ate all the food he could from the jettisoned pile, and then took his consolidated pack with him as he made one sweep move around his camp site to try to find the other horse. He finally saw horse prints, but they ended near a stream with hard rocky soil on the other side. Plus, the animal was headed back the way he had come, and Vlad was not about to travel in that direction. In all, the search was a futile effort, as the horse had circled and returned the way it had come to try to escape the storm.

Vlad collected himself the best he could and walked down the mountain's southeastern slope. He decided he would walk until he absolutely could no more and then fall down and sleep. He had to keep things basic in order to survive; unfortunately, his necessities weighted him down. He took the gold, the bear skin, the rifle, powder, flints and ammunition, knives, some food, and a variety of small items that he thought useful. When combined, they were very heavy. He could have taken twice as much weight in necessities without truly having enough. As he walked, he kept a careful eye out for anything shadowy on either side of his route. His rifle stood ready to fire on his impulse. His dark somber mood was only countered by his high anxiety and fear. He still had his survival instinct, and he did not want to become dinner for a wild animal. He had to stop and rest a lot more frequently than when he alternated riding the horses. In fact, as the day wore on, he had to stop and rest every few hundred yards. He kept pushing onward, despite his dark mood and fatigue.

He was bound and determined to reach some non-Russian person, even if they were hostile to him. If he were to die here alone, he would have died on his own terms, and that was better than dying of starvation, injury, or disease in a Russian camp. Still, he would have died without accomplishing his main goal. He had to keep pressing.

Vlad stopped to take a drink from a creek. He ached and hurt all over. The bitter cold water tasted almost sweet. As he guzzled it in, it began to quench his deep thirst. It satisfied and comforted him. The water rushed over the nearby rocks as he drank, making a loud noise. Since his sense of hearing was impaired by the noise, he frequently stopped to look around. He drank for about three minutes in all, including breaks to check his surroundings and to allow the water to go down. The cool feeling in his core felt good, but the water was so cold that it gave him a headache. As it began to quench his thirst, he felt bloated and no longer found the water's taste desirable.

After drinking about a half-gallon, he decided to make it to some higher ground, look around, and find a campsite for the night. He pressed onward for about a half mile, then saw some boulders. He climbed them to the top and could see about a quarter mile, so he got his general bearings from watching the sun and rested, soaking in the beautiful scenery. Something about the protection of high ground on top of boulders made him feel more at ease.

Vlad reflected upon the beautiful scenery he had seen on his trip. He wondered how much farther he had to go before he would encounter a human settlement. He wondered if he would ever encounter a settlement. He figured that as vast as the wilderness was, he could walk in large semi-circles until some beast killed him or until he got injured or sick. He figured that he should be getting close, but he had thought that for a few weeks now, and he really did not know. He only knew that death was behind him.

As Vlad took in the scenery, he felt a dread of having to climb down. He wanted to stay on top of the boulders and sleep there. Unfortunately, they were not at all comfortable for sleep. With exhaustion and fear, he returned to the forest floor and walked for another mile.

Finally, too tired to go any farther, he gathered wood, placed it a few feet high in a circle around three large trees, and dug a hole for a fire. He started the fire with some difficulty, then collapsed into sleep with his gun at the ready. When he woke up a few hours later, the fire had burned down to embers. He threw a few small logs on the embers, and it started going again in about 20 minutes. Vlad listened to the forest noises, and imagined dreadful beasts. He could sleep no more. He had three and a half hours of sleep after having walked for sixteen hours. He would need more for the day ahead, but the fear in his mind kept him from it.

Vlad's psychological condition was growing worse with every mile. He could not bring himself to believe that the Russians were not still following him. Just when he thought that might be true, he imagined that giant bears were lurking behind every tree. Vlad had lost 40 pounds of muscle and health. He was highly susceptible to disease or injury. Still, he pressed ahead; he had no choice.

Chapter 20
First Contact

After a week of anxiety and depression, Vlad came to a river. He just could not bear another wet and cold river crossing. He thought that he would rather walk five miles to avoid even wading chest deep for ten yards. He had a large and heavy pack that could drown him if he stepped into a deep hole in the river, and there appeared to be an animal trail that ran beside the river. It was easy walking, so he followed the trail upstream. He was still dreading his usual practice of crossing the river at a rocky place or at a point where the trail turned into the water from an animal crossing. Although that crossing should be shallow all the way, he would still get wet -- at least below the waist -- and cold all over.

Vlad was beginning to think that he had headed in a hard north-northeasterly direction, even though he had used the sun for direction. He estimated that he had traveled farther than he actually had. Disbelieving even the sun's location, he was beginning to get disoriented and confused.

As he walked along the trail, he saw human footprints in the mud, but he did not comprehend them at first. He had seen thousands of footprints in the mud before. Then, it hit him: they were human footprints. However, he was startled at first and reached for his gun for protection. He wondered if they were made by a Russian looking for him. He did not know whether the men who had followed him earlier had gotten in front of him as they had before. He then thought it may have been made by an Indian. He was reminded of the stories about Indians and how some would kill white men. He could see the imprint of a heel; like the heel of a boot. From the stories he had heard of Indians, though, he reasoned that Indians did not wear boots with a thick heel, and the overall impression was different from Russian Army boots. He slowly began to get optimistic, but he was still very concerned.

Vlad decided that the best way to find out the identity of this person was to go into the woods and wait to see if he returned. He waited for over an hour, and finally got tired of being afraid and waiting in the woods. As his fear subsided, he was ready for human contact, friend or foe. He decided to follow the path farther, and he saw the footprints of different people wearing different types of boots and shoes leading to rocks strategically placed for crossing the creek. After about fifteen minutes, he saw smoke in the distance. He crossed the creek cautiously and circled around. He neared a small village from the east side. He heard a strange language being spoken, and he saw men and a few women tending gardens and washing clothes. He thought it was English they were speaking, and he did not hear any Russian.

Vlad placed the slinged gun across his shoulder so that it would not threaten the people he encountered. He quietly began walking out into the open and then called out, "Hello!", keeping his hands where they could be seen and smiling, as a disarming gesture. The villagers looked a bit apprehensive, and one of them took a step closer to a nearby gun, but stopped and looked at Vlad. Vlad was absolutely filthy. He spoke to them in Russian, but no one understood.

Hearing a commotion, a missionary minister named James Tedder came out of a cabin and walked over to Vlad with his hands raised to show he meant no harm. The minister could see that Vlad was in horrible condition and knew immediately that he had been lost in the woods a long time. He spoke in English pointing to himself, "My name is James," with emphasis on his name. After several tries, Vlad understood that the minister was saying his name. In response and pointing to his own chest, Vlad said, "Vladimir." Vlad then spoke the only English sentence he had ever learned. His father had taught it to him as a young boy on a warm Russian summer day. He said, "Love is patient and kind." James smiled and, beaming with joy, repeated, "Love is patient and kind." He then placed his arms around Vlad, surprising Vlad at first. Then, Vlad broke down and cried. A flood of emotions from the ordeals that he had been through these many months overcame him. He had survived so much, from the capture, to the trial, to Siberia, to Alaska, to escaping, and to being hunted. He survived going through uncharted wilderness for weeks on end and living off the land. He could barely communicate with the villagers, but the caring heart of the minister broke the language barrier.

The minister took him home and fed him hot chicken and potatoes. Vlad ate bread brought by other villagers and drank fresh milk. The villagers brought food and milk more out of curiosity and to have a better look at him than anything else. Three of the village women boiled water and brought him soap. He took a long cleansing bath. James collected clothes for him to wear and gave him a pair of shoes. The clothes and shoes were well worn, but extremely valuable given the difficulty of obtaining such items in the far Canadian west. Vlad looked at the shoes and understood from such a generous gift that these people meant him no harm.

As the days passed, Vlad came to understand that the village was called Fort St. John. It was a supply center and fur-trading post located on the Peace River in what is now Northeastern British Columbia. Fort St. John was about 570 miles in a straight line from Skagway. Vlad had wandered many more miles than that as he went around mountains and rivers and avoided the Russians.

Vlad worked chopping wood and carrying anything heavy for the villagers. He more than earned his keep. He stayed with James, and he helped the minister keep fire wood. Vlad cut and stacked about three months' worth of firewood, which was no easy task, since the fire burned always, summer or winter. He fished and hunted. He shot elk, field dressed it, and brought it back to camp. In fact, he shot and cleaned three elk in one day, and cooked them for the villagers to show his gratitude for their help. The villagers made side dishes, and they all had a huge feast.

While he could not yet communicate well with the villagers, he began to learn English words. He found that the language was almost impossible to understand when spoken rapidly by the villagers, but he could speak words. James taught him the alphabet at night and read passages from the Bible.

Vlad was concerned that word of his escape had spread to the other Russian settlements. He feared that the Russians from his camp or another would eventually come to the village, since it was a trading outpost. He desperately wanted to communicate with James that his life was in danger. He learned more and more English and then, one evening after working especially hard that day on learning English, Vlad was able to communicate both that he had escaped from the Russians and that he was concerned that they might kill him. At first, James thought that Vlad actually wanted to make contact with the Russians and explained that they usually did not come this far east. Rather, there was a trading post village about thirty five miles to the west where they sometimes traded. Vlad learned the word "danger" and kept saying "Russians danger."

After hours of talking, well into the early hours, the minister figured that Vlad was not trying to contact them and that his life was in danger by staying in the village. There were plenty of fur traders and merchants who traveled between the two posts, and, eventually, one of them would see a Russian in the other village and communicate Vlad's presence at Fort St. John. James was part of a missionary group sent by the Methodists. There were other missionaries in villages east of there, so he decided to arrange for Vlad to travel to Henry Clark, a missionary friend in Grande Prairie, an outpost town located in what later would become the Province of Alberta.

The following day James sent a letter to his friend Henry Clark by a merchant leaving that day for Grand Prairie. He described Vlad's plight, as best he understood it, and asked the missionary to respond with news of whether he would help. Within ten days, James received a reply from Henry by a returning merchant. James was to send Vlad to the missionary via a merchant traveling to the village or any other way he could get him there. Henry promised to write to the other missionaries in other outposts east of there, and they would move Vlad a few hundred miles east for his safety.

James thought that Vlad's plight was similar to that of escaped slaves that other ministers back east had assisted in escaping from the southern United States. Also, James decided to pen a letter of greeting for Vlad to show to the other missionary-ministers on his route east. The letter described Vlad's flight as comparable to escaping slaves and asked them to assist in saving Vlad's life. It mentioned Vlad's hard work, too. James knew that most of the missionaries despised slavery and would be willing to do their part to keep Vlad from returning to the work camps or being killed.

In the meantime, Vlad continued to work very hard chopping wood and even using mules to haul long sections of timber from the woods into town. He virtually kept the town supplied in firewood, for which the townspeople admired him. He was tall and had gained muscle from eating the nutritious food that the villagers fed him and from chopping and hauling wood. In exchange for chopping and stacking wood for a barber, the barber cut and shaped Vlad's dark hair, and gave him a close shave. The barber placed a hot wet towel on Vlad's face, which was pure luxury to Vlad. Vlad was so relaxed and comfortable that he almost fell out of the chair asleep.

Vlad worked especially hard during the last few days he was in the village. He repaired fences as well, and continued to add to the supply of firewood. The villagers' gratitude overflowed, and most of them did not want him to go, but they gave him generous portions of salted elk meat and dried beans for his trip. Some even gave him a few pelts to help him keep warm and to sell to generate a bit of cash when he got to a new home. None of them knew of the gold that Vlad had kept hidden in different places. That gold now was securely around his waist in a belt and in a carrying sack, which never left his side.

Vlad thought about the gold, especially the gold that he had stolen in Poland and Russia. He thought that he needed every ounce to establish himself when he got to America. However, he felt guilty about the stolen gold. James spoke of his wanting to stay at Fort St. John, but he was running out of supplies and had no funding. Vlad knew that James would not accept stolen gold. Vlad also knew that he could not return the stolen gold to the rightful owners, but he wanted it to go to good use. Vlad thought how James had saved his life and had done a lot of good in Fort St. John. Vlad decided to hide the gold in James' cabin and only tell him of its presence as he left. He took out the gold and separated the stolen gold from the many nuggets he had found. Remembering a Bible passage that he had read with James while learning English, Vlad took ten percent of the nuggets and put them with the stolen gold. He felt right about doing this and hid the gold in a cupboard, placing the turkey fan, which had sentimental value to him, over the gold to conceal it. Since he could not return the gold, he thought this was the next best thing.

Chapter 21
Close Calls

Early on a Friday morning, near the end of August, Vlad and a merchant named Louis Minton were set to leave for Grande Prairie. Before leaving, Vlad spoke with James at length, thanking him for everything he had done. In broken English Vlad told James, "One hour I gone, look in cupboard. Promise you wait, one hour." James looked strangely at Vlad, but then smiled and, shaking his head, said, "I'll wait. I promise." James thought that Vlad had carved a present for him, like a special bowl. James would later find the gold and be astounded. Given how frugal he was, it would keep him at Fort St. John for years, which meant that he could keep serving as a missionary to people who desperately needed ministering in the wild and hard life of a frontier town.

Vlad and Louis set off for Grande Prairie on a trading path that initially led east out of town before it turned southeast. They both sat on the wagon, which meant a slow and bumpy ride. Vlad was very sad to leave James, who had saved his life, but he was thankful to be putting further distance between himself and his former countrymen. He and Louis rode for several hours, then they stopped to water the horses, drink cool, refreshing mountain stream water, and eat a bit of salted meat.

Louis was not sure what to think of his Russian acquaintance; he could hardly communicate with him.

He looked down on Vlad as an inferior, but he also felt a little sorry for the Russian. He tried to imagine what life would be like on the run. He understood that Vlad had basically been a slave of the Russians in an Alaskan camp, and that Vlad had been a soldier who was sent to Siberia and then on to Alaska. Louis had no idea that Vlad had a small fortune in gold nuggets stashed away, or else Vlad's life would have been in jeopardy from the opportunistic Louis.

As they rode throughout the day, Vlad kept an eye on the surrounding woods. He watched, as would any good soldier, for any sign of danger, keeping his hand near a pistol that Louis had entrusted to him for their protection. Vlad still had his long gun, but a pistol could be aimed at something much quicker, such as a bear or a robber. Louis thought that once they stopped and camped, bears would be the greatest danger they faced. However, using a pistol could inflict a nasty wound that would simply enrage a bear. Just as with a rifle, the bullet had to hit the brain or spinal column. Even a shot through a major artery might not kill a bear before it could seriously injure or kill someone. A shot to the gut or even to a lung would eventually kill the bear, but it too would do little to stop the attack. Although not as powerful as a rifle, the pistol offered repeated shots.

Vlad and Louis rode throughout the afternoon. They stopped about one hour before dark, took care of the horses, built a fire, and set up a comfortable place to sleep. They were careful to eat their food and then replace it into tightly tied thick bags to stop the smell from permeating through the woods and attracting bears. They kept the fire large and their weapons nearby. Vlad knew that he no longer had to worry about the smoke from a large fire attracting the Russians. With that concern strongly decreased, they built an extra-large fire to keep away bears; however, Vlad's wary nature was not convinced that he was totally free from the Russians. Occasionally, he felt free, and there were times that he truly wanted to let down his guard, but whenever he tried, his anxiety would return. Now, he was again facing the threat of bears. The threat of death, no matter the source, was enough to reignite his anxiety.

Sure enough, during the first night, a massive female brown bear took interest in their food, which she could smell through the bags. The bags did not stop the smell from reaching her powerful nose. She wandered around the edge of the woods just inside the wood line from the small clearing in which they had set up camp. She made a low growling noise, which Vlad instantly heard. He said, "Louis . . . bear!" He and Louis had agreed to take watches throughout the night for their mutual protection. Every two hours, they switched, so that the one standing guard did not become complacent and fall asleep or fail to keep a good lookout. The bear could smell the food, but the roaring fire signaled danger to her. Vlad caught a glimpse of her and aimed his rifle, but she disappeared before he could fire.

When the bear finally got downwind of the men, she turned and walked quickly away, making a large racket. Vlad said, "I think she's leaving," which gave him some comfort that she might not return.

The night passed without further incident, although neither Vlad nor Louis got any sleep after the bear sighting. When morning came, they ate breakfast consisting of a few eggs given to them before they left and salted meat, which they cooked like bacon. They drank fresh, cold stream water and filled their water jugs for the day's journey ahead. They kept a good watch for the bear as they moved around. They moved out about an hour after first light. They had a total of 130 miles to cover between Fort St. John and Grande Prairie, and they just wanted to get to Grande Prairie as quickly as possible.

Back at Fort St. John, a group of Russian soldiers arrived two days after Vlad and Louis had departed. Fur traders had told them of the powerful Russian man in the village. James avoided the Russians, but the villagers misled them into thinking that Vlad had befriended them and then stolen a fast horse. They said that he had spoken of traveling southwest towards San Francisco in hopes of catching a ship home to Russia. They also told the Russians that he was traveling alone and that they had no idea exactly which route he would eventually take, except to first go along the trading path that led southwesterly out of town. Believing the story, the Russians headed southwest for a few days, then simply gave up and returned home by another trading path. Vlad was finally free of them, and he did not even know it or of the close call.

Had Vlad stayed in the village for just a few more days, he would have been a dead man. The Russians would have held the townspeople at gunpoint, taken Vlad outside of town and killed him to prevent him from escaping. If nothing else, they would have brought back his head as proof of his death. His head would identify him, and it would be easier to transport that his entire body.

As Vlad traveled, he kept one eye towards the rear, just in case Russians were following. He had suffered much emotionally over the past months. Even with the care he had received at Fort St. John, he was paranoid, anxious, and simply shattered inside. His hands shook, and he was in need of a long rest. However, rest was something that had been eluding him. He had worked hard in the village to impress the villagers. He needed their food and comfort. He knew that he could not have lasted long in the woods. As soon as fall and winter came, he would have died, and he knew it. He had used the spring and summer months to escape and get to a new place. Now that it would soon be fall, he must get somewhere safe for the winter and then think of traveling farther east next spring: the spring of 1857.

As they traveled, Louis tried to teach Vlad some more English words. Louis would point to an object, like a tree or rock, and pronounce its name. Vlad would repeat it. Unfortunately, there was not a huge array of objects around for learning, but the men did the best they could, and Vlad learned.

Chapter 22
Grande Prairie

After another three days of traveling, Vlad and Louis reached Grande Prairie without any more bear sightings. Louis took Vlad to the local mission where Vlad met Henry Clark. Vlad spoke broken English to Henry and was able to express his gratitude to Louis. He returned Louis' pistol to him and gave him the rest of the salted meat that some of the people in Fort St. John had given to Vlad. After wishing each other well, Louis then left to continue on his route southward towards Hinton. From there, he planned to go to Jasper, across the Yellowhead pass, and westward back into British Columbia.

Vlad found that constant immersion enabled him to learn English quickly, although it was still quite difficult. Vlad would lay awake at night trying to think only in English. It was frustrating, and he felt like he was drowning. He felt stupid for forgetting words he had already learned, which reminded him of the monumental task of learning a new language. He not only had to learn new words, but also grammar and an alphabet far different from his native Cyrillic Russian alphabet. Spanish, Italian, and French derived from Latin to a large extent, so many of their words could be understood by speakers of any of those three languages. Likewise, English had many Latin root words, but it also had many similarities to German. However, Russian was not similar at all to English or to French, which he also could expect to encounter further to the east in Canada.

Vlad hungered to succeed at his new language. In his broken English, Vlad spoke to Henry about his willingness to travel east. He wanted Henry to know how he would work to earn his keep until then. Henry could see the enthusiasm in Vlad's eyes. He invited Vlad to join him in a hearty meal of fresh chicken and vegetables in the mission house.

While a motherly cook named Mildred prepared the food and table, Vlad fell asleep in a large soft chair, with his feet propped up on a stool. Henry fell asleep in an identical chair. Vlad was exhausted from chilly northern nights keeping watch and bumpy roads that were more like rutted animal paths through the forest. In about an hour, they were awakened by the cook to enjoy home cooked biscuits, chicken, potatoes and gravy, carrots, and cabbage. Both men ate until they were stuffed, and then discussed Vlad's desire to work his way east. Later, Henry showed Vlad to his room, where Vlad slept soundly until the next morning.

When they had both awoken and were at breakfast, Henry told Vlad, "Usually, our guests just stay a day or two and then continue traveling west. However, I would be delighted to have you stay longer. You could work around the mission to earn room and board while we plan where is best for you to go. What I am trying to say is that you are welcome to stay for as long as you'd like." Although this mission was more established and better funded than James' outpost, Henry showed Vlad many projects needing completion. Vlad repaired the steps leading into the mission house and re-roofed a stable.

As the days passed, the mission's firewood supply reached an all-time high. Vlad worked hard by day, ate heartily, and slept soundly at night. Henry and a few of the villagers taught Vlad more English, and he learned a bit every day. The nourishing food, the social companionship from the English lessons, and even the hard work with an accompanying sense of accomplishment helped to heal Vlad's frayed nerves and mental problems. It returned a sense of balance, security, and order to his life. The missionaries also taught him about prayer. Vlad became a Christian, and he prayed earnestly to understand God better and for God's help.

Chapter 23
An Opportunity

A few weeks after Vlad's arrival, it was early October of 1856. Henry returned from preaching and rode up to the mission house. He would set out for two weeks every month and ride a circuit, preaching in a different town, village, or outpost every day. On this trip, he had gone all the way to Edmonton to get extra supplies needed for the mission during the upcoming long winter. Henry called Vlad from his work to come to talk with him in the mission house. As they sat down by the fire, Henry told Vlad that during his travels preaching, he had met a farmer near Edmonton who had recently lost a son in a logging accident; a tree fell and crushed him while he was clearing trees to make crop land. The farmer had another son and a couple of daughters, but needed extra help on the farm right away. Vlad wanted to go, so that he could begin working his way east.

Henry explained, as best he could, that the farmer would feed, house, and clothe Vlad during the long winter and spring. After the crops were in the ground, the farmer would pay Vlad a small amount of money, but most of Vlad's pay would be room and board. After the spring planting was completed, Vlad could leave, or he could choose to stay should he and the farmer come to an understanding, which would be completely between the farmer and Vlad. Henry started to worry about the farmer taking advantage of Vlad, but one could look Vlad in the eyes and know that for all the goodness in his heart, cheating him would not be wise. From the stories Vlad had told Henry of his escape, Henry knew that enslaving him would be impossible.

Henry also told Vlad that the farmer's wife had been a French teacher back east. Although she could not speak Russian, she understood how to teach languages, and she could help Vlad learn English. After about fifteen minutes of explanation, Vlad finally comprehended the gist of it. Henry talked with Vlad for another ten minutes to make sure that Vlad understood. Vlad was amazed at the charity that the missionaries had shown him. He saw them as being people who gave to him without taking or even expecting anything in return.   Their actions motivated him to want to work to help them, which he did around the missions in both Fort St. John and Grande Prairie.

Vlad saw the human side of the missionaries as well. They were people with faults and flaws, but something more motivated them. They tried to put the interests of others above their own. The fact that they had faults and flaws and still helped so many people impressed him even more. These people had left homes and families and traveled to the middle of nowhere to minister to people living in the wilderness. They had given up so much and, yet, they were so happy. Through giving, they had found inner peace, and that made an indelible mark on Vlad's life.

Vlad agreed to go work for the farmer. Henry told Vlad that Vlad would need to travel to Edmonton, and there was a group traveling there in about five days. Henry would write letters of introduction for Vlad and also letters for him to give to the head minister in Edmonton so that he could contact the farmer. During the next five days, Vlad worked as hard as ever at the mission. He single-handedly finished cutting enough firewood for the mission to have plenty for the entire winter. His strength and stamina had increased from the hard work and nutritious food. Proper nutrition had been a missing component of his life in Russia, but now he was in the best physical shape of his life.

Henry gave Vlad an old Bible and continued to teach him English from it until Vlad left. Although old, it was very valuable because books were scarce in Western Canada. Vlad had been a quick study as he learned to speak and read. However, even for native speakers, the "King James" version of the Bible that Henry had given Vlad was not easy to read. The original draft was written in the early seventeenth century in England. While it was considered a highly accurate translation of the original Hebrew, Aramaic, and Greek, it was written in English that was spoken 250 years earlier in England. The difference between that style of English and the English spoken in Western Canada in the mid-nineteenth century was vastly different, especially with the accents of the Western Canadians. Their pronunciation of certain words made the words sound entirely different to Vlad. That difference made it even more difficult for him to learn English, but he did learn it, slowly but steadily. Many portions of the Bible were beautifully poetic to Vlad. He found the "love is patient and kind" verse that his father had taught him and that he had repeated to James when he first entered Ft. St. John. However, in the King James Version, it read, "Charity suffereth long, and is kind."

Finally, the day of Vlad's departure arrived. Once again, he was saddened to leave and humbled by the kindness that Henry had shown him. Henry hugged Vlad and thanked him for all he had done around the mission. He also introduced Vlad to the members of the party, who were all trusted parishioners of Henry's. The journey went quickly, but still took ten days. The weather turned colder, and they had their first snows. Vlad had his bear skin to keep himself warm, and the group built roaring fires each night with huge blown down logs that Vlad hauled to the campsite.

When they finally arrived, the head minister, George Carlisle, immediately sent word to the farmer through an assistant pastor heading that way to preach on circuit. The church at Edmonton was made of stone and also had a small stone parsonage and barn on the grounds. It was a permanent establishment, rather than a missionary outpost. The farmer arrived within a few days. In the meantime, Vlad did odd jobs around the church. Vlad also explored some of Edmonton. He was amazed by all the supplies for sale. George introduced Vlad to the farmer, whose name was Luke Smith. Luke was impressed by Vlad's height and build. He asked Vlad some basic questions, and after Luke had rephrased a few questions, Vlad understood and answered them to Luke's satisfaction. Luke told Vlad that he had to return to the farm immediately, but the farm was several hours away and the sun was very low in the mid-afternoon fall sky. George insisted that they spend the night and get started at first light.

Something about Luke did not sit well with George. George told Vlad, "If you would prefer, you are welcome to tell Luke that you plan to stay and work here. You have been such a big help, and you are welcome to stay and work at the mission." Vlad declined, saying in broken English, "Luke son died. I want be like James and Henry." Vlad added, "But, I talk with Luke tonight to see if I see a problem."

Vlad spent the evening getting to know Luke. Luke showed a friendly, even gregarious side. He completely disarmed Vlad of any concerns he might have had. Vlad thought they would become fast friends, as close as he and James and Henry had been. However, George stayed nearby watching Luke closely. He made a mental note to have one of the circuit riders stop by Luke's farm occasionally to check on Vlad. In the morning, Vlad left with Luke in an open wagon. The ground had frozen, which made the trip bumpy, and it started to snow with the wind in their faces.

Chapter 24
Luke's Farm

As Vlad and Luke left town, Luke spoke to Vlad about the work that needed to be done. "You'll need to work sun-up to sundown clearing the trees and stumps to make fields for planting. You'll also need to milk the cows before and afterwards, and clean the barns once a week. You'll have part of Sunday off, but only if you finish everything that I've told you to do during the week."

Vlad did not understand much of what he said until they stopped and Luke drew on the light snow covering the hard ground. Vlad still didn't understand that he would be doing hard manual labor about 80 hours per week. Luke also expected Vlad to do all of the dangerous work. Luke had no intention of losing another son. There was very little law and order in these parts, and Luke knew it. He thought he was the law, at least as far as Vlad was concerned. Had he known that Vlad was wanted, he would have used that to try to enslave Vlad further. Even without that knowledge, he figured he could do what he wanted because Vlad was a foreigner who didn't speak the language well. Luke also knew that he could keep Vlad a virtual prisoner because Vlad could not travel across country in the winter. He did have some neighbors, though, so he had to be a bit careful.

After a couple of days traveling, they arrived at Luke's farm. Vlad met Luke's wife Sally, his daughters Nancy and Victoria, and his son Joseph. Luke showed Vlad the barn where he would stay in a storage room. Luke told Vlad that in Vlad's spare time, he could put in an old stove. They moved a bed into the room and Sally brought in a few quilts. It was already cold, and Vlad would need much more when winter came. Vlad ate with the family, and Luke spoke more about all the work he had planned for him. The first order of business was cutting the felled trees from the cleared field into fire wood. Vlad understood some of the words, but was lost as to Luke's meaning and intentions.

Before supper, Vlad went with Joseph to see the farm. Joseph showed Vlad a mule and cart that he could use for hauling firewood. With harvest over, Joseph and Luke would be busy repairing equipment and fences, tending to the animals, and winterizing the farm, including the house. Luke asked Joseph to make sure Vlad understood not to become romantically involved with Nancy or Victoria. Vlad understood that plainly. Since these were two of the ugliest young women Vlad had ever seen, he thought to himself that Luke had nothing to fear. After seeing the farm and eating supper, Vlad then retired to prepare his room for the night. He thought how he would use some of the wood to build an outer wall and fill it with corn stalks and wheat chaff to insulate it from the cold winter winds. He also would use bark from firewood he cut and anything else he could get, including mud.

Vlad looked at the old stove, which had a hole in it, and he wondered how he would make it work without filling his room with smoke. He planned to cut a hole in the ceiling for the smoke pipe and to insulate that area with sand or dirt to prevent fire. Vlad then made his bed and went to sleep. He was tired from the bumpy trip and the soft worn out old bed felt good to his body. He piled the quilts and his bear skin on top of his bed to keep himself warm during the chilly night in his unheated room.

Luke woke Vlad very early the next morning, long before first light. In a grumpy tone, he told Vlad, "Go milk the cows and then get to the felled trees and begin sawing them for firewood right away." Vlad asked, "What about breakfast?" Luke snapped at him, "Get to work and quit being so lazy. If you don't hurry, I'll make you clear twice as much as planned!" Although Vlad did not understand all of Luke's words, Vlad resented Luke's tone, and Luke's facial expressions and demeanor conveyed what his words could not. Vlad planned to work hard without being told, but he did not like being ordered about like a slave. Vlad got dressed and milked the cows. Then, with just a lantern for light, Vlad hitched the mule to the cart. By the time he finished that, a gray milky colored eastern sky gave him enough light to head towards where he would work. After only a hundred feet or so, Vlad stopped at the well to draw up a large drink and to fill a bucket for the morning. The water partially quenched his hunger, but he still wanted breakfast and needed energy to work hard. He saw Luke eyeing him with contempt, and Vlad wondered why. Vlad thought that he would only take so much, but he wanted to make this work well, so he held his tongue for now.

Vlad went out to the field and cut a cart load of wood from the downed trees with the crude saw in just over two hours. He planned to bring the sawed logs back to the barn and split them with an axe. He finished the water and was very hungry. He returned to the house with the cart full of wood, and Sally called him to breakfast. Joseph and Luke had fed the animals. Luke told Vlad not to eat too much. Vlad ate anyway. In response to Luke's statement, all the promises that Vlad had made himself about trying to hold his tongue evaporated. He decided right then that he was going to do what he thought best and if Luke tried to mistreat him, he would have none of it. Luke gulped down his food. Before Vlad could finish, Luke was finished and told Vlad, "Get back to the field before I whip you!" Vlad looked at Luke with a cold stare for about 10 seconds. The look was full of hate and death. It made the rest of the family nervous. It took Luke a few seconds to see it. When he did, he asked Vlad what he was looking at and repeated his command. Vlad quickly stood and told Luke to go outside with him.

Luke went and, once outside, Vlad and Luke looked each other in the eyes. Luke started to swing at Vlad, but Vlad hit Luke so fast that Luke could not avoid the blow. Vlad hit Luke so hard, the family thought Luke was dead. Joseph went towards the house to get a gun, but Vlad grabbed him by the arm and told him not to do it. Luke started to moan, and Vlad spoke to the family. Against his better judgment, he told them of his hardships with the Russians and of his escape. He told them of what he had endured for freedom and that he would never again be enslaved. Vlad told his story in broken English, but he knew enough words to convey part of the horror of what he had experienced. When he finished, he told the family that he would get his belongings and leave.

Sally stopped him. She told Nancy and Victoria to look after their father and told Joseph not to harm Vlad. She asked Vlad not to leave; they desperately needed him. She promised him that if he did not leave, she would make sure that things were different. Sally apologized for her husband's actions, explaining that he had been different since the death of their other son. Vlad told her that he wanted to stay and would be a big help to them. He promised to work hard, but he needed to be treated properly. She promised that he would be well treated. She told him to return to the field, and she would make things right with her husband.

Vlad did not have many options. The prospect of leaving the farm in a hurry and having to watch his back for Luke was not appealing. Vlad figured that Luke would tell his neighbors some fictitious story of how he had tried to rape his wife or one of his daughters, and a group of farmers would trail him and try to kill him. He would not even be safe back with George in Edmonton because the law would believe Luke and arrest him there. Winter was fast approaching, and it was too cold to set out east without anywhere to go.

Vlad left to go to the field with a heavy heart, keeping an eye on his back the entire time. Vlad also kept a pistol with him, hidden at all times. While in Edmonton, he had taken a little of his gold to the assayer's office there and sold about £50.00 British Pounds' worth. From there, he went to a gun shop, traded his rifle, and bought a nice Colt black powder six-shooter. He liked the pistol that Louis had leant to him, and he wanted a nice American pistol of his own. This one was a bit expensive, but it was state-of-the-art. If Sally was unpersuasive and Luke and Joseph came after him, he would need it.

Sally spoke with Joseph again, and got his solemn promise not to seek revenge. She told Joseph that she saw a fire in Vlad like that of her father, and he had killed two men when she was young who had mistreated their family, which was why her family had fled so far west. She told Joseph that his father was in the wrong, and no good would come from seeking revenge against a man who had acted to protect himself. Joseph thought like her and agreed to give Vlad another chance, and he promised to work to change his father. However, he told his mother that if Vlad ever laid a finger on his father again, he would kill Vlad.

When Luke came to, Sally spoke to him harshly about mistreating Vlad. She told him that Vlad was protecting himself and that Luke had treated Vlad like an animal. She told him that Vlad was out in the field even now working hard and that he only wanted to be treated well. She told Luke that things would be bad for him in her eyes if he did not act like a gentleman towards Vlad. She also told him that Vlad would surely kill him like her own father would have if Luke tried anything else. Luke's pride was hurt when he agreed to act differently.

During the following weeks, Luke and Vlad slowly worked at getting along. Luke occasionally spoke in an overly authoritative tone, and Vlad tried not to allow it to bother him. Vlad worked hard, and the entire family was impressed by what he accomplished. Still, Vlad did not feel comfortable there. He wanted a different situation where he admired his boss, and he wanted to continue going east in hopes of someday reaching America.

Vlad worked hard at night to fix his room, even though he was exhausted from the day's work. Soon, his room was well insulated with the stubble and chaff of grasses and wheat that had been discarded after the recent harvest. He coated the outside and inside boards of the wall cavity with mud for wind-proofing. The mud made the room look terrible, although it resembled a stucco cottage. He also made a type of ceramic out of clay from a creek bed that he heated super-hot. He used that to fix the stove and to protect the flammable wall and its contents from the hot stove pipe. It was crude, but it worked very well. Vlad placed an old quilt in the rafters and placed straw on it. He created a well-insulated space. When he burned small dry pieces of wood, he could heat the room to close to 90 degrees, even when it was bitterly cold outside. However, he knew that he had to be careful, because the stove would glow red hot and make noises that sounded like the iron or mud ceramic might crack. He did not run the stove that way very often, but got it toasty warm for a couple of hours when he had finished working for the day and let it die down before he went to sleep. He sat in his room reading maps and relaxing by the light of an oil lamp. While Vlad tried to make it wind-proof, there were some cracks that allowed fresh air to enter the room. Those cracks added fresh air to an otherwise stifling room.

The family did not visit the inside of his room, so they did not know how warm and cozy it was. Luke had forbidden the women from entering it, and he and Joseph had no reason to see it. Luke wanted to stay ignorant of what he thought were Vlad's difficult living conditions. The family stayed in the farm house thinking they were better off than Vlad. However, the house was drafty and cold. They had to pile under quilts on top of their beds to sleep comfortably. Even so, their faces were cold from the frigid air, and the tips of their noses hurt from the cold. If they had to get up in the middle of the night, they would shiver for a minute or two even after they had returned to their beds.

During the long winter, Sally taught Vlad English and a little French. Vlad studied hard and learned quickly. She had saved her written lessons from her teaching days in Edmonton, and they helped her to teach Vlad. He learned to read and write more words and even to write paragraphs. Sally taught Vlad well enough so that he was able to write letters to James, Henry, and George. In the letters, Vlad again thanked them and he told them how he was doing and of his future plans. Once, on a trip to Edmonton, he delivered one to George personally. He gave the other two letters to a fur merchant who was leaving shortly to travel to Fort St. John through Grande Prairie. He agreed to deliver the letters for a small fee, which Vlad gladly paid him.

After a long winter, the weather broke for a day or two at a time, with intermittent cold spells, until spring finally arrived. Vlad had cleared, sawed, and split an amazing amount of wood. With the help of a couple of mules, Vlad, along with some assistance from Luke and Joseph, had removed stumps from over five acres of land, which now could be planted. When time came for planting crops, Vlad worked very hard at it. Just as soon as the seeds were all planted, Vlad had completed his obligation to Luke, and at dinner he told the family of his intention to leave. He packed his belongings that night and got ready to leave the following morning. However, Luke was not about to let him go.

At first, Luke told Vlad that their deal was for him to stay through harvest. Vlad told him that was false and that they could easily resolve the matter by contacting George Carlisle in Edmonton, who had helped broker the deal. Luke knew that George would side with Vlad, and he knew that the two preachers who had visited the farm over the winter and asked about Vlad had been sent by George to check on him. Luke made other excuses, but then simply asked Vlad to stay. Vlad said that it was time for him to leave. This would always be the Smith farm and there was no real future for him here. Plus, now was a good time to leave because the crops were all planted, and with summer approaching, it was the best time for Vlad to travel unknown distances east; it gave him ample time to find another farm to work the harvest and stay over the winter much farther east.

The next morning, Vlad said good-bye to the family, and he especially thanked Sally for teaching him English and a little French. Vlad traveled about two miles on foot away from the farm when Luke came after him on horseback. Luke had a gun in his hand and was intent upon forcing Vlad to return. Vlad saw him approach from about a half mile away and knew it meant trouble. The road curved as it went into the woods. Vlad hid in the woods and let Luke pass, making certain that his own pistol was ready to fire. If Luke confronted him, there would likely be shots fired. Vlad was again in an awful predicament.

Vlad decided that he had come too far to allow Luke or anyone else to stop him. He climbed a tree over the trail and waited for Luke to return, knowing that Luke would realize Vlad could not have gone too far and turn around. It did not take long for Vlad to see Luke riding cautiously up the trail towards him with his gun drawn. Luke was looking all around him, but not up. When Luke was under him, Vlad jumped and hammered Luke, who dropped his gun from the startling impact. Vlad jammed his pistol into Luke's neck and cocked the hammer. Vlad told Luke, "Coming after me with a gun? You want to make me your slave. I bet if I don't kill you, you'll go into the next town and make up some story about me. Why shouldn't I just kill you now, hide your body, and take your horse?"

Luke trembled with fear and begged for his life. Vlad hit Luke under the eye with the barrel of his pistol, and the skin over Luke's cheek bone immediately swelled. After several seconds of begging, Luke finally pushed Vlad and reached for his gun, which had fallen nearby. Vlad yelled at him to stop, and Luke froze. He eyed the gun and then Vlad. His body stayed poised ready to grab the gun. Vlad slowly walked over to the gun and kicked it away.

Vlad knew that he would have to kill Luke to ensure his freedom. However, he just could not do that to Sally and the family, and he was tired of killing. He told Luke that he would put the guns away and the two would fight to decide if Vlad stayed through harvest or left. If Luke won, Vlad worked for room and board through harvest. If Vlad won, Luke would let Vlad go and give him his gun. Luke arrogantly agreed, but planned to shoot Vlad if he got a gun in his hand. It took about ten seconds of pounding for Luke to cry out for Vlad to stop. Luke had suffered a terrible beating of at least ten blows to the head and body. He felt the tremendous force of Vlad's strength and realized that he was not to be taken lightly. It sobered Luke to the reality of Vlad; a person who could not be enslaved just because Luke thought that he was inferior. Vlad had once again fought for and won his freedom; he briefly thought how hard it is to be free.

Vlad picked up Luke's pistol and told him, "If you follow me, send another after me, or lie and tell anyone that I've done you wrong so that they come after me, I will hunt you down and kill you!" Vlad took additional pains to describe that he would do to anyone Luke sent to come after him. Vlad also told Luke, "I'll return to your farm to kill you when you least expect it." Vlad made a convincing speech. He did not want to do it, but he hoped that persuasive words following such a sound beating might prevent Luke from trying anything.

For the next several days, Vlad watched his back carefully. He slept off the trail and walked parallel to it when he could. When he neared towns, he circled them instead of going through them. By doing this, he was able to avoid making contact with anyone. If Luke followed, there would be no witnesses in town to testify as to which direction Vlad had gone. They would be clueless. For anyone following, each town offered multiple directions that Vlad could have traveled.

After traveling over 200 miles on foot, Vlad arrived in Battleford, a village in modern day Saskatchewan. There, he sold Luke's gun and bought some food and a good pair of socks and boots, which were very expensive but needed. He still had plenty of gold nuggets, and he again set out east. He walked for three weeks, catching rides with people on wagons between towns as he went.

Chapter 25
Saskatchewan, Manitoba, and Western Ontario

As Vlad traveled, he reaffirmed his plan to go as far east as he could that summer of 1857. He remembered that James and Henry had both told him that the West was more lawless than the East, and that was true of both Canada and the United States. People in the West were so far removed from the cities and established government of the East that they more often took the law into their own hands and created their own rules. Luke was an example of this. Being an immigrant who was not yet completely fluent in the language, he was a natural target. Also, a number of immigrants, including Russians, were arriving in New York City, and Vlad thought that he could more easily fit in there. He decided to try to get north or northwest of New York State in Canada and spend the winter of 1857-58 there before heading down to New York City during the spring of 1858. He wanted to learn the language better and save some more money before he tried to establish himself in New York. Plus, if he got to New York City in the spring and things did not work out, he would have time to travel somewhere else and find employment before the next winter.

Since harvest was still a few months away, he decided to work a few days to make some money. He could earn at least enough to pay for his food as he traveled, which would prevent him from depleting his money or having to cash in more gold nuggets. Vlad spent the rest of the spring and most of July of 1857 traveling across Saskatchewan and into Manitoba. He worked for a week in Saskatoon at a general store loading wagons. It was hard work, but it paid reasonably well. From there, he was able to join a company hauling wagons loaded with fur pelts to Winnipeg. This offered him free travel, food, and small wages. From Winnipeg, he traveled to Fort William, now Thunder Bay, in Western Ontario.

In Fort William, he found work at a general store, loading wagons, stocking shelves and doing everything else he was told to do. While loading a wagon especially fast and efficiently one day for a farmer, the farmer told him that he needed someone like Vlad on his farm. Vlad had wanted to leave the store because it was a seven-day per week job; he ate, slept and lived at the store, and he barely earned enough money to offset his expenses for things that he desperately needed. The farmer lived farther northeast around Lake Superior, about five days away, and he offered Vlad good terms. With the summer waning, Vlad decided to go work for the farmer, so he quit the store, collected his last wages, packed his things, and left with the farmer, whose name was Daniel Joseph Green. The store had constant turnover, anyway, so the loss of Vlad was no big concern. In fact, another man took his place that same day.

Daniel was a no-nonsense but fairly kind man. He was worried about his getting his crops harvested in a couple of weeks. The two left by wagon that afternoon and rode well past dark. Vlad was concerned that they would wreck as they rode after dark because he could not see a thing. They finally stopped to rest. At the crack of dawn the next morning, which was just after 5 a.m., the farmer woke Vlad, gave the horses a quick bit of food and water, hitched them, and they all left, riding as long and as far as the horses could stand. After another two days of travel, they finally arrived at the farm near Cameron Falls, Ontario.

Daniel asked Vlad, "Vlad, you unload the wagon while I unhitch and care for the horses." The horses needed much caring for after the hard journey. Daniel's wife, Mary, his two sons, and his three daughters all came out to greet them. The two sons had managed the farm while Daniel was gone to town for supplies. Daniel introduced Vlad, and they were glad to have a new face to help on the farm and to tell them new tales. The two sons helped Vlad unload the wagon, and they all went into the house to eat. They then showed Vlad where he would sleep, and he began work the next morning.

Vlad had Sundays off. He went with the family to church in a nearby crossroads community. He spent Sunday afternoons readying his small shack for the upcoming harsh Canadian winter. As before, he insulated it with straw and dirt. He even placed plenty of straw above the ceiling to insulate it and propped up boards in the room from floor to ceiling to reinforce the ceiling. It was unsightly, but very functional. The whole family helped him and gave him odds and ends to use.

Vlad worked hard and got along well with Daniel and his family. The family was easy to like. Daniel was all business concerning the harvest; it was life or death for his family, and a good harvest meant a comfortable winter. However, he was not selfish like Luke. Vlad worked long days, but so did everyone else. They tried to have fun doing it, they got the crops harvested, and they had enough to sell a good amount at the market back in Fort William.

During the cold winter, Daniel's wife Mary helped Vlad with English. She also helped him turn his bear skin into a fur coat with an old blanket cut and sewn into a lining. This coat kept him warmer than the bear skin alone as he worked outside doing the chores that could be completed with snow on the ground. The family included him in Christmas and taught him many Danish customs that Mary's parents had brought over from Denmark. This included special pastries that the children loved to eat. While some of the customs were a bit young for Vlad since they were geared towards children, Vlad still enjoyed them. Although the youngest of the Green children was twelve and the oldest twenty-one, they all enjoyed the customs, too. Vlad especially appreciated being included in the family and learning how loving families interact.

One of the daughters flirted with Vlad, and he was attracted to her. She was fourteen, and Vlad was mindful not to ruin this good situation by letting it go anywhere. He was not prepared to marry, and only bad could come to him if he pursued her affections and they did not marry. However, he was still a young man, and he thought of her a lot. In fact, one time she was alone with him and they kissed. He enjoyed every minute of it, but told her he had to leave that spring. They were alone a few more times and again kissed, and it was all Vlad could do not to go further with her, but he knew she was not what he wanted. He did not want to treat her as Elena had treated him, so he finally made sure, as best he could, that he was not alone with her anymore.

When spring finally arrived, Vlad was torn about leaving because the family had been so nice to him. He even stayed on and helped a week after completing the spring planting and then, with extended goodbyes, he left to go towards Quebec. Daniel had been generous in his pay. Vlad thought about the difference between Luke and Daniel. He worked hard for both, but they were so vastly different in how they viewed and treated other people. Daniel was full of love, and his family reflected it. Luke was full of strife, and his family suffered because of it even though Sally often rose to overcome it.

Chapter 26
A Business Deal in Ottawa

Vlad caught a ride with a neighbor who attended church with the Green family and who had business in Sudbury, Ontario. Vlad reaffirmed his plan to go into the United States through New York State, because it was more populated and offered the best opportunities.

From Sudbury, Vlad bought a ticket on a commercial coach to Ottawa. He thought of how easy his trip would have been had there been commercial coaches like this one running from Alaska here. He arrived in Ottawa and got a nice but relatively inexpensive hotel room. He then set about looking for work by going to the farming supply stores.

At one store in Ottawa, Vlad was talking with the owner about possible farmhand jobs when a farmer overheard them. The farmer approached Vlad and asked about his experience. Vlad told the farmer about his journey from Russia to Alaska and how he had worked on farms across Canada. He omitted the part about escaping from a Russian prison camp because he did not want the farmer to think he was a criminal, or for anyone to think he was wanted by the Russians. He told the farmer that he was willing to work for room, board and standard wages for boarding workers in that area. He said, "I will work during the summer, through the winter, and until after the spring crops are planted and the weather is good for traveling." He and the farmer spoke for a while to get to know one another, and they even talked of their experiences in the armies of their respective countries.

The farmer's name was John Harris. He was a widower with three daughters, Mary, aged 17 (almost 18), Rachel, aged 16 (almost 17), and Edna, aged 15. He had gray hair and wrinkled skin. The sun and bitter cold winters had weathered him both inside and out. His wife, who also was named Mary, had died delivering Edna, so the girls did not remember her. John had no sons, but a late cousin's son, William Jones, lived at the farm and helped him. William had no other close family. John was getting older and needed more help than William and the girls could provide. John told Vlad that the farm was located a couple of miles east of Rockland, which was on the Ottawa River about 25 miles east of Ottawa.

John was careful to screen Vlad as best he could to make sure that he was not bringing a criminal into his home. He read the now tattered letters written by Henry Clark and Daniel Joseph Green. Vlad could not show him the one from James Tedder because it spoke, albeit poignantly and favorably, about his escape from the Russians and his ordeal getting to Fort St. John. John was impressed by Vlad's work ethic, which was mentioned in both letters. John laid down strict rules for Vlad. Vlad could eat with the family and even visit in the house after supper. However, Vlad must not touch his daughters. John warned him that if he were caught even kissing one, he would be forced to leave that minute, regardless of the weather. John said he would watch him like a hawk.

Vlad never agreed because John did not ask for his agreement; this was a stern warning.

John was extra careful. His daughters were gorgeous, and he knew it. He could not help but notice that they were well developed and that most young men in the area found them pleasing to the eye. Although he knew that they were all fairly self-controlled, he feared that his daughters were at an age where their curiosity might overcome their judgment. However, without a doubt, he knew a young man like Vlad would need little enticing from any of them. After all, he had met their mother while working on her family's farm, the same farm for which he was now hiring Vlad to work.

John would not have hired anyone, but he had too many acres of land to be worked for himself, his daughters, and William alone. William was not a great deal of help, anyway. John knew he simply must have more help, and Vlad seemed perfect for the role. As for Vlad, he had not yet seen the girls, and his thoughts were on work and making a living. Besides, he figured the girls looked like their father, and he did not want to get tied down to a rural Canadian farm when he was so close to New York and fulfilling his dream. He could work one more year and be in the United States with enough money to establish himself by late spring.

John had more business to attend to in town before he went to stay at a friend's house, so he told Vlad, "Meet me right here tomorrow at 8 a.m.," to which Vlad agreed.

Vlad went back to the hotel and packed. He awoke at 6 a.m. and paid for a hot bath. He got dressed up and even slightly slicked back his full, black hair with some lotion. His cold steely eyes and strong features made him look even more impressive. Vlad thought that his appearance would make John feel confident about hiring him. At 7 a.m., Vlad ate a hearty breakfast and checked out. He arrived fifteen minutes early, but John was already there waiting as if Vlad was late.

Chapter 27
The Harris Farm

When John saw Vlad, he told him, "Ah, I, ah, I've been having some second thoughts about this." Vlad was crestfallen, but not overly worried. Vlad told him, "I'll find another farm. Goodbye." John stopped him and told him, "My second thoughts are that . . . , well, never mind. You're welcome to work for us, and, ah, please come and get aboard so we can get started towards the farm." The farm was a couple of miles east of Rockland, so they had almost 30 miles to travel.

They arrived late in the afternoon, and John went inside first to prepare his family for their new guest. John then brought Vlad in to meet everyone except William, who had left the farm without saying where he was going or when he would return. Vlad met Mary, Rachel, and Edna. When Vlad first saw Rachel, his eyes locked on her. She was thin, with thick black hair that laid close to her head and tapered down her feminine neck. She had soft blue eyes and creamy porcelain skin. With just a glance, he could tell it was incredibly soft. She had a length of hair that always fell over one eye. She tried to brush it back, but it fell just the same. It made her even more beautiful and desirable.

Rachel glanced at him, turned away, and quickly looked back. Their eyes met for what seemed like ten seconds, which felt awkward, but they could not tear their eyes away from one another. They finally did for fear that the rest of the family would notice. Vlad could not help himself. He was infatuated, if not in love. He had fallen hard, and he did not even know her. It did not matter. She was infatuated too, and she could not help herself either. They were introduced, and were distantly courteous to one another, not wanting their facial expressions to betray their thoughts.

After the introductions, the entire family, except for William, worked to set up a bunk in an outer building for Vlad. John and Vlad cleaned out the furniture and other belongings that the family had stored in the modest one-room structure. Mary, Rachel, and Edna swept, placed linens in the room, decorated it, and tried to make the room comfortable. However, they made it a bit too feminine, as if they were decorating it for a female guest. Vlad did not mind. After months on end being out in the cold, spitting sleet and rain and exposed to bears and rattlesnakes, linens and lace were very welcome, as was the girls' thoughtfulness.

John and Vlad placed an old stove in the room. They cut a hole into the wall near the ceiling and ran a stove pipe through the hole. They insulated it with thick clay from the creek, which would harden when dried, and placed small flat stones into the clay on the outside to help deflect water. Mary and Rachel placed a small table and chair in the room, and Edna placed an oil lamp on the table to give Vlad light for reading during the night. Edna also placed a pitcher for water and two bowls, one for washing and the other for relieving one's self during the night so that a cold nighttime journey to the outhouse would not be necessary. It was a small room, but it was very cozy and comforting. Vlad had a bed with sheets and quilts, so he put away his bear skin coat that had kept him so warm on many frigid nights outdoors.

Just before supper, William returned to the house and was furious with John for hiring someone without consulting him. John reminded William that this was his farm. Although John had never led William to believe that he would inherit it all rather than John's daughters, William thought that he had earned that right. John told William that Vlad would help them until the crops were planted the following spring, and then he was heading to America. This made William less angry, but he was still upset that John had not consulted him first.

During supper, William looked at Vlad and questioned him at length. John and the girls frequently interrupted, as they wanted to learn all about their new friend. Vlad was still in his new clothes and looked very handsome, unlike his farmhand and frontier trapper appearance of the past three years. After Vlad, the girls and John spoke of their backgrounds; John talked about the work needing to be done, what would be expected of Vlad, and the house rules. He spoke of the house rules more for the sake of his daughters than Vlad, since he had covered them with Vlad the day before during the ride home. Vlad was not allowed in the back portion of the house, which was where the girls stayed. John warned Vlad not to even think of touching his daughters, and

William echoed that statement. Vlad told John that he was simply grateful for the opportunity to have a job and such a nice place to live. He spoke of the hardships of Russia, but was careful not to discuss his imprisonment and escape from the Russians. He did not trust anyone, as he thought, if nothing else, they might want to collect on a bounty. He had regretted mentioning it to Luke's family. He was able to avoid that part of his life story, as he had excellent credentials, of which John told William.

Vlad had truly worked hard and had not taken advantage of his former employers. He gave them honest work, and did even more than was expected. He was modest; he simply allowed his hard work to speak for him, and it always did. Vlad sincerely wanted to make a good impression and did not want to cause any problems. He knew that he would need the family's respect to survive during the long winter. Even so, his eyes meet Rachel's a number of times. She was all he could think about at the table and that night when he went to his room.

During the next day, Vlad chopped down three trees, then sawed and split them into several weeks' worth of firewood. He brought the firewood to the detached kitchen building and stacked it to dry for later use, as the family would first use wood previously cut. He worked from very early until the third time he was called for supper at the end of the day, stopping only to eat breakfast and lunch when called. Vlad made a great impression on John. When the sun finally started to go down, he ate with the family. He thought that Rachel had grown more beautiful during the day, and he was embarrassed about how sweaty and dirty he was from working, especially in his work clothes. Rachel often wore a white dress, which she had made, and she had her full, dark hair pulled back, showing her high cheek bones and blue eyes. Vlad stole several glances at her, and she at him, but both were careful, though Rachel was less careful than Vlad. His sweaty muscles showed through his shirt as he ate, and she was even more attracted to him. Her frequent glances caught the attention of William. Although he was her second cousin, he had his own designs on her. He was suspicious, and began to watch both of them.

Vlad felt a warmth that he had not experienced in years. The awakening feelings inside of him gave him the kind of happiness that people remember for the rest of their lives. He felt a tingling sensation, and desire for Rachel crossed his mind frequently. Her beauty was intoxicating. Out of the corner of his eye, Vlad saw Edna looking at Rachel and him, so he was careful not to look at Rachel again for a few minutes. Rather, he ate heartily. He had plenty of fresh vegetables and bread still warm from the oven. The variety of good foods appealed to him. He joked with John and William. He complimented and praised the girls' cooking, and he meant it; it was wonderful.

After dinner, John, William, and Vlad spoke briefly of the next day's work. They would wake up near 4:30 a.m. during that month of June when the sun rose early and set very late. They would eat breakfast, and then Vlad would travel with John to the lower fields to begin preparing them for planting. That day was particularly long and hard, and Vlad was exhausted. He bid the family goodnight, took a candle, and went to his room, which now looked like a small cottage.

When Vlad entered the cottage, it smelled faintly of perfume, the kind that Rachel wore. Rachel had sprayed some in his room to sweeten his thoughts of her. She had snuck into the cottage after supper on her way back from the outhouse, which was the most convenient excuse she had for slipping out of the house without raising suspicion. Like everything that was shipped in from afar, perfume was expensive in Canada, even what some people would consider cheap perfume. Any perfume was a luxury to a rural farm girl. Rachel had saved for it by helping a neighbor with her chickens. She was paid with eggs, which she sold to another neighbor who worked mainly with cattle. Rachel appreciated the few luxuries she had. Had Vlad understood how much work went into Rachel being able to purchase the perfume, and what it meant to her to spray even a little of it, he would have known the depths of her feelings.

At 16, Rachel was of marrying age. In a different time, people would consider such 16 year old girls fickle, frivolous, and incapable of making important life decisions. However, this was a different world where young people grew up quickly and were often middle aged before they turned 25. With so many women dying during childbirth, Rachel could have already lived well over half her life at age 16. In fact, about half of the girls she knew her age or a year older were already married and one or two had a baby on the way. By the time they reached their teenage years, their mothers had taught them how to run a country household. Rachel and her sisters did not have a mother, so they learned from a grandmother, John's mother, who had lived with them until she passed away about three years ago.

Vlad used the candle to light a lantern and prepare his clothes for the next day. He gathered his thoughts as he sat on the bed, during the time that some people would read before going to sleep. He thought of Russia and what lay ahead of him now. In the past, hard times were all he ever really knew. In the future, he figured it was best to forget about his plans to move south for the short-term and concentrate on making himself a success in his current job. Even with his gold nuggets, he feared he was only a few meals away from starvation. In order to eat, he needed some place where he could trade gold nuggets for food.

Vlad pulled back the crisp top sheet and blanket and fell into a soft feather bed, with two overstuffed feather pillows onto which Rachel had sprayed a little more of her perfume. Vlad quickly detected the scent and thought of her. The mattress had been hand-stuffed by John's mother years before; it was full of goose feathers and soft down. In addition to the pillows and crisp clean sheets, Vlad had three hand-quilted patchwork blankets.

The luxury was not lost on him. Since his days in the Russian army, he had spent many nights on the hard ground or against boulders, passed out from sheer exhaustion. While he had slept in beds since meeting James Tedder after his escape from the Russians, none had been this soft.

He grew accustomed to the faint scent of Rachel's perfume, but thoughts of her stayed on his mind. He thought of the curve of her face, her neck and shoulders, and of course her eyes. He imagined what it would be like to hold her. His thoughts drifted as his imagination unfolded into an ideal fantasy. While the warmth of the fantasy filled his body, reality tugged at him. He thought that touching her would be risky, and it impaired his fantasy. John would surely throw him off the farm, and he would have nowhere to go.

John could do worse to him, after all, since no one in these parts knew Vlad. Vlad could disappear and no one outside the family would know what had happened to him. A Russian who had come from nowhere could disappear. Even if someone asked about him, they would have no reason to question a passing answer that he had simply left to go further south. Vlad thought that John was no murderer, but he still thought the safest course was to develop a careful friendship with all of the family and not spend too much time and attention on Rachel. Even so, Vlad wanted to be with her. He felt compelled to have her, and he could not help his feelings. His fantasies about holding her left him unsatisfied, and he was bothered to the point that it took a long time for exhaustion to overcome him.

Rachel helped Mary with the dishes and went to bed herself. She and Edna shared a bed in the house. Rachel thought of Vlad and how his strong face was so handsome. She thought of him holding her tightly, and she felt warm and secure. Her thoughts of him turned less inhibited than Vlad's. She desired him. He was constrained by the fear of losing his job and possibly his life, but she was not. She knew her family, so she thought, and she did not even think that a relationship with him would cause her father or anyone else to harm Vlad. She thought that if she wanted him, everyone else would accept him too. If they would not accept him, then she would run away with Vlad. After all, he knew the world; he had traveled half way around it. They could set out to see big cities together. She wondered what lay beyond Ottawa. She had not traveled more than fifty miles from the house, in which she was born. She wanted to see the world, and that desire was more than just a passing fancy.

There were several young available men in that area. Rachel had her pick -- some of the men even thought that her father would give her to them in an arranged marriage -- but she wanted Vlad. Strong-willed since birth, she decided that night that she would have him for her husband. She was immovable in her determination.

Rachel had more than a school-girl crush. She could feel something deep inside. They were almost seven years apart, but there was a sense of timelessness about what they were beginning to feel. There was something different about the way that Vlad felt for Rachel, too. It was not yet as strong as his feelings had been for Elena while she was alive, but it was different. It was deeper, and it seemed so right.

At dawn the next morning, John came for Vlad. Vlad dressed quickly, and the two men went into the house for breakfast. They ate eggs and bread with real farm-made butter, drank fresh milk, which Mary had just extracted from the cows, and talked further of the day's plans. As they were finishing, William came in from feeding the chickens and hogs.

William looked at Vlad and took an even stronger disliking to him. He could not pin down the reason, but he hated foreigners, although it did not dawn on him that he had been born in New York City, and his own parents had arrived there from England. He was too narrow-minded to appreciate the hypocrisy of his own prejudice. William was quite jealous of Vlad, although he was not sure why. He had lost his fiancé to a man in town who talked of riches in Alaska. His fiancé had run away with the man, and no one had heard anything from them since. It had been a lonely life for William during the past three years since she had left. He had his mind set on Rachel, although she never thought of her second cousin as anything but family.

During breakfast, Rachel came around with a pitcher of fresh milk and filled everyone's cup. When she got to Vlad, she reached across his left side to get his cup. As she did, her arm brushed his shoulder and her long hair fell onto his left cheek and neck. He could feel his heart pound from the excitement of being close to her. When everyone had finished breakfast, the three men got up and set out to weed a lower field. They started at one end and moved down the length of the field. Vlad got ahead of the others, really proving his worth. John looked over Vlad's work expecting to see a half-completed job, but realized that Vlad's work was thorough. He was efficient and hardly missed any weeds. William waited until Vlad was further ahead and away from him to criticize Vlad's work. He pointed to the few weeds Vlad missed and told John of the sloppy work Vlad was doing.

After finishing that field, the men started on another, and then another. They cleared many acres of weeds before lunch. Each time William had the chance, he would criticize Vlad to John. Vlad sensed William's dislike, but there was little he could do. He simply did not know why William disliked him. Vlad truly had done nothing to William. That someone could dislike another person for no apparent reason was one of life's unexplained mysteries. At first, Vlad believed that William's dislike of him must be well grounded because he seemed like a man of reason. Vlad wondered what he could do to befriend William and felt a bit helpless. Here was a man who could cause him to lose his job. He thought of how John had defended him so far. Then Vlad reasoned that differences of opinion are often meaningless and based on personal biases. It is as though people filter their thoughts and feelings. Still, Vlad did not need an enemy.

As the work progressed and became tedious, Vlad's thoughts quickly turned to Rachel. Her lovely smile and body entranced and distracted him from the monotony of hoeing weeds. He thought of her brushing against him and speculated as to how her perfume had gotten on his pillow. He wondered if she felt for him anything like what he felt for her. He wondered about her faults and her interests, and if she was thinking of him.

Around noon, Rachel volunteered to take the men their food and drink with Edna, while Mary sat down and relaxed in rare solitude in the house. Rachel and Edna rode down on a cart pulled by a stubborn mule. It took the better part of a half an hour to deliver the food and drink. Rachel was quick to suggest the idea shortly after breakfast. Mary and Edna wondered why, as Rachel usually did not volunteer for such work, and often quarreled with Mary over who had to do it. As the youngest, Edna always was forced into it by her older sisters.

As the girls came upon the men, the men stopped and walked over to the wagon. The men ate and drank well. Vlad talked with Rachel. He told her of Russia, and how he had once seen the spires of what would later be known as the Kremlin. He told her of the vast Russian plains near Poland and how Russia spread nearly halfway across the world to the Pacific Ocean. He told her of going to Siberia and into Alaska. She listened intently, as if the trip were a first-class pleasure expedition.

While they spoke, John, Edna, and William sat on the other side of the wagon talking. They were so engrossed in their conversation that they could not see or hear Vlad and Rachel. Vlad and Rachel looked into one another's eyes with a depth of compassion and feeling that only two persons falling in love know. Somewhere during that otherwise trivial conversation, true love bloomed for them. They would both remember that day and that conversation for the rest of their lives. Vlad was simply amazed at how beautiful Rachel was as he noticed more of her features and got to know her personality. Rachel thought that Vlad's strikingly handsome features grew softer, but more handsome as she saw glimpses of his past experiences. In fairness to her, Vlad begin to talk of the difficulties during his life and travels in Russia. However, his disclosure only made her love him more as a sympathetic figure; it brought out her nurturing and compassion. She had an overwhelming desire to hold him and be held by him which was so strong that she started to reach for him, but was quickly drawn away by a loud hawing sound made by the mule.

Since everyone had finished lunch, they all simultaneously rose and packed up. The men went back to work, and Edna and Rachel drove the cart back towards the house. As they went, Rachel looked at Vlad repeatedly over her shoulder. Vlad spoke with John about the afternoon chores as the girls left.

Excited from the encounter, Vlad worked hard all that afternoon. He did back-breaking work that only a young man can perform continuously. When he finished for supper, he rode back to the house with John and William. The men stopped at the well to wash before supper. Vlad took extra care to clean the sweat and grime off of himself, to the point that his shirt was soaking. He would dry fairly quickly in the refreshingly cool breeze of the Canadian summer.

The men sat outside and dried off as the last preparations for supper were made. They spoke of tomorrow's work and of the many tasks to be done during the short summer months. Working 12-14 hour days took its toll, but there were always many months of long nights during the winter in which to rest. The winter had its own chores, and the cold was brutal, but it was not as grueling as the summer's work.

Rachel came out and called them into the house. Her freshly washed and brushed black hair was again pulled back to show her high, pretty cheekbones. She led the men to the table. Once seated, John led them in saying grace. The family dug into the food as if they had not eaten all day. Vlad ate potatoes, beans, fried chicken, and fresh bread that was so hot it instantly began to melt the butter smeared across it.

After everyone finished eating the chicken, vegetables, and bread, Rachel presented a freshly baked cake with icing made from sugar and berries growing nearby. Everyone ate to the point of discomfort. After dinner, they all sat around the fire telling stories of events past. Vlad spoke of Russia and of years of feast and famine. He described the daily brutality of a Russian peasant's life. Rachel hung on his every word, and her respect for Vlad grew.

Vlad also mentioned that he had been learning English, and wished to continue. Rachel had completed seven years of school, including three years in Ottawa. She had learned to read and knew basic math. She was bright and had common sense. Had she lived 150 years later, she certainly would have completed college and graduate school. She also had good judgment, which made her intellect even stronger. She proudly announced to everyone, "I am going to teach English to Vlad. We'll begin every night after dinner." John wanted to object, but Rachel's strong will always had a way of overcoming his objections. Vlad gladly agreed because he could spend time close to her and learn more English, too.

Chapter 28
Rachel's Visit

About an hour later, as the last few rays of sunlight disappeared, Vlad retired to his room. He dressed for bed and was just getting under the sheets when he heard the creak of wood from someone or some animal on the porch of his small cottage. The door slowly opened, and Rachel came partially into the room. She asked, "Vlad?" "Yes!?!," he answered. She replied, "May I come in?" "Yes, Rachel," Vlad said. "I want to hear more about Russia," she said. He immediately saw through her pretext for coming to him. He reached out and took her hand, then pulled her to him and embraced her.

After the initial rush from that first embrace, each pulled back so that they could look into one another's eyes through the flickering lantern light. They simultaneously moved to kiss one another, and embraced in a kiss that made their hearts pound fast. Vlad's hands felt the warmth of her back and waist. He relished this first kiss with her, full of excitement. His insides were more upside down than during any of the fights he had fought. However, the emotional turmoil was exhilaration, not fear. While he held her, he felt the way a man feels when he holds his newlywed wife and the mother of his children. It was not mere lust or just physical passion. While he could not put a name to it, because it was beyond description, it felt right to the core of his being.

After that long kiss, they embraced again. He whispered to her, "I've longed to kiss you since I first saw you!" She too said, "I've wanted you to kiss me!" Right then, they both heard Mary calling for her. She raced out of the cottage and circled around to the outhouse, arriving just in time to lead Mary to believe that she had been fixing her undergarments after a visit to the outhouse. She returned to the house and promptly went to bed thinking of the brief encounter, the memory of which would last her a lifetime.

Vlad laid back down, his ears listening for evidence that they had been caught. His mind switched between thoughts of how to explain Rachel's presence and the ecstasy of their brief moments together. It was June 28, 1858. For him, it was a date that would be as memorable as any national holiday.

Try as he may, it was 3-4 hours before he could fall asleep. The thought of Rachel with him was more than he could bear. The thrill and wonder of the moment overpowered his exhaustion. Finally, after getting up and walking around a couple of times, he laid down, and the exhaustion from the hard work done that day allowed him to sleep.

The following morning he got up after the rooster had crowed several times. He was happy and content, but his body and mind were still in need of sleep. He needed to sleep until 10 a.m., but 4:35 a.m. was all he was allowed. He went and feed the chickens and milked the cows. By the time he had finished, washed up a bit, and dressed for the day's work ahead, breakfast was ready.

To wash up, he drew cold water from the well and used a broken bar of lye soap. Since he had no comb, he used water and a towel to at least give his hair an attractive shape. His thick black hair required little upkeep other than washing and cutting, which was fortunate since he had no means of taking much better care of it. He did have a dull razor, which he used to shave his face. The lye soap he also used for shaving cream was abrasive in the cold well water. Still, the water felt refreshing against his tired skin and woke him even more.

He went into the house for breakfast. Rachel had not fallen asleep at all. The thought of the encounter, her first, thrilled her young body and mind. She laid in bed semi-conscious all night thinking, if not actually dreaming, of Vlad. As the first rooster crowed, she was quick to arise. Edna thought nothing of it, except gratitude that she would not be the only one working on the first of three big meals made completely from scratch with a wood-fired oven and stove.

As Vlad sat down for breakfast, William and John came in and sat down. After John said the blessing, the family tore into the biscuits, eggs, sausage, sausage gravy, roasted potatoes, and fresh milk. Vlad particularly liked the biscuits. This morning, Rachel had placed a hunk of cheese into about half of them, which made them plump and round. Vlad bit into the melted cheese in the middle, enjoying the intense flavor. He reached for a glass of milk to cool the hot cheese in his mouth.

After checking to see where everyone was looking, Vlad finally got the courage to look over at Rachel. At first, her expression did not betray her thoughts or feelings. She looked stern, almost mad, and he was concerned that she deeply regretted their brief embrace. Then, she met his eyes, and her face brightened. She smiled and then quickly looked away, afraid that her expression would give her thoughts away to any of her family who looked. William did see her as she turned, but did not see the entire event. He looked over at Vlad, who had just turned to pass the biscuits around the table. William was troubled by what he saw, but because he did not understand it, the feeling quickly passed.

The family finished eating, and the men got up to go to the fields. Vlad allowed William and John to leave the room first. He tried to speak to Rachel, but the other girls stayed near her. She looked at him and smiled, then finally came over and walked him towards the door. She looked him in the eyes and took his right hand. She placed a handkerchief with her perfume on it into his right hand and then closed it with both of her hands, looking intently into his eyes as if to tell him to keep it hidden. She smiled and went to kiss him, but Mary called for her just then. Vlad quickly placed the handkerchief into his pocket and left to join John and William.

Vlad met William on the steps as William was heading back to tell him to hurry. William asked him what he and Rachel were doing, and Vlad said he had simply passed her in the hall and had thanked her for the breakfast. William was unconvinced because he caught a glimpse of Rachel looking as though she were about to kiss Vlad and heard her get called away. The glare from the sun shining on the slick and worn wooden railing of the stairs had blocked his view of the handkerchief.

Chapter 29
Boiling Point

During the entire trip to the fields, William looked jealously at Vlad. Vlad felt uncomfortable, but he dared not say anything because of the repercussions for Rachel and himself. Once they had arrived, William immediately laid into Vlad. He accused Vlad of stupidity and carelessness. Vlad took it because he had no choice, but he wanted to hammer William, whose chin stuck out like a dazed prize fighter before the knockout blow. John was weak and did not defend Vlad, but he did not criticize him either. He simply changed the subject and got the two to work separately. Vlad eyed William with a look that should have sent chills up his spine, but William did not look Vlad in the eye. Vlad had taken human lives in self-defense, although he regretted doing it. However, at this particular moment, his face looked like that of a killer.

Vlad spoke the language better every day, but he was still in a foreign country. The winters were cold and long, and he knew he might not survive if he fled during or close to winter. The fact that it was still summer gave him some confidence, but he did not want to lose this position, which would mean losing Rachel, too. Still, he would only take so much from William.

The men separated to do the work that John assigned them. Vlad went to do the hardest physical labor. He worked all morning without any breaks. Finally, he got the call about 12:30 p.m. for lunch, which was much later than he had hoped. He rode in a cart back to the house, ate baked chicken and freshly cooked vegetables, and drank the cold well water that Rachel had just drawn. As soon as he finished, he slumped slightly. William took his relaxation to imply that he had been lazy that morning and not working hard. Vlad recoiled and let William know exactly what had been done. William accused him of having a temper, and Vlad knew he could not win. Rachel quickly defended him, and John told her it was not her place. William decided that he had better move quickly to take her for his wife, and her defense of Vlad only fired up his jealously.

After lunch, William tried to talk with Rachel, to flirt with her. However, she knew how he treated Vlad, and she told him, "You disgust me!" William was furious. He accused her, "You're attracted to Vlad, aren't you? I'm going to tell John for him to get rid of Vlad!" She said, "You do whatever you please, but leave me alone! You leave Vlad alone, too, or you'll regret it!" She marched off with her back arched and her nose high in the air. She feared no one; certainly not William.

William was left to go to the fields with his temper high and continuing to boil. He was not thinking rationally, and he wanted to kill Vlad. Mary and Edna came along and saw that William was upset. Although both were becoming suspicious of Vlad and Rachel, they did not relate that to William's anger. Being straight-forward farm children, without the hesitance of their contemporaries in the big cities of the United States or England, Mary and Edna simply asked him what was wrong. William quickly said, "Vlad is polluting the mind of Rachel and you'd better watch him to protect her!" Both were startled and in disbelief.

William continued making accusations against Vlad, but the statements were not logical. The accusations made Mary and Edna uncomfortable, but because they were not logical, neither Mary nor Edna knew what to say to William. They had assumed that, if given the chance, Vlad would be untrustworthy with their pretty sister, but they would have thought that way of most single twenty-something year-old men who stayed at their home. He was also a foreigner, with different customs, which made them uncertain as to what to believe about him, but they also liked Vlad. They themselves found him attractive. They thought he was a great help to their father, who had worked himself far too hard their entire lives. Ultimately, they each concluded that William was jealous, possibly over nothing. They had not been impressed with William because he could have done more than anyone to take the burden off of their father these past several years as their father had aged. Plus, they suspected him of wanting their inheritance.

Mary and Edna quickly found a way to separate themselves from William. They went about their chores during the rest of the afternoon, William's words weighing heavily on the hearts. They separately dissected each phrase. Soon, however, their thoughts turned to their own boyfriends. Mary was engaged to be married later that fall. Edna also had been seeing a farmer's son, who was 19, for almost a year. Edna and the boy planned to announce their engagement that Christmas.

William worked for a short while, but his temper continued to boil. He went over to where Vlad was working. He approached Vlad from behind, planning to get the first vicious blow with a shovel. He thought he could incapacitate Vlad and then threaten Vlad to leave the farm or else something worse would happen to him. It was a hastily devised plan. William thought he could strike easily, but he was unaware of the extent of Vlad's military combat and wilderness experience.

As with anyone who could survive long-term combat and a trek across the wilderness, Vlad had the proverbial eyes in the back of his head. In actuality, Vlad had a habit of frequently checking his surroundings. He developed that habit in the military, and it was further sealed by the bear attacks in the wilderness. It was an unconscious habit, which Vlad seldom even realized he was doing. It was a part of who he was. Also, he knew of William's feelings, which made him extra sensitive when William was around. Vlad caught a glimpse of William's approach; that was all he needed.

Vlad was digging a long narrow ditch to funnel water from a creek to a field. He gathered a scoop of pebble-laden soil, while catching a few glimpses of William approaching. When William got about three steps away, he raised his shovel with which to strike Vlad. Right when he was about to bring it down against the back of Vlad's skull, Vlad swung around and threw the dirt and stones hard into William's face. The dirt got in William's eyes, while the pebbles hit him with a shocking effect. Vlad then quickly swung his shovel back-handed and popped William in the head, dropping him to the ground.

Vlad used the energy from the contact and follow-through of his swing to stand and move away. In a split second, Vlad went from being bent over to standing over William, and William went from standing over and behind Vlad to being flat on his back on the ground. Predator became prey. Vlad impulsively raised the shovel up to deliver a fatal blow with the blade. He was going to try to cut William's head off with the blade or dig it into William's neck or chest, but he stopped. His heart pounded in his chest, as his killer instinct was about to end William's existence on this earth. However, Vlad was moved not to kill as he had been trained to do. He just stood still with the shovel ready to strike and with pure death in his eyes. Vlad delivered a cold hard stare while his muscles began to quiver with energy, his mind and conscience fighting a battle that would decide whether William lived or died.

William rubbed his eyes clear with one hand while trying to shield himself from another blow with the other. Then, he moved his hand from his eyes and placed it upon the bump above his temple. He groaned as he rubbed it and focused on Vlad. Vlad's voiced trembled as he told William in simple English, "You try anything again, I kill you!" William felt genuine fear as he looked up at Vlad and slid backwards away from him.

William thought that the foreigner would be easily intimidated, but from then on, William viewed Vlad differently. Vlad, tired of death and conflict, simply told William to leave. However, to teach William that he was serious, Vlad turned the shovel and swung it towards William's ribs, striking him in the arms with the flat side. William had raised his arms to block the swing towards his ribs. With lightning speed, Vlad switched sides and swung again, hitting William's arms again. The blows did not break any bones, but were designed to inflict pain and send a message of dominance. Vlad asked William, "Why shouldn't I go ahead and kill you and bury you here?" William cried for mercy and promised he would leave Vlad alone. Vlad then pulled out his pistol from his pants, cocked it and pointed it at William. Vlad did not say another word.

After covering his face for over a minute waiting for the fatal shot, William finally started to slide further back. He slid several feet and then slowly got up. He walked backwards as he moved away, slowly at first and then briskly, keeping an eye on Vlad with every step that he took. Vlad thought that William might go and get a gun, so he ran after him. William fell to the ground and begged Vlad, "Please don't kill me!" Vlad told William, "From now on, I will carry a gun, day and night. If you ever try to harm me or even look like it, I will shoot you. I was in the Russian Army and was taught to kill an enemy that could return to hurt me later." Vlad's compassion and desire for a new life again returned, and he told William, "Now leave and tell no one of how you were injured or of our words." Not truly meaning it, but wanting to keep William from convincing John to make him leave, Vlad added, "If you get John to send me away, I will come back and kill you in your sleep!" William quickly fled, but from that moment forward, Vlad was on full alert.

Chapter 30
Vlad Finds His Home

At dinner, Vlad sneered at William as William told everyone, "I was trying to take a pebble out of that mean brown horse's horseshoe, and it showed its gratitude by kicking me!" Even Rachel felt sorry for William's supposed misfortune. After dinner, William quickly left, and Vlad helped Rachel clear the table with the gratitude of Mary and Edna, who had plans that evening with their boyfriends. When William left, Vlad kept a close eye on him to make certain that he did not double back. Vlad and Rachel finished clearing the table and washing the dishes, but John was around them. Vlad then found himself briefly alone with Rachel while she began his English lesson, and he told her what had really happened. As she taught Vlad, John entered the room and sat nearby to observe. When they finished, John when into the next room, and Vlad softly asked Rachel if he could see her in private. She said that she would meet him at the well in fifteen minutes, when it would be completely dark. Vlad then left to go to his room, making a pronounced exit for John's benefit.

After waiting by the well for at least thirty minutes, Rachel appeared. She said, "It took me longer than I had expected to slip away because dad wanted to talk. I couldn't appear anxious to leave, so I waited a bit before sneaking out to make certain he had finished talking to me. I'm certain that he doesn't suspect anything." They made certain that they could not be seen from the house, and then they embraced and kissed passionately. Vlad could feel that her body was more of an hour-glass shape than her heavy practical clothes revealed to the eye. He kept kissing and holding her close. She let her passion for him go momentarily unchecked, and she pressed herself against him to feel his body close to hers.

As she kissed him, she could not help but slightly exhale, which caught Vlad by surprise with a little puff of her breath entering his mouth. It did not bother him. Rather, her kiss showed him how desperately she wanted him. He felt the same, but knew that her absence from the house would soon be noted. Sure enough, her father called for her, and she said, "I'm at the well, dad. I had to go to the outhouse, and I'm getting some delicious cold water to drink." She quickly dropped the bucket, raised it, and drank using a ladle kept at the well. Vlad crouched down and hid behind the well, holding the outside of her thighs wanting her to stay and not go. Rachel reluctantly tore away and went towards the light her father had in his hands to keep him from coming to her and discovering Vlad.

After Rachel left, Vlad circled around to check out his room. He wanted to make sure that William did not lay in wait. After checking from the window, Vlad gathered his pillow and quilt, and he went to the barn to sleep. He thought it more practical to miss a soft night in bed than to be ambushed by William. Vlad laid down so that he could watch his room for either William or Rachel.

William was angry, but his sore head reminded him that death awaited him if he tried anything.

Vlad watched the house, too, and saw William return and go in. Vlad watched until all the lights went out. A short time later, the moon appeared from behind some clouds and lit up the yard. Vlad watched for an hour to see if Rachel would come. She did not. He had trouble falling asleep, thinking that she might come. He finally fell fast asleep and slept until the rooster crowed. He then got up, ate breakfast, and worked all day. He could not find a time to speak privately with Rachel that day. All they could do was exchange glances. She was able to tutor him for about fifteen minutes, but so many people were around that they could neither talk nor concentrate on the lesson. Both Mary's fiancé and Edna's boyfriend, who was well known to the family, had supper with them and stayed around to spend time with the whole family talking.

Vlad went to bed early that night. He decided to sleep again in the barn, but he set string around his room tied to cow bells that he set up near him. If anyone approached the place, they would trip his makeshift alarm. It could be Rachel or one of her family members or it could be William. Thankfully, though, William did not come, and Vlad slept soundly all night. In a few days, Vlad returned to his room. He kept his gun ready and set trip lines around the place for a few weeks, but William never came. Rachel tripped them a few times to come see Vlad. He was always careful not to point the gun for fear that he may shoot Rachel by mistake. It placed him at a disadvantage had it been William, but Vlad would rather risk his life than risk shooting Rachel by accident.

As the weeks passed, Vlad proved his worth to John through his solid hard work. During that time, Edna and her boyfriend got engaged. Almost every night, Rachel taught Vlad from the books from which she had studied in Ottawa. Rachel and Vlad's love grew. As harvest time neared, Rachel was more open with John about her feelings for Vlad. John was not pleased at first, but he had come to like Vlad and respect him. Finally, John called them together out in the yard in private and told them, "I know that you two have strong feelings for each other. I've known that for some time. I almost let Vlad go when I first sensed it, but I needed Vlad, and I didn't want to upset Rachel. Also, Edna and Mary have fallen in love – all my girls have. I guess you all picked the same time to grow up. By the time Rachel began speaking with me about her feelings for you, Vlad, I already knew your character was strong, and Rachel needs a person of strong character and will. I don't know of anyone else who seems so right for Rachel for a lot of different reasons."

Rachel hugged her father and told him, "I love you, daddy!" Vlad told him that they would continue to respect him and act honorably. John told them that William would cause trouble for them, but he would speak with William provided that they wanted him to. Vlad told him that he did not want him to speak with

William, but Rachel wanted her father to ask William not to try to harm Vlad. She thought John could smooth things out between them, but Vlad knew better.

When harvest time arrived, the entire family worked in the fields. It was the one time that everyone was needed. For lunch, the family ate hard bread prepared in advance and salted meat. It reminded Vlad of his traveling days. Rachel and Vlad were so tired at the end of each day that they did not spend as much time together in the evenings, and Rachel canceled their tutoring sessions because she was too tired. Rachel also felt that she smelled from the sweaty work, and she wanted to bath before she got near Vlad.

Finally, harvest was complete. The days were getting rapidly shorter, and the nights were a little bit cooler. Once the crops were harvested, the entire family worked storing grain and preserving fruits and vegetables in jars. It was continuous hard work. When that was finished, the family sold much of their harvest, John paid Vlad what Vlad had earned, and the family planned a huge feast to celebrate the end of another successful summer. They invited friends from neighboring farms and had a dance. Vlad and Rachel danced together, while William renewed his jealously and hatred towards Vlad. Everyone was so busy that Vlad and Rachel slipped away without being noticed. William got drunk, mouthed off at some neighbors' wives, and passed out before their husbands could harm him. He made a fool of himself in front of everyone.

Vlad and Rachel went to behind where the grain was stored. Earlier in the day, Vlad had spread and piled some hay there for them to lean against and had hidden a blanket for them to spread to keep the prickly hay off of them. Rachel had bathed and put on extra perfume. Her fragrant body was quickly in Vlad's arms. Her soft and creamy porcelain skin had returned with the long bath. Vlad had also bathed, and he wore his best clothes. Surprisingly, John had even given him some cologne to wear. Mary had trimmed Vlad's hair, and he was more handsome than Rachel had ever seen. They spent hours talking, kissing and holding one another under thousands of stars in the clear, cooling Canadian night sky. Vlad thought if they married, he would spend his life here on this farm, and he would be perfectly happy doing so as long as Rachel was with him. He had finally found a home; it was wherever Rachel was.

Chapter 31
A Death in the Family

About two weeks after the dance, the work was down to winterizing the farm. The work hours were fewer, and there was a lot more leisure time. Rachel tutored Vlad for hours on end, and they took more walks together. As they spent more time together, they grew even more confident in the special nature of their love. John was able to take it easy, allowing Vlad and William to do most of the work. Vlad had saved his summer wages. John had been generous to him because the harvest was abundant and the market in Ottawa had paid better prices for their excess crops than in years before.

One morning, John did not come for breakfast. Edna went to check on him, and he was not breathing. He had died of a heart attack during the night. The entire family was greatly grief stricken, except for William, who seemed sad but peculiar. Vlad comforted Rachel, but was very sad himself. Vlad had come to love John as a second father. A minister and a number of neighbors began visiting. The funeral service was poignant, as the preacher had plenty of wonderful things to say about John. John had only lived 48 years, but he had meant so much to his family and to the people in the area.

After the funeral, John was buried in the family cemetery on the farm. It was a small field surrounded by fruit trees and a wooden rail fence. He was buried between the graves of his wife and his mother. His three daughters were devastated at the loss of their father and their grandmother, who had raised them as a mother, in just a few years. John's father had also died when he was young, and he was buried on the other side of John's mother.

The night following the burial, the family sat around the kitchen table just staring down at it, except for William, who was in and out of the house. When he finally entered the kitchen, he began speaking as though he was now in charge. He said, "Girls, you're going to need to start working more in the fields. Vlad, you can stay a week or two to help me finish winterizing the farm, but after that you're no longer needed." Simultaneously, all three sisters spoke out in protest. Mary told him, "You're not in charge. All three of us sisters will make the decisions about running the farm!" William told them, "I've worked hard on the farm for years, and I'm the son your father never had. Your father meant for me to run the place if anything happened to him." He then turned and left as the girls continued their strong protests.

The next day, Vlad saw William at breakfast, and William did not say a word until they had finished and started walking outside. He ordered Vlad, "You work in the back field clearing stones for grazing cattle next year. I may want to plant crops there." It was an isolated field, and no one other than Vlad heard what William had said. Vlad figured it was a set-up, so he carried his pistol and a shotgun. When William saw him packing a shotgun, he told Vlad, "I may hunt some squirrels for supper, so I need that shotgun." Vlad told William, "No. I don't trust you. I'll keep the shotgun, and if I see you anywhere near the back field today, I'll take this shotgun, shove it into your rear-end, and pull the trigger." With one hand, Vlad gripped the shotgun just behind the trigger housing and pointed it at William. Vlad did this more out of fear than meanness because he knew that William had something planned, and he wanted to nip it the bud.

William waited for Vlad to lower the gun. When Vlad did, it appeared to William that Vlad had taken his eyes off him, so William stepped forward and swung his fist at Vlad. Vlad blocked the swing by swinging the gun up and to the left so that the barrel met William's fist. Vlad used his right elbow and right foot to push and kick William to the ground, and William landed to the left of Vlad. Vlad then kicked William very hard in the ribs and placed his boot on William's neck. Vlad was a hair's breadth away from stomping down, but he could not do that.

Instead, Vlad said, "Today is the day that you will choose to live or die. If you get within 100 yards of me while I'm working, I'll kill you!" Vlad also told William, "You are going to work the back field today, and I am going to work near the barns." Vlad pressed down on William's neck, choking him slightly and asked, "Do you have any problem with that?" William choked out, "No." Vlad let off and said, "Git!" William scrambled away in fear that Vlad was going to shoot him.

After William was out of sight, Rachel ran to Vlad. She had seen everything. Vlad told her, "I must leave because William will try something again. If I don't leave, then either William will ambush and kill me or else I will be forced to kill William. William will not allow me to stay here in peace. I fear for you, Rachel. Not just for you, but for Mary and Edna, too. I don't want to leave without you, and we cannot leave your sisters to whatever William sees fit to do to them." Rachel hugged Vlad and told him, "I won't let you leave without me. I never want to be apart from you." Overcome with emotion and almost in tears, Vlad asked, "Will you marry me?" Rachel immediately said, "Yes! Absolutely!"

They decided to force William to leave for good. However, they had no idea of how to get rid of him. William had taken up residence there with John's permission and had worked there for years. Rachel said that she would talk with Mary and Edna while Vlad worked. They kissed, and he left to begin his day working.

Chapter 32
Grave Danger

As Vlad walked away, Rachel knew that his life was in grave danger. She knew that if William forced him to leave without her, her own life would be one of enslavement to a man whom she did not love. William would mistreat her because she could never truly love him. With her father dead and her sisters engaged, she knew that there was nothing requiring her to stay. She would miss her sisters terribly, but she knew they would be concerned with their own families once they married, and she would rarely see them once they had babies and multiple small children to care for.

That night, William was not at supper. Vlad left the house and went to his room. William came home later. When he arrived, he staggered drunkenly to his room. Rachel snuck out of the house and approached Vlad's room. She signaled him by throwing two stones at the side of the structure and waited for Vlad to appear from the barn. He had been watching her approach, but he waited to make certain that William was not following her. He called for her quietly, and she came to him. They embraced, and he took her by the hand and walked quickly behind the barn. Vlad told her, "I've been watching my room from the hay loft because I know William is about to strike." Rachel told him, "I'm so thankful that you're taking precautions. I couldn't go on without you, Vlad!"

Rachel looked Vlad squarely in the eyes. She could see his strong eyes in the full moonlight, and he could see her beautiful eyes, although the light of the moon was not bright enough for him to see the deep blue in them. She told him, "I love you deeply and want to be with you forever, beginning now." He told her, "I love you, and I always want to be with you, too. I fell in love with you when I first met you, and getting to know you only proved what I already knew." Neither one needed to say anything because they loved each other so strongly. Vlad also told her, "You make me the man I want to be, and you're more than I ever dreamed a woman I loved could be."

Rachel told him, "Let's leave right now. We could take a wagon and two of the best horses. We could ride by my sisters' fiancés' houses and warn them of William." Vlad replied, "I'll hitch the horses to the wagon while you pack, but Mary and Edna need to go with us. Then, I'll return with those two men to resolve matters with William. You should go pack, and pack very quickly and quietly."

Rachel went back into the house and packed. She told her sisters that she was leaving, and they all cried together. She asked them to prepare to go to their fiancés' houses for protection. She told them, "William may harm you once he discovers I'm gone." They all got dressed, and Rachel packed everything. She placed her belongings near the door, so they could be moved into the wagon when Vlad drove it close to the door.

Just as she finished, William came into the room. He had heard everything Rachel said by quickly sneaking into the next room and listening. He looked at her belongings, all packed and ready to go. He walked over to her and hit her, cussing at her the entire time. Vlad saw this through the window as he approached the house. Vlad grabbed a shotgun from the wagon and quickly entered the house. Rachel got up and William pushed her back down; she fell, just missing an end table. William told her, "Tonight, you'll sleep with me, you whore! I know you've been loving that dirty Russian farm hand. From now on, you're going to earn your keep with me!"

Vlad heard her make a sound as she lost her breath hitting the floor to William's right by an end table. He also heard what William had said to her. Vlad immediately entered the room and was ready to beat William to a pulp with his bare hands. However, when William saw Vlad, he reached for a gun in his belt. It caught on his shirt for a second as he began cocking the hammer. Vlad lowered the shotgun and quickly pointed it at William's chest. Just then, Rachel fired a small pistol that she had retrieved from a drawer of the end table. She had grabbed it just as Vlad opened the door.

William fell to the side and then backwards, hitting the wall. Vlad immediately went forward, ready to fire to take away William's gun from him. William was mortally wounded and paralyzed, but conscious. His lungs, spine, aorta and heart were hit. Both of his lungs filled with blood. He tried to finish cocking the pistol, but his hand could not obey his thoughts. Vlad grabbed the pistol, pointed it in a safe direction and twisted it while he pressed his boot against William to separate William's hand from the pistol. William struggled and gasped for air. His muscles contracted involuntarily as life left him. Finally, his body was still, and blood was everywhere.

Mary and Edna all screamed in horror. They shook and cried; their noses ran and their hair fell into their wet faces. As Rachel hugged Vlad, he watched William carefully. Rachel said, "I had to shoot him. He was going to rape me tonight." Vlad said, "I know, sweetheart. I was late trying to pull the trigger because I was going to beat him with my fists. I was afraid that he was going to shoot me first or at least a tie, which would have killed us both. He would have killed me and then harmed you and your sisters had you not shot him." Vlad shook at the thought that he had failed to have the shotgun ready, choosing first his hands over the shotgun so as not to accidentally shoot Rachel or her sisters.

Rachel and Vlad then embraced Mary and Edna until they calmed a bit. Vlad took them into the kitchen to sit down and then returned to the room where William lay dead. Vlad knew that William was dead, but he still approached him with caution. He kept William covered with the shotgun and kicked him in the ribs to make certain that he was dead. When Vlad kicked William, William let out a low gurgling sound, which sent chills through Vlad. Vlad kicked again and was finally certain that William was dead. The amount of blood alone should have convinced Vlad of William's death.

Vlad grabbed some sheets and put them over William. Then, Vlad wrapped William in those sheets and dragged him over to the window. He opened it and pushed William through the window to minimize the blood leaking over the house and to avoid the girls having to see the body again. Vlad then went to Rachel and told her he would dispose of the body. She offered to help, but he asked her to get cloths for him to use to wipe up the blood. With William's death, Vlad figured he had at least a few more hours before they had to leave. He asked Rachel's sisters, "Will you pack enough clothes for a few days? I'd like to accompany you to your fiancés' houses to stay, but wait before leaving. Go out the back door and crawl through your windows so you don't have to see the blood until I can get it cleaned." He moved the wagon over to the other side of the house so the sisters would not have to see the blood. Rachel then began loading it. He asked her to pack enough food for several days and to bring whatever money, gold, or other wealth that was rightfully hers. Although Vlad had plenty of gold and some cash, they would need plenty of money to get to another place and establish themselves there.

Vlad then took William to a well on the other side of the barn. The family had dug another one closer to the house, and this well was seldom used. Vlad decided that he did not have adequate time to dig a proper grave, so he found three large stones and placed them inside of

William's clothes. Vlad then lifted William up and dropped him down the well. Vlad heard a splash and William's body sank to the bottom a few feet below the top of the water. Vlad then returned to the house and used water and more sheets to clean the floor and wall. It had a reddish hue, so Vlad got some lye soap and scrubbed some more until it was passable. Once dried, he moved a rug over the floor and a bookcase to cover the wall.

Vlad spoke with Rachel about the importance of her sisters not telling anyone of William's death until they had left. To make certain that no one blamed the girls for the death, Vlad hand wrote a letter stating that he shot William in self-defense. It was hardly readable because of Vlad's poor English, so Rachel re-wrote it detailing what had really occurred, and Vlad signed it believing that it implicated no one but himself. Rachel added adjectives and adverbs and emphasized the defensive nature of the killing. Anyone reading the account would believe it was self-defense, or at least would have no evidence to the contrary. While Vlad was outside again, Rachel counseled her sisters to emphasize that it was self-defense. She schooled them on their accounts and had them rehearse them over and over again.

To keep her sisters from arriving at their fiances' houses too quickly and to give herself and Vlad extra time, she went to the barn and freed the horses they would ride so that they could graze in nearby fields. The horses loved to graze there. They would eventually return to her sisters or the girls could track them down, but either one would take hours. Walking also would take over an hour. Rachel and her sisters then tearfully hugged one another as they talked, knowing that they were never going to see each other again.

Vlad washed his hands with water drawn from the other well and then secured Rachel's belongings in the wagon. He packed his own belongings and went for Rachel. He hugged her sisters and thanked them for their kindness to him. He asked them, "Please allow Rachel and me time to leave before reporting what happened. Also, ask your fiancés not to report it or to at least give us 24-48 hours before going to the constable. The girls promised that they would tell their fiancés not to report it. Each girl said she was upset, but they knew that William was going to rape Rachel, he would have shot Vlad, and he would have imprisoned and probably raped all of the sisters eventually. William had already told their fiancés not to come to the house anymore. They saw him for what he was and promised, "We see no need to contact the law."

Chapter 33
Vlad and Rachel Flee

As Vlad and Rachel packed and got ready to leave, the sun was beginning to rise. Vlad had packed all of his possessions, including the Bible that Henry had given him, his bear skin coat, and his gold. He loaded Rachel's and his possessions very carefully into the wagon. Vlad saw Mary's and Edna's horses leaving to go towards the fields, and he retrieved and saddled them for Mary and Edna. They appreciated what he did. He asked if they wanted Rachel and him to accompany them so he could explain what had happened. Rachel strongly objected, and her sisters said that they would be alright. Vlad wanted to make certain no blame would fall on Mary and Edna, and they convinced him that they would be alright. They showed Vlad his written and signed statement, and he believed that would keep them out of trouble. The group said its last goodbyes, and Rachel and Vlad headed off into the pale light.

As he drove, Vlad asked Rachel, "Would you please cover our belongings with a couple of quilts you brought? If people see the quilts as we pass through the town of Rockland, they at least will not know what's in the wagon." "Good idea," Rachel answered. As Vlad and Rachel approached the town, they became very nervous. Rachel held Vlad's arm tighter and tighter, until Vlad mentioned it to her. They entered town and had to travel about 300 yards to the turn that would place them on a post road leading southeast to Casselman.

Rockland was amazingly quiet. They only saw one or two people, who looked for a moment and waved before going about their own business. Vlad softly said, "They must believe that we are going to the store and on errands." She simply nodded. They made the turn and continued on for about 400 yards until they were out of town. Rachel could not help but look back. When she did, she saw no one following or even looking at them. Rachel and Vlad knew that the town's people would have no reason to suspect what had occurred. Still, they were nervous about getting caught and possibly executed for William's death, even though it was in self-defense.

Vlad had wanted to take a different route to the post road, but there simply were no others that did not lead through town or across someone else's property. If they cut through someone's land, the landowner would want to know where they were going and the details of their travels. There just was not very much else to do other than to get into other people's business whenever one felt like he or she had a reason for doing so.

Vlad motioned the reins and made a sound for the horses to increase speed as they cleared the town. Slow-moving had kept their noise down, but now Vlad wanted to put as many miles behind them as possible before nightfall. Rachel had traveled to Casselman several times before, and it was about 22 miles from Rockland. She knew that the road led from Casselman to Cornwall, a border town on the St. Lawrence River across from New

York State. From there, they hoped they could catch a ferry across the river.

The roads were in good condition from summer repairs, and the horses were fit and well-fed. Rachel had packed a basket full of breads, honey, hand-churned butter, and roasted chicken. She had brought milk and cold well water from the clean well closer to the house. Vlad thought of the ease of this departure compared to his flight from the Russian camp. Riding on a wagon and eating delicious bread sure did beat salted meat eaten between attacks from men and bears. Still, they had only just begun their trip. Once William's death was reported, anyone who saw them in Rockland or Casselman would be key witnesses for a search party in pursuit of a slow wagon on a main road.

Vlad thought that they had better try to make Casselman and, if possible, go a bit farther. Rachel said that it usually took a full day to get there, but that was when the family took their time and stopped to picnic at a favorite spot near a river ford. Other than an occasional trip to Ottawa, the family had used trips to Casselman as vacations. Vlad thought that if the horses were tired, and they likely would be, they might be required to stay in the town to allow the horses proper food and rest. He had lost his horses in British Columbia, at least in part by pushing them too hard. It had cost him dearly because he had to jettison supplies and carry a very heavy pack rather than ride. He thought they could at least find a comfortable place to stay and try to leave as early as possible.

As they rode, the sun continued rising and crossed the sky to the west. Vlad noted it, as he noted many things in nature because of his prior travels. He and Rachel discussed their plans, including where in the United States they would go. Rachel wanted to see New York City or Philadelphia, but she said that she wanted them to find some land on which to settle and have a farm. Vlad told her that he wanted the security of home and family, but, above all, he wanted to be with her and to make her happy. He said he could adjust to anything so long as she was with him. She kissed his cheek and assured him that everything would be alright. He believed her, and he felt safe.

They made excellent time, stopping only a few times to allow the horses to rest; they arrived in Casselman just after 3 p.m. Vlad found a stable and placed the horses there. He decided to stay in the wagon to protect their belongings. He insisted that Rachel stay in a local hotel, but she refused with an iron stubbornness that he knew he could not overcome. Vlad gave the stable owner some extra money to allow them to park the wagon inside of his stable and stay there for the night. Vlad and Rachel also saw a map that the owner had, and they memorized the route they should take. However, in case the stable owner was later questioned, Vlad talked as though he needed directions towards the southwest, and the owner gave him those directions. Rachel told him,

"I'd love to see Chicago," which was true. Vlad and Rachel had a picnic in the stable and talked while they relaxed on a pile of hay. As the night chill came upon them, they cuddled close to each other, but the surroundings, the excitement of the recent events, and the concern that they get on their way early precluded any romantic time together.

Both were able to fall asleep with a couple of quilts wrapped around them and the bear skin coat over them. When the owner entered the stable at first light, they awoke, then hitched the horses to the wagon and drove out of the stable. They headed out of town and were on their way before the sun rose completely above the horizon. Vlad discussed the mental notes he had made from the map. They had enough information to get them to Cornwall and into New York State, but once they arrived in New York, they would need further directions. Since the stable was out of sight of the fork where Vlad and Rachel headed southeast rather than southwest, anyone following them who spoke to the stable owner should believe that they were heading towards Smiths Falls instead of Cornwall. The stable owner and the owners of the town's two hotels would be the first people with whom anyone following would inquire.

In the meantime, Rachel's sisters had arrived at Mary's fiancé's farm. They were anxious and scared. They told him of the events mostly as Rachel had advised them, except they said that Vlad shot William.   The girls reported how William said that he was going to make all three his "wives." Also according to Rachel's instructions, the girls emphasized that William had not touched them, but was about to do all sorts of things. They then said that Vlad had spoiled that plan, so William had tried to kill Vlad, and that is when Vlad shot William. They were adamant that William had drawn his gun first and that Vlad had acted in the defense of his own life and of their honor.

The girls repeated the same story, basically word for word, to the other fiancé. Their fiancés believed them because they loved them and would not question their young loves on such a point of honor. Their blood boiled at the thought of William attempting such a perverse thing. Rachel knew that making the fiancés slightly jealous and angry at William was the best way to protect Vlad and herself. Sure enough, both boys were mad enough to have killed William themselves and said they would have had Vlad not beaten them to it.

The girls went further and told how Vlad had hidden William's body in the outer well and had signed a letter so that no one would blame them for William's death. They said that Vlad also said that no one would believe that the girls had been able to carry William's body so far, lift it, and dump it into the well. They further told of Rachel and Vlad leaving to go to the western United States to start their lives together in California and to try to make it rich in gold. In all, Rachel had devised clever additions to what had actually occurred. The story was convincing enough to bring the fiancés, and later their families, into the conspiracy.

One of the most convincing points that Rachel had not mentioned in her haste, but that was equally persuasive in gaining the fiancés' assistance, was that the girls would have clear title to the farm. William could no longer claim that it had become his through his work or that John had intended for him to have it. While William's claim would have been hard to win under Canadian law, the fiancés did not know that. They just knew that he was out of the way. They did not speak of that fact, but it was a thought that had occurred to them independently of the other, and they each felt a little guilty for thinking it.

They all agreed to wait a week to report William's unfortunate fall and drowning in the well. They would first claim that he had disappeared right after Vlad and Rachel moved west. They would say that they had thought nothing of it at first because William was notorious for leaving for days at a time to go to Ottawa to drink and visit various establishments. Next, when he did not return after several days, they began asking around. When no one had reported seeing William, they conducted a search and saw some faded foot prints in the dirt near the unused second well. They then checked the well and saw a shoe. The boys snagged him with a hook on a rope and pulled up his body, which was damaged when it fell numerous times. William's body was quietly buried in the family cemetery, a good distance away from John and other beloved family members. The girls claimed that William must have been drinking heavily the night following Rachel and Vlad's departure and gone outside. He was in a foul mood, which was typical of him when he drank, and everyone at the house thought that he had ridden off; again, to go to Ottawa. They added that he had bidden Rachel and Vlad a fond farewell and that Vlad and William had made amends before their departure. However, he was still very sad about Rachel leaving, as he had wanted her for his wife. It was a complex and well-thought plan, and it worked. Vlad and Rachel were safe, and they did not even know it.

As the morning wore on, Vlad and Rachel put a dozen more miles between themselves and Rachel's former home. She reflected on probably never seeing her sisters again, and that made her sad. However, she also thought of her love for Vlad and her new life, one of which she had always dreamed. They could go practically anywhere; they were free. They had some gold and silver, which they took time to hide more carefully in case of robbery.

When they went through Monkland, they found a general store that had maps of Eastern Ontario and New York. At around 4:00 p.m., they neared Cornwall, but did not believe they could make it through town and across to New York before dark. They decided to head a couple of miles east and camp for the night, in case they were being followed. They thought they could approach the town from the east the next morning and see if things looked alright. The road crossed a large stream at a rocky ford. It had some small pools about 100 yards from the ford, and they parked nearby, allowing the horses to graze in the succulent grasses along the stream's edge. Rachel undressed and bathed out of sight around a bend, washing with some lye soap scented with herbs that she had made a month before. Vlad washed with a bar of that soap nearby, but away from her. They decided not to consummate their love until they were married; they planned to marry as soon as they reached the United States.

They dressed separately and ate supper, then laid down on a quilt in a field of autumn flowers and watched the sun set. It was a tamer place than the wilds of the Pacific Northwest. Vlad felt at ease, although he kept one eye on the woods and road, and one hand near his pistol. Rachel laid her head upon his other shoulder and they kissed. It was all Vlad could do not to press Rachel to go further, but he knew that waiting was important to her. He wanted to do what was right, too. He had done so much wrong during his life that he wanted to live the rest of his life honorably. He could wait for her.

The sky slowly darkened, and the two fell soundly asleep. In the early morning light, Vlad awoke, collected the horses, and hitched the wagons. Rachel helped pack and make breakfast, which included some cheese she had purchased in Casselman. They approached Cornwall and saw nothing suspicious, although they wondered if they would even if there were danger there. They stopped at the first store, purchased some more supplies, and gauged the owner's response to them. Their presence did not seem to alarm him. As they moved through town, no one seemed to think anything of them. They then rode to the river and paid an exurbanite sum to cross the St. Lawrence River on the ferry. On the other side was New York State.

As they boarded the ferry, Vlad could not help but look back towards Canada, even though he was busy watching their wagon and horses being loaded onto the ferry. As the ferry pulled away from shore and crossed the river, Vlad kept looking back at Canada instead of across at America. He thought of all the years that he had dreamed of coming to America for freedom, and he now was about to realize his dream. Only during the past few days had he realized that he had already been living his dream of freedom in Canada. With the benefit of hindsight, he realized that he had been free since he last had contact with the Russians, even though he had thought he would not be free until he reached civilization.

Vlad thought of James Tedder at Fort St. John, Henry Clark at Grande Prairie, and George Carlisle at Edmonton. He thought of the late John Harris, and now of Rachel. Canada had become his home, and he was free there. He knew Rachel wanted to see New York City with him. He wondered if life in America would be truly better or if he and Rachel should return to Ontario once she had her fill of the big city, and purchase a farm away from Rockland and any problems caused by William's death. He did not know. For now, though, he was about to set foot on American soil and start the process of becoming an American. As the ferry neared the other side, he looked at America. He was about to take a step that would be a milestone in his life and complete a dream of his: to reach America. Still, he could not deny that he regretted leaving Canada.

Chapter 34
The United States

Vlad took a deliberate step onto American soil. Then, he became very busy helping to get the horses and wagon safely off the ferry and going to a customs house. When they entered the small wooden government building, a bored clerk was waiting behind a counter. He hardly looked at Rachel and Vlad. Rachel tried to do all of the talking so as not to give away Vlad's nationality from the remnant of his accent. There was little paperwork for them to do, but the clerk did ask Vlad a couple of questions. Vlad imitated the late John Harris' accent. Since Canada was somewhat diverse, the clerk did not suspect anything.

One of the things they needed to do was to put down their names. Vlad and Rachel moved to the other side of the room and spoke about the forms. Vlad said, "Rachel, My Russian name – Petrov – it would hurt our being accepted in a largely English-speaking country. Let's use your last name of Harris." Rachel beamed with joy. She had always liked her last name, although she would have been proud to share Vlad's Russian name with him had he desired to keep it. Vlad decided to keep his first name, and Rachel said, "Yes. Please keep your first name, Vlad. Don't give that up. If you do, you'll regret it later." They gave the forms to the clerk, and he did not even question the Russian sounding first name. He had ten other people to process along with Vlad and Rachel, and he wanted to get back to doing nothing until the next ferry full of people arrived.

Once Vlad and Rachel left the building, they were truly Americans and were free in the United States. They felt even freer because they thought that Canadian laws did not apply there. In truth, it would have been all but impossible for any Canadian legal authority to reach them in the United States, but had there been an issue at the border, the United States clerk would have denied them entry. In that case, they would have been required to return across the St. Lawrence River to Cornwall, Canada.

Just to be safe, they immediately rode about 25 miles into the United States. They came to the small town of Malone, New York. There they went to the first church, a Baptist one, and found a preacher. They talked him into marrying them immediately. It was a small wedding, just them, the preacher, and his wife as a witness. The sun was setting as they said their vows with the long shadows from the autumn sun shining into the church. Rachel wore a dress she had made, and Vlad wore a suit that he had purchased when he had gone to town with John to sell some of the harvest. They received a marriage certificate from the preacher, paid him with two silver coins that John had given Rachel just before his death, and ate dinner with the preacher and his wife. That night, they stayed in the nicest room in the small town's quant inn. They each washed separately and then came together. Rachel had packed a gown that she had sewn years earlier for her honeymoon. It now fit her snuggly, as she had filled out nicely since making it. It accentuated her incredible curves.

Vlad held her and the two finally shared the passion that had been burning in them for what seemed like forever. They spent all night exploring one another, and holding each other in between. The sun rose without the two having slept at all, and they felt tired but excited to be husband and wife at last. Afterwards, they fell asleep in each other's arms and didn't awake until lunch time. They went downstairs, and Rachel felt as if the entire world knew what they had been doing. She was embarrassed, but very happy as they ate lunch together. They could now plan their route, not only in safety from Canadian authorities, but as husband and wife. Today would be a day of celebration and rest from travel. It was October 1, 1858.

Chapter 35
Vlad and Rachel Travel through the Northern United States

As Vlad and Rachel traveled through New York State, they found they were distrusted as outsiders, but particularly Vlad because of his accent. Also, even though teenage girls often married older men in those days, some people stared and commented upon the age difference. By now, Rachel had turned 17, and Vlad was 26. However, her girlish looks made her appear even younger than 17, and Vlad's chiseled face, worn by the years of harsh survival, made him appear closer to 30.

Vlad asked Rachel to help him lose his accent. She told him, "Vlad, I love your accent, but I'll help you with it if that's what you want." She really did love his Russian accent, but she was concerned that Vlad would continue to have a difficult time because of it. She said, "It makes your appearance even stronger, and, to me, it's part of your overall charm and being." He could see the love in her eyes by the way she looked at him. Her eyes softened and her pupils enlarged whenever she spoke to him.

She worked through different words and common sounds used in the English language as they rode for a few hundred miles over many days. Vlad learned quickly, but still had difficulty with a few sounds. With those, he would slip into his Russian accent without realizing it. Rachel worked to make those sound German or Scottish.

Although very different, there were many immigrants from Germany and Scotland, and even a mixture of those accents would be more acceptable than Russian.

When they arrived in New York City, they found it expensive. They rode around town and found an affordable place to stay that would house them, their horses, and their wagon. They then toured around the city and saw the sights. Rachel enjoyed the excitement of the city, but she quickly realized that it was not a place where she could live and raise a family. For all the dreaming she had done about it, the city was just not for her. She needed a farm in the country. Vlad was willing to stay or to go, whatever she wanted. She was his family. That night, she said, "Vlad, I'd like to go to Philadelphia. I'd like for us to consider moving south from there to a climate that's warmer, but that still has some winter." Vlad said, "Yes, I agree. I'm sick of long winters, but I guess I do like some things about winter. A lot of warm weather sure would be nice."

The next morning, the two left early and were in New Jersey before lunch time. They traveled down the state and found that it became very lovely with more and more farms as they got farther away from New York City. They spent the nights along the road at camp sites, and they made friends with fellow travelers. They even traveled to Philadelphia in a group of their new-found friends, which made the trip safer, more enjoyable, and seemingly faster.

When they arrived in Philadelphia, they said goodbye to their new friends, who traveled on to Baltimore. Vlad and Rachel went to see the Liberty Bell and Independence Hall. They thought of their own struggles to be free and what a free country meant to them. They felt safe from Russians and anyone in Canada seeking to imprison them because of William. They found a comfortable hotel and stayed for a week.

Chapter 36
Vlad and Rachel Move to Southeastern Virginia

One day while walking near their hotel, Rachel bought a newspaper to teach Vlad to read better and to read for her own interest. While reading it, she saw an advertisement for farms in Greensville County, Virginia. A local bank in Emporia, the county seat of Greensville, was advertising low interest loans for farm land it described in large print as "Land so rich, you can grow money on it." Rachel discussed the advertisement with Vlad. After discussing, she concluded, "While it grossly exaggerates the quality of the land, this may be an opportunity. I am concerned, though, that if the land is so good, then why would the bank need to advertise, and why did the bank own it in the first place?"

Vlad said, "We need to go somewhere, and a farm that's affordable is very appealing, so long as the land looks good. And, we can buy many acres of land that are already cleared." Rachel agreed. Rachel and Vlad understood the value of cleared land from the amount of work necessary to turn woods into a field.

Rachel said, "Well, we could go down there and at least see it. The ad says that the railroad goes there. We could see it, and if it doesn't look good, then we could travel back here, perhaps look at farm land in Pennsylvania, or we could travel down into North or South Carolina. The growing season is longer in the South, and it would be nice to live in a warm climate."

The advertisement mentioned that Greensville County had mild winters. They did not realize that the price of the mild winters were incredibly hot and humid summers, which neither of them had ever known growing up in the frigid climates of Russia and Canada.

The next day, they packed their bags and took a train headed south. As they traveled, they stopped for a few days in Baltimore and Washington, D.C. In Baltimore, they enjoyed the harbor area and ate delicious crabs from the Chesapeake Bay. In Washington, they enjoyed seeing the Capitol and the White House; they were able to go right up to the front door of the White House and walk around in the yard. They were careful with their money, using only enough to supply their needs, with a few occasional purchases to make their life easier and more enjoyable.

Rachel knew about Vlad's gold nuggets, but they had not needed to cash them yet. They hoped to trade them for farm land or cash with which to buy land and other goods to set up their household. Before leaving Washington, they decided that they might get the best price for the gold there, rather than in a small town; they could at least find out how much they were worth. They checked with a few banks, and, after finally finding a place with the best rates, they decided to sell some of it. Their gold was assayed and proven to be genuine. They received United States currency and then traveled south out of the city on the railroad. They saw the Capitol dome as they headed towards the Potomac River bridge. They stayed in and toured Fredericksburg, Richmond, and Petersburg as they headed towards Emporia.

Once they reached Emporia, Vlad and Rachel went straight to the bank that had advertised the land. They met a young man named Dave Hawley, who was between their ages. Dave said he had left West Point near the end of his second year after getting injured. His dad had always looked after him and bailed him out of trouble. Dave got the job at the bank because his dad owned it, but his dad closed all the deals. Dave was anxious to make a sale. At first, he was prejudiced against them because of their youth and Vlad's accent. He reasoned that they did not have any money. Dave said, "This is good land and, while priced to sell, we must make certain that potential buyers can afford it. Are you sure you're able to afford the land?"

In response, Vlad produced about $500.00 in cash, and that gained Dave's attention like nothing else could have. Vlad found that money overcame a lot of prejudices, at least on a superficial level. In all, Vlad and Rachel had collectively over $1,700.00, plus gold, and did not feel safe carrying that much cash or their gold. They thought of opening a bank account, but they might not stay in this town, and they did not want Dave to know how much money they had; they believed it would influence the price of the land.

Dave said, "I'll meet you at 7 o'clock tomorrow morning and take you in my carriage to view a few farms." He recommended a hotel in town, which his father owned. Vlad and Rachel found it, checked in, and went to bed early. They were tired from traveling, but Rachel bathed and sprayed herself with perfume.

Early the next morning, Dave took them to see the land. Vlad explained, "Dave, We appreciate your showing us the land and all, but we want the honest truth about why the bank has so many farms for sale." Dave explained, "The bank was owned by someone who made many risky loans. There was a drought a couple of years back, and the bank had to foreclose on the farms now for sale. The bank was nearly bankrupt last year when my dad bought it. Dad then consolidated it with his other banks around Greensville County and the surrounding area. The drought is over, and most of the farms around Greensville survived. We live up near the town of Purdy and have a large farm outside of town where we grow all kinds of crops. We also have a small bank there. Should you buy land around here, we have convenient, secure banks all over."

Vlad and Rachel saw a couple of farms, but none seemed quite right. The land seemed too worn out to grow good crops. The next day, they met Dave again and saw a farm near Purdy. It had a good wide stream running through it, with trees along its banks. It had ample crop land overgrown with lush weeds and some woodland for cutting trees for lumber and firewood. It seemed perfect, but the price was $650.00. Vlad and Rachel returned to the bank to negotiate with Dave and his father.

Dave's father, David Hawley Sr., was a United States congressman. He was as crooked as a dog's hind leg and pretty much ran the town and the entire county. He took an instant liking to Rachel and spoke to her as if Vlad was not even in the room. Before Vlad could express himself bluntly, Rachel took his hand and reminded the Congressman, "Vlad and I are *married*, and we're looking for a farm on which to raise a family." She squeezed Vlad's hand and gave him a nervous look and smile, which Vlad understood to mean not to hit this man, or worse.

After a bit of haggling, they agreed to a price of $562.50 for the land, which was contingent on the deed giving them good title and the description matching the boundaries on the survey they were shown. The couple put down $100.00 as a deposit. In two days, Dave Jr. showed them the newly drafted deed and took them to walk the property to make certain that the surveyor and lawyer had not made an error in either side's favor. Everything checked out as far as any of them could determine, so they rode back into town and closed the deal. The next morning, Vlad and Rachel checked out of the hotel and moved to the farm. First, they set about making the old farmhouse livable. Then, they bought some farm animals, such as cows, chickens, pigs, sheep, and goats.

Vlad and Rachel both worked very hard to make the farm prosperous by putting in long days of heavy physical labor and doing household chores. With only two of them, they both had to do a bit of everything. Vlad even cooked while Rachel was busy delivering a calf, a skill she had learned from her father. They were a partnership and a team. They worked hard, but they tried to have fun in their work. Vlad taught Rachel to ride a horse better, and she taught him to tie all kinds of knots that her father had taught her. They both knew how to shoot and enjoyed competing in target shooting contests with each other. With her mother gone, Rachel's father sometimes treated his girls like boys, and they were well-trained in many skills not usually taught to girls in the mid-nineteenth century. Although it was early winter, the high temperatures were often in the low 50's or 60's, which seemed like spring to them.

After getting the farmhouse and farm in order, they decided they needed some help. Although it was still winter, they were told that spring would come much sooner than in Canada. They would plant their first crops, but the fields badly needed plowing after a couple of years of not being worked. They saw an advertisement for a slave market in Richmond, but both abhorred slavery. Rachel was raised to believe that it was wrong, that people should be paid for their work. Vlad particularly had strong feelings against slavery because of his imprisonment at the work camp in Alaska, which would have been slavery for life. They decided that they would hire laborers and pay fair wages. They could not afford to pay much, but providing room and board would make up the difference. They asked around in town and posted a notice for farm laborers on the community board.

Chapter 37
Runaway Slave

Before they could hire anyone, Vlad was cleaning out the barn one day when he saw movement in the haystack. He slipped away quietly and went to the house to get his pistol. He made sure it was ready to fire and circled far around to approach the barn from the opposite direction. He entered the opened back door and saw a young black man looking towards the front. The man was shaking and scared. He was about ready to run out the back door towards Vlad, when he turned and saw Vlad pointing the pistol at him. Vlad asked him, "What's your name, and why are you here?"

The young man said, "A-a-a, Aaron, sir. I'm, ah, lost." Vlad immediately knew that he was a runaway slave. Since runaway slaves could be beaten so badly that they died, Vlad knew that Aaron would try anything to escape, so Vlad kept him covered with his pistol. Vlad told Aaron, "I know you're a runaway slave, and you'd better answer the rest of my questions honestly, or else." Aaron trembled with fear.

Vlad asked Aaron, "Where are you from?" Aaron said, "I've come from Enfield, North Carolina. I was, I am a slave on the Jones farm there. Please, sir, let me go, and you'll never see me again! If you return me, my master's slave managers will take me into the swamps, tie me to a tree, whip me good, and leave me to die slowly!" Aaron vividly described two others who had died in such a way.

Vlad thought of the man in the Alaskan work camp who had tried to escape and immediately believed him. That man had been beaten and left outside overnight, where a bear killed and partially ate him. The slave owners may have used slightly different methods from the Russians, like dehydration and exposure, but it was the same old cruelty. Vlad's mind raced with curiosity and questions, so he asked him all at once, "Why did you escape if you thought you'd be tortured and killed upon recapture, and why did you think you could get very far in the first place? Where did you plan to go?"

Aaron said, "The crops have not been good for a few years and the chief slave manager was under pressure to get more crops out of us slaves. He pushed us harder and harder, to the point that several slaves died, so the chief slave manager pressed us even harder to make up for the lost labor. Then, just a week before, I was going to wed another slave. She was a couple of years younger than me, and she was very pretty. The chief slave manager heard of the wedding and took the girl from the fields, raped her during the day, and beat her to death." Aaron began crying from his fear and remembrance of his love. He hesitated to tell the rest, but Vlad told him in a commanding voice, "Please finish, and tell me the truth." Aaron replied, "I am telling you the truth! That night, when a group of us slaves came in from the fields, I found her. Her younger cousin saw the whole thing and told us what he'd done. I was so upset that I ran away that night."

Vlad said, "Was that after you killed the slave master?" Aaron asked, "How did you know that?" Vlad said, "Tell me what happened." Aaron didn't want to, but figured it didn't matter now that he was captured, unless Vlad felt sorry for him and let him go. "During the night, I snuck up to the chief slave manager's house, broke in, and attacked him. I didn't carry any type of weapon. I should have, but I wasn't thinking clear. It looked like he had passed out from drinking, so I jumped on him and strangled him to death for raping and killing my girl! I had no choice but to leave. You can do with me what you will, but ask yourself what you would have done!"

Vlad asked, "I know exactly how I'd feel and what I'd do, but how did you get from near Enfield all the way here? The Roanoke River, swamps, fields, and towns are between here and there." Aaron further explained, "I crawled out a window of the house where the slave manager was, and I just started running. I didn't go back to get nothing. I traveled through the woods, swamps, and fields of Halifax County. I crossed the Roanoke River over a railroad trestle at Weldon very late one night and was able to make it across Northampton County and into Virginia. I thought that if I kept traveling north, I could reach a non-slave state. I've heard there were ministers and others who were against slavery who might help me along the way, but I don't know who to trust. Sir, will you please help me by letting me go?"

It was such a painful story that Vlad frequently looked down so that his emotions would not betray him. Vlad saw Aaron's calloused feet, which were practically white from the thick dead skin and dirt upon them. Vlad was reminded that slaves did not get shoes, and their feet were always in rough condition.

As Vlad listened to the story, he was impressed with Aaron's honesty, and his escape and travels reminded Vlad of his own flight. Although Aaron's journey was shorter than Vlad's, he had made it almost 50 miles across populated counties with much open cropland without being caught, which was impressive. Vlad saw a lot of himself in Aaron, and told him, "I'll give you some food before you leave if you promise that you will leave at nightfall and never tell a soul who helped you, regardless of whether or not you make it to the North. If you get up there and run your mouth about who helped you, I could get sent to prison or worse." Aaron said, "I promise! I'll never breathe a word, no not a word, but I won't forget you the rest of my life!"

Vlad knew that Aaron stood little chance of making it into the next county, let alone across Virginia and Maryland. Still, Vlad had made it across the Alaskan frontier and most of British Columbia alone. Vlad told Aaron, "Stay in the barn and out of sight while I go get the food." Vlad walked away without waiting for a response. As Vlad left, it occurred to him that Aaron probably did not trust him. Without saying anything to Rachel, who was busy sewing in the house, Vlad went to the kitchen and got some cheese and biscuits. Since kitchens tended to burn, they were built as separate structures away from the house, so Rachel didn't hear him. Vlad wrapped the food in a piece of cheesecloth and went back towards the barn. He entered cautiously by a different door in case Aaron was so scared that he attacked Vlad.

As Vlad entered the barn, Aaron was sitting on the floor crying. Vlad moved closer to him and placed the wrapped food down on a bale of hay, then backed away. Vlad again told Aaron, "For helping you, I could be severely punished, perhaps even lynched. Do you understand how important it is that you stay out of sight until dark before you leave?" "Yes," Aaron said. Vlad also told him, "Throw away the cheesecloth once you finish the food, so there will be no trace of assistance in case you're captured." Aaron agreed.

Aaron asked Vlad for directions. All he knew was that he should go north. Vlad then retrieved a map from the house. While he was there, he got an old pair of shoes, which he had bought in Edmonton, and a new pair of homemade socks. Vlad thought that if Aaron was captured, the shoes and socks might signal assistance, but he also thought that the captors would probably think they were stolen, and there was nothing in them that would lead anyone back to Vlad. When Vlad gave Aaron the shoes and socks, Aaron hugged him and cried with relief. Aaron knew that anyone who would give him shoes and socks would not harm or betray him. Vlad told him, "Say nothing of it." Feeling awkward and embarrassed by his own generosity, Vlad said, "Now, let's look at the map."

While they looked at the map, Vlad told Aaron of the railroad nearby that ran to Petersburg. He told Aaron, "Follow it, but stay off the actual tracks during the day, because you could be seen for over two miles on the straight portions. Be careful following the tracks into Petersburg, and go around all cities and towns, if possible. From Petersburg, the tracks go to Richmond and then to Washington, D.C." Vlad could see and smell that Aaron had been through the swamps. That was no small feat with all the water moccasins and mosquitoes, but traveling through there certainly had saved Aaron's life by keeping him away from people and dogs that might have tried to track him.

Vlad told Aaron, "Your clothes look like those of a slave. I'll get you some newer ones of mine. You'll look like a freeman. But, if you are ever questioned about them, you must claim that you got them off a clothesline or something. You will be killed if you're captured, anyway, so admitting to stealing clothes will not increase your final punishment." Aaron shook as he thanked Vlad again for his help. Vlad then went to the house and got some slightly worn-looking dress clothes and a hat, which would give Aaron the appearance of a free black man trying to appear well-off. He went back to the barn and gave the clothes to Aaron. He told Aaron, "Take your old clothes with you and throw them away far from here."

Vlad then went back to the kitchen and got some chicken left over from lunch. Vlad knew that meat would give

Aaron energy, and Vlad thought of how the wild game he had killed and eaten had sustained him through his horrific journey through British Columbia. He wrapped it in cheesecloth, brought it back, and told Aaron to save that food for supper. Vlad also gave him some fresh milk full of rich cream to drink right before he left because it would soon spoil. He told Aaron to get some sleep, if he could, and that he would wake him in about 5 hours, right before dark. Aaron ate and lay down in the hay. He got up once or twice to look out towards the house where Vlad was working. Aaron knew that there was a bounty on runaways, and he began to worry again, but for the most part, he trusted Vlad. After all, Vlad had him at gunpoint and could have taken him in when he first encountered him.   Plus, Vlad gave him shoes, clothes, and food, and he could be punished for that. Still, Aaron's fear of trackers coming to the farm was hard to completely overcome.

After a while, Aaron finally felt comfortable enough to fall fast asleep. He was so exhausted that he truly could not help it. It was the first time that he had felt at least a little comfortable in days. A few hours later, Vlad came and pointed him in the direction that he should go. Vlad said to be sure not to leave until dark, then Vlad left and went inside to eat supper. Rachel had cooked a small supper with only a baked chicken, collards flavored with ham, sweet potatoes drizzled in freshly churned butter, and buttermilk biscuits with honey. Vlad had worked hard that day, and every day except Sunday. He needed a lot of food to fuel him, and he ate until he was full.

During dinner, Vlad spoke of his work that day and what he planned to do the next day. He asked Rachel about her day, and made sure he kept the conversation away from why he kept coming in and out of the barn, kitchen, and house. In case he was ever questioned, he wanted Rachel to be able to say that she had not seen Aaron at their place and that Vlad had nothing to do with him. After dinner, Vlad returned to the barn, woke Aaron, and gave him a bit more food to go along with the chicken and milk.

The next morning, Vlad checked the barn and Aaron was gone. Vlad cleaned up so that there was no sign that Aaron had been there. Vlad needed to go into town, but he did not want to leave Rachel alone, so he asked her to come along. She was delighted to go into town with him. She usually insisted on coming along anyway, even when she knew that Vlad was only going there for an important purchase and needed to get back to the farm quickly. She did not mind slowing him down. She dressed up, brushed her hair, and wore the silver hair comb that Vlad had bought in New York not long after their wedding. She cherished that silver comb; it reminded her of their wedding.

Vlad and Rachel rode into town, and Vlad stopped first at the hardware store. He asked about any news, and all of the fellows were talking about an escaped slave from North Carolina who had drowned trying to cross the Merriman River. Vlad was extremely sad. They said that he had murdered his master's slave manager for not allowing him to get married. They spoke of what a great man the manager had been and how he had been too benevolent towards the slaves. The other men agreed that kindness towards slaves is always repaid with violence or slothfulness.

Vlad's blood boiled. He quickly changed the subject to the crops being planted and expected weather. He then bought what he needed and returned to meet Rachel. She was not yet back at the wagon, so he went into a women's store where he knew he would find her. She was busy admiring a dress, which was too expensive, but he did not even protest or try to steer her mind towards something less costly. He simply asked how much and pulled out the money. Vlad knew it was Rachel's money, too.

Rachel was excited the entire way back, but he was sad. She asked him, "What's wrong, Vlad?" Figuring that he had nothing to lose and that she would not be in danger by knowing, he told her of Aaron, his helping Aaron, and the news of Aaron's death. She sat silently at first, horrified over the drowning. Then, she hugged Vlad and gave him a kiss. With a tear in her eye, she told Vlad in a broken voice, "What a wonderful compassionate man you are. I'm so proud of you!" She added, "You know, you could have trusted me to help, but I understand that you wanted me to be able to say convincingly that you were not involved in case you were suspected of helping that poor man."

She sat close to him as they rode and smiled at him often. She said, "I knew that your character was strong when I first got to know you. I just knew it." Changing the subject, she said, "You know, I feel guilty about the dress and I wish I hadn't gotten it now." Vlad stopped her, "You don't have enough of those dresses, and you have sacrificed so much so we could be together. I wanted to get you something like that long ago and I'm glad that you felt comfortable enough to buy it. After all, it's your money, too."

When they returned to the farm, Rachel went into the house to try on her dress again and then to hang it carefully so that it would look great for church on Sunday. Vlad went to the barn. He walked in and looked at the place where he first saw Aaron and where Aaron had slept while waiting for nightfall. He was concerned that his making Aaron leave at night may have caused him to drown because he could not see a good place to ford the river. Vlad thought it strange that Aaron had been found so quickly and that news had spread so fast. Even though the river was fairly close by, how could they have identified Aaron so quickly? Vlad figured that none of that really mattered, because they seemed so certain.

Vlad was about to turn around and leave, when he saw a portion of the suit he had given Aaron sticking out of the haystack. Looking puzzled because he remembered Aaron wearing it, he walked over to it and touched it. Aaron sprung up quickly, and Vlad was both shocked and glad to see him. Vlad smiled and said, "Aaron, You're alive!" Aaron was afraid that Vlad would be mad at him for returning. Vlad explained what he had heard in town. Aaron said, "Please don't be mad with me. I got to the railroad tracks last night saw lights approaching fast! I hid and armed men on horses with torches passed by me on the tracks. When they did, I knew I couldn't go north along the tracks. If armed men were looking for me in the country, I wouldn't make it through Petersburg or any towns along the way. I came back to the farm and slept in the barn. I was fixin' to go ask you for another way to travel when you and your woman left, and I then fell asleep, hiding in the hay."

Vlad told him that he was welcomed to stay for a few days until Vlad could be certain that he was no longer being hunted. That would also give Vlad more time to figure out how to get Aaron past Petersburg and Richmond, so that he could make a clear run for the North. He told Aaron that he was concerned for his wife's safety and that Aaron should not go near her, the kitchen, or the house. Aaron agreed. Vlad told him, "I'll bring you some food in a little while."

Aaron asked Vlad, "Maybe I could be your slave? I promise to work very hard." Vlad stopped him and said plainly, "I came from what was basically slavery with the Russians in Alaska and I never want to own slaves!" Still, Vlad thought he could use a hired hand around the place. Vlad said, "If you're willing, I may be able to hire you, but we need to wait and see what happens regarding the drowned black man. I'll check in town in a few days, and if no one is still looking for you, we can work something out."

In reality, a group of angry white slave owners had lynched a free black man because he had been talking publicly about how slaves would be freed soon by the United States government, which would make the Southern states free the slaves. He had spoken boldly and tried to make himself appear important and authoritative. After lynching him, they carried his body about 25 miles southeast until they reached the Merriman River, stripped him, and dumped him. They then went back home, denying any knowledge of his whereabouts and speculating that he probably went back up north from where he had come – "Good riddance," one of them declared. They had not heard of the escaped slave from North Carolina, as news had not traveled that far. They were more tied in to the Petersburg and Richmond news centers. When local men had found the man early the next morning while fishing, they assumed that he was the slave from North Carolina that they had heard reports about.

Vlad went into the house and told Rachel the news. She was very happy for him. They discussed whether or not they could trust Aaron. Although he seemed harmless and honest, he had killed someone. Vlad thought that had anyone raped Rachel, he would have surely killed that man without any second thoughts or regrets. Plus, Vlad had killed a number of men, and his own darling

Rachel had shot William in self-defense. Vlad decided that he would tell Aaron he could stay, but warn him again not to approach the house. Experience had taught Vlad not to trust people until he knew them well. Vlad always slept near his pistol. He knew how to use it, and time had shown that he needed to know how to use it. Even so, he was not as concerned about Aaron because he knew that Aaron needed him too much. Vlad just wanted to be careful.

Vlad gathered some chicken, cheese, biscuits, and milk, and went to Aaron. He and Aaron had a long talk and reached an understanding. Aaron again promised not to go near Rachel or the house. Vlad agreed that Aaron could do some chores around the barn at first, which would cover his food and lodging. He would help Vlad fix up an upper part of the barn for him, which would be comfortable and out of sight. If the heat had truly died down, then Vlad would consider hiring him for other more visible duties around the farm. Vlad thought that after harvest, he could possibly reward Aaron's work with a train ticket north to Philadelphia and find out how to draw up some papers showing that Aaron was free. Aaron could earn enough in working for Vlad and Rachel to be able to afford that. Vlad would not own a slave, and Aaron would not have to trade one plantation for another, smaller one.

In the coming days, Vlad learned that the body of the free black man had been buried unceremoniously outside of town and that news of the runaway slave's death had been sent back to Enfield. News of an escaped slave drowning in the Merriman River finally reached the men who had murdered the free black man, but it reached them two weeks later. It also sounded as though it had just happened and it was not the man that they had dumped in that river. In any event, they were not going to ask any questions. Even though they would not have been prosecuted for his murder, much less convicted, they thought of themselves as upstanding men in their community, and they did not want anyone thinking negatively of them. After all, that would be bad for business.

After a couple of weeks, Aaron began helping Vlad in the fields planting crops. Vlad knew that sooner or later someone would see Aaron and ask where Vlad had gotten him. Vlad, Rachel, and Aaron conspired to say that Vlad had gotten Aaron from a slave market in Fayetteville, North Carolina. Vlad would say that he went there because his wife had family there and one of her cousins could get him a good deal on a slave because he worked at the large slave market located there. Vlad and Rachel even came up with names for her Fayetteville cousins.

Since Rachel could read and write, she forged papers for Aaron. She spent a few evenings practicing copying and redrafting papers from similar ones she had seen at other women's houses in town when she went to her sewing group and at the Register of Deeds Office, where slave transactions were officially recorded. She had made a point to discuss possibly buying a slave and asking about the details of how to go about it. Her friends were glad to show off their slaves' papers as a way of bragging about their wealth. Rachel was even able to keep the ownership forms for a slave who had died. After a few evenings of careful work, she had altered those forms to the slave that had died to cover Aaron. She used Aaron's first name, but kept the last name of the deceased slave, so as not to have to alter too much of the document and because using Aaron's prior last name, which was the name of his former slave owner, was too risky.

Rachel and Vlad debated whether trying to record them at the Register of Deeds Office was too risky. They decided to do so as soon as possible, so that some time would pass before they filed the ones necessary to make him officially free. They had to file slave ownership papers to be able to file papers granting Aaron his freedom. If they filed those papers too close to one another, they would raise suspicion. Rachel and Vlad hated the idea of officially owning a slave, but it was the best pathway to Aaron's eventual freedom.

In a few months, and with Aaron's help, Vlad could harvest and sell the first crops of the season. As more crops matured and were harvested, Vlad should then have ample funds to provide for Rachel and himself for the winter, with plenty of funds left over to buy Aaron a train ticket and provide him with some cash in repayment for his very hard work. It was the summer of 1859.

Chapter 38
Rumors of War

As 1859 passed into 1860, Vlad and Rachel continued to build their farm. They filed papers officially recognizing Aaron's freedom, and he stayed on to help. As 1860 wore on, rumors of the Southern states leaving the Union became public talk, along with the Presidential election. Virginia and neighboring North Carolina were not strongly in favor of succession, while South Carolina, Georgia and other states in the Deep South were in favor of it. Vlad and Rachel attended meetings in Purdy and Emporia. They listened intently, and Rachel asked Vlad, "If it happens, I wonder what it will mean for us and our new farm." Vlad, fighting the urge not to be pessimistic, but wanting to always be honest with her, said, "Probably war and a lot of suffering that no one is talking about."

Finally, when Abraham Lincoln won the election, succession seemed sealed. In early 1861, Vlad attended another meeting in Purdy, but instead of simply listening, he got up and addressed his neighbors. Vlad told them of how he struggled for survival in Russia. He even partly mentioned Alaska and leaving there to go to Canada where he met Rachel. He omitted the details about being a prisoner and escaping. He told them about how he and Rachel had traveled through New York and Pennsylvania, not knowing where to go until they saw an advertisement for land here and had liked it so much that they wanted their home to be here.

He told them how he and Rachel poured their heart and soul into the land. It was their home and how they thought of the people of Purdy as their new family. Vlad told of the bloodshed he had seen in the Russian Army. Despite what some said about the Northern states not having the will or means to fight, Vlad told them his perspective from his days in Russia. He knew that the Russian way was to fight and fight brutally, and the North would fight just the same.

He also said that he hoped to live out his days with Rachel farming the land and raising a family in peace. He spoke of how he had agonized over whether to support the United States, because he had dreamed of coming here for years and the freedom that it represented, or to support Virginia should it secede from the United States. Vlad told them that his country was where Rachel and their farm are located. If Virginia seceded, then he would fight to protect the woman and land that he loved. But, he warned, they would all lose loved ones from the tragedies of war. They could lose their homes and possessions, too, everything they had worked for their entire lives. He told them to view war soberly despite all the rhetoric.

As Vlad sat down, the people present cheered and hollered in support of his speech. They only heard that he would fight for Virginia because that is where his love and home are. The crowd lusted for war. Vlad sat expressionless with the stark awareness that a brutal war was coming. When he heard the cheers, he regretted that his speech had not conveyed to the crowd the meaning of the plain words he had used. He figured there would be a war, and he prayed that Rachel and he could survive it. He did not want to fight. He simply wanted to live in peace. He wished he could just flee with Rachel. Fleeing is easy to think of doing, but extremely hard to actually do. He realized that he should have pressed Rachel to return to Ontario or some other part of Canada when she had her fill of the big eastern cities and wanted a farm.

As other speakers worked the crowd into a further frenzy, Vlad sat there motionless knowing that he could not sell his farm. If they ran, they would lose everything, and where would they go? They both might be wanted for murder in Canada over William's death. Plus, neither Vlad nor Rachel was the type of person to walk out on their responsibilities. They were citizens of Virginia; it was their home, and they would act accordingly. He had to hope that cooler minds would prevail and peace would somehow be kept. He had killed and seen so many violent deaths already during his life. Vlad then placed his face in his hands and wept while the others cheered. He thought that they were fools, but he knew in his heart that they would know the terror of battle and the pain of death all too soon. Rachel placed her hand on his shoulder. She sat frightened and in disbelief that the crowd wanted war.

Vlad and Rachel rode home quietly that night. Vlad had certainly endeared himself to his neighbors, and that would help Rachel should he have to leave to fight. She respected him for saying what he did. Part of her now wished that they had stayed in Canada. However, at the same time, she realized that Southern Virginia was their home, and she felt that strongly. They had built a wonderful life together. They had roots there, however new they may be.

Rachel broke the silence by saying, "Vlad, we fled once because we had to, and to build our lives together. If we flee now, we'll be the type of people who run every time there's a problem. We'll lose everything we've worked so hard to build. It's not just about the material things, but about our lives together. If we run this time, we won't be true to who we are. I believe we are meant to stay here and continue making this our home. Also, where would we go? The entire country may be at war soon with nowhere being safe. We may or may not make it all the way back to Canada. With talk of war, people do lawless things, and that could make it even more dangerous to travel there. The only place we really could go there would be back to my old home. While I'd like to see my sisters again someday, there's nothing else for me there. If we did go there, would you or I be wanted for murder? If so, I'd lose you. There's nothing there for us!"

Still, a tall mountain was right in front of both of them. They both knew that they would have to climb it, together at times, but alone most of the time.

Chapter 39
Vlad Joins the Confederate Army

In about a month or so, news of the battle at Fort Sumter reached them. Simultaneously, Vlad heard that a number of his fellow Greensville County residents were organizing a cavalry unit because so many of them thought they were good at riding horses. They also thought it would save them from the discomforts of the walking foot soldier. Vlad was surprised that he had a choice, as he thought he would be conscripted into an infantry unit. He knew he could not avoid service, so he went to one of the meetings. He thought it best to explain his prior experience and rank. For the first time, he discussed in some detail his prior military service to his neighbors, but omitted the parts that might reflect badly upon him. He thought it best to try to be a leader so that he would have more freedom and options.

In describing his prior service, he emphasized his rank, horsemanship, and overall abilities. He characterized his service as a defender of the Russian border from Polish attacks, which was the basic function and responsibility of his old unit. The Clarksville men were impressed and voted him a sergeant. Their latent fear and prejudice of foreigners kept him from being a lieutenant or captain.

They voted a rich man captain. He was David Hawley, Jr., a son of the banker and the young man who had shown Vlad and Rachel several pieces of property for sale. Dave got the position because he went to West Point for almost two years, although he left under hushed circumstances, claiming to have been injured to the people of Greensville County. The injury to Dave's back, the family claimed, meant that he could no longer meet the physical requirements for an Army Commission and graduation from West Point. Since his father had been a United States congressman, the real reason for his departure had been covered up. Anyone disbelieving the injury story simply assumed that Dave had been caught cheating and expelled.

The family now spoke of his full recovery to secure his rank. Vlad remembered when he first met Dave how Dave had walked perfectly fine around the farms and later checked the boundaries of the deed to Rachel's and his farm. Dave also rode to and from the farm on a bumpy road without any complaints. Other people had seen him around his family's farm riding hard. He even competed in horse competitions in Richmond and had won or placed second or third on a number of occasions. He was hardly a man physically unfit to be in the Army. His knowledge and tactical abilities were what worried Vlad.

Captain Dave Hawley quickly chose Vlad as his primary aide, based upon Vlad's experience. Dave realized that he did not know tactics as well as the other men had assumed he did. The first two years at West Point were full of math, science, English, physical training, and drilling, with only a small amount of tactics. He needed a man who had real combat experience. Vlad knew that Dave was chosen because of his family, his wealth, and his status in the community. Vlad was scared that such a man would get them all killed. He knew that he needed to get Dave to trust and listen to him. Remembering that Dave was friendly when Rachel and he had looked to buy land, Vlad tried to develop a friendship and made certain not to upstage him. Thankfully, Dave needed Vlad more than Vlad realized. Also, while Dave had a bit of an elitist attitude, he was very personable. He wanted too badly to be accepted by people to stay a snob all the time.

Chapter 40
The Battle of Fredericksburg

Vlad's company trained and trained. It practiced shooting pistols and rifles while riding. Vlad was already good at this from his days in the Russian Army, and he helped to train the others. The company also practiced hacking targets with sabers while riding, and it practiced all types of riding skills. Vlad taught them tactics, which he had to think through to put into words because they were second nature to him. Then, the company was ordered to move north to patrol around quiet parts of Virginia between Richmond and Fredericksburg, protecting the Capital City against federal raids. Vlad and Rachel had only one day's notice. They held each other all night and said a long goodbye early in the morning, each not knowing if they would ever see the other again.

After quickly moving out, the company went through Richmond and north to patrol near Richmond. After countless months, the group received new orders. It was the summer of 1862, and they were sent to Fredericksburg to help defend it from a probable Union attack. They practiced with other units and got very good at cavalry tactics by learning from other cavalry companies. Confederate General Lee had excellent commanders under him, and his army was full of men ready to fight. That would change over the course of the next two years, but for now, they were ready for the Union Army.

In December of 1862, the Union attacked. Despite all of Vlad's pessimism and hatred of war, he was primed and ready to fight. Just like old times, once Vlad was in the fight, he did his job and did it well. He and his company fought with tenacity. They ambushed a Union cavalry company that was disorganized and improperly led. Vlad's company hacked and shot them to pieces. Vlad personally killed their commander with his saber by cutting most of the man's head off in one blow. The image of the dangling head of the rider as the horse carried him away was one more image forever seared into Vlad's brain. The body stayed in position on the horse for what seemed like a minute, spewing blood as the commander's heart still pounded. He fell off in a few seconds, but the time between the blow and the fall seemed a lot longer to Vlad.

Despite the horror of the kill, Vlad pressed on. He had to because the battle was raging and someone could be eyeing his neck for a similar result. Close to dark, both sides returned to their lines for protection. They were tired, hungry, and very dehydrated. As night fell, the entire battle started dying down, with only the cries of the wounded being heard.

The Confederate Army handed Union General Burnside his men's heads at Fredericksburg. Vlad thought that Burnside must be an idiot because of the way he threw his infantrymen into heavily fortified positions. The Confederates tore them apart. Wave after wave of the Union soldiers were shot down as they marched in tight and exposed lines of men to their deaths. For the first time, Vlad became optimistic that the South had a real chance at beating the North. Vlad thought that if the North continued to fight by exposing large numbers of men to heavy fire from protected elevated positions, it would run out of soldiers. He knew better, but he needed the relief, and he savored the victory with his fellow countrymen. He felt a part of the Confederacy and of Virginia. They were his country and his state.

Vlad's company yelled excitedly over the victory. However, it was more out of relief that the battle was over and they had survived. It was also out of having beaten an opponent who was supposed to have crushed them nearly two years ago, within a few months of the start of the war. From the commander on down, his company celebrated the win the way young men seventy-five years later would celebrate after a football victory. Vlad celebrated as loudly as any of his comrades. He enjoyed the mental relief of a mass celebration. They all did. They feasted on roasted chickens from a local farm and drank homemade whiskey. They celebrated without any thought for tomorrow, until tomorrow dawned.

Vlad awoke at dawn after four hours' sleep realizing that they had won one battle and not the entire war. He walked dazed from exhaustion around a hospital where young men from both sides lay slowly dying or realizing that their lives would never be the same again after hastily performed amputations. Despite the Confederate victory, thousands of Confederates had been wounded or killed. He had lost five men in his company alone, fellow Greensville County farmers who would never go home to their wives or parents. He knew that this was war, and it would not go well even if the South won. If the Union Army sacrificed its men in such a way, it would not give up without taking a whole lot of Confederates with it. Vlad no longer thought that General Burnside was an idiot. He thought he was cold and calculating. Any General who would send his troops to slaughter the way Burnside had done lacked a heart, and an enemy general without a heart was the most dangerous enemy of all. Vlad was scared.

As Christmas approached, Vlad's company was ordered back to north of Richmond where they took relief from the winter's cold in a railroad town called Ashland. Vlad told Dave, "We're only about 80 miles north of Emporia, but it feels ten degrees colder up here than it would back there." Dave agreed, "I've heard there's a weather line just north of Petersburg." The group was quartered in houses throughout the town and had a number of days' rest, as the lines were far to the north of them. They felt relatively safe, although they still posted guards and took precautions. Vlad thought of Rachel constantly.

Vlad was staying with a family who cooked great food and extended their hospitality to him. They were required to house him, but they seemed to enjoy having him there. It was a great time for Vlad. He slept in a soft warm bed with a fireplace nearby. It was a stone fireplace, and once heated, the rocks would give off heat that warmed the entire room fairly evenly. Twice a week, he bathed in the owners' bathtub. First, he would eat a delicious supper. Then, he would warm water over the fire and place it into the tub. He would soak for a half an hour, periodically adding hot water heated by the nearby fire. When finished, he would get out, dry off, and put on a fresh night shirt that had been washed that day. Sometimes, he would crawl into freshly washed sheets. His bed had warm quilts on top of a down-filled mattress.

The usual life for a cavalryman was to camp in the open where, as in Russia, half his body would be roasted by a campfire in the winter while the other half would be frozen from the night air. Although, the cavalry had its own risks, like getting ambushed easily or cut off and trapped, Vlad knew that he had it better than the infantrymen. Dave Hawley stayed in the house next door and set up his command post there. Vlad was his adjutant, so he spent most of the day indoors with Dave in his command post, reading and occasionally playing cards.

As 1863 dawned, Vlad's company was ordered northwest of Fredericksburg to near Warrenton and Culpepper, both of which were practically ghost towns from all of the fighting in and around them. Prior to leaving, a few dozen men from near Norfolk were assigned to the group, and Vlad received a promotion to Lieutenant. The circumstances there were very different from Ashland.

The company had to watch its every move to avoid a deadly ambush. Throughout the late winter and spring of 1863, they patrolled and engaged in a few skirmishes. They moved farther north and spent time keeping lookout on a foothill near Paris, Virginia. Finally, they received orders to join forces moving north to bring the war to the Union. It was Lee's great plan to live off of northern farms and raid Yankee villages.

Chapter 41
Gettysburg

In the weeks that followed, they crossed into Maryland and then into Pennsylvania. Dave Hawley rallied his men, "Soldiers of the South! This is a great opportunity – our opportunity – to defeat the Yankee Army and then maybe swing around, destroy Philadelphia or Washington, and end this war!" Vlad thought of the wonderful times he had with Rachel in Philadelphia, Baltimore, and Washington.

It was early July of 1863 when the days of traveling suddenly stopped, and the battle quickly began. They had arrived late and quartered their horses away from the lines, thinking they would be held in reserve. However, they were quickly called up to serve as infantrymen in an area where the line had been breached. There was no time to retrieve their horses, anyway. The company lost half of its strength the very first day. Many were killed, wounded, captured, or just separated from the others in the terrible confusion of the battle. Dave and Vlad were both cut and badly bruised. They tried to hold the group together, but there were so many people and so much confusion on the field. You could look beside yourself and see a Yankee soldier fighting another Confederate.

Not long into the battle, Vlad grabbed a rifle from a fallen soldier, an 1857 Enfield. However, when the enemy got close, he did not have time to reload it. Vlad then used the bayonet at the end of the rifle until he ran it into a Union soldier's stomach. The blade had lodged in the man's spine. Vlad pulled very hard, and the rifle separated from the bayonet, which remained lodged in the dying man. With no time to reload in the man-to-man fighting, Vlad began using the rifle as a club. The stock broke, but Vlad continued swinging the broken rifle until it flew out of his blood-soaked hands. He watched it spin out of control, narrowly missing a Confederate soldier.

Remembering his pistol, Vlad quickly unholstered it and carefully fired all six shots. Not having time to reload, he holstered it and drew his saber. He even used a butcher knife that he had borrowed from a cook that morning. In close quarters, the butcher knife was highly maneuverable. Vlad stabbed a Union soldier with it, but cut his own hand, although not seriously, as he plunged the knife into the soldier and his hand slid down the handle onto the blade. It was hot, and all the soldiers on both sides were winded and dehydrated. Dave stayed close to Vlad, as did a few of their men. They tried to form a pocket to protect each other.

As night fell, the armies finally separated. Back at camp, Vlad and Dave discussed the orders for the following day. Each thought that it was a miracle they had survived that day, and they both figured tomorrow would be their last day on earth. Instead, the following day went better for their particular group. They retrieved their horses and served in more of a supporting role. They kept together the remaining men of the company and others who had joined them. Still, one man from their company lost a leg to a bullet that shattered his shin bone, and seven suffered minor wounds.

That night, they went over their orders for the following day. The next day seemed like it would be the decisive final battle. Knowing that any plan would be abandoned as soon as the fighting started, Dave and Vlad spent more time praying with their men than planning. They then passed out from sheer exhaustion. Had it not been for the lack of sleep during the previous nights and their tremendous physical exertion, they would have been too afraid to sleep that night.

The following day broke with a Confederate attack. During the massive confusion, Vlad got separated from his company. He saw three Yankee soldiers walking beside a creek with one man closer to him than the others. Without thinking, Vlad charged them on his horse. To try to scare the men into thinking he was part of a large group, he yelled, "Attack!" He shot the closest one in the face with his pistol, killing the man instantly. As Vlad continued to charge the two remaining soldiers, they both hastily aimed and fired their rifles at him. One bullet hit Vlad's horse in the chest, penetrating into the arteries of the heart and the right lung. The other bullet smacked a leather strap of a powder and shot bag slung over Vlad's shoulder, hitting at an angle on Vlad's left collar bone and deflecting off the bone into the top of his shoulder. It broke Vlad's collar bone and damaged the muscles around his left shoulder. The wound was not far from where he had been hit while raiding Witowo, Poland.

The round bullet and the low powder charge used by the soldier in his haste to reload the day before kept the bullet from penetrating more than a half-inch. The thick strap had almost stopped the bullet. Earlier during the combat, the soldier had spilled about half of the powder for the charge as he reloaded, cramming down the ball in a hurry without properly seating it. Still, the wound was debilitating and Vlad would be in recovery for months, should he get out alive and without an infection.

Almost simultaneously with the shots fired at him and his horse, Vlad fired two shots at the two remaining men, wounding both of them badly. Vlad had plenty of experience shooting while riding and under fire, and he was a good shot. Both men ran off and one died while he ran, leaving a trail of blood until he fell. The other man kept running until he reached a creek. He stumbled across it and passed out on the opposite shore.

As the horse faltered and finally fell, it threw Vlad several feet. Vlad landed in a smaller ditch that led to the creek near which the third Union solder had passed out. Vlad hit his head and was knocked out cold. He was hidden by high weeds along the ditch. The blood from his cuts mixed with the blood stains from other men whose blood had spattered on him during the previous two days of fighting made him appear dead to anyone who could have seen him. The battle continued to rage with Vlad unconscious in the tall weeds of the ditch. He was invisible to both Southern comrades and enemy troops as each group passed during the next few hours.

Finally, Vlad woke up and gradually came to his senses. He slowly crawled up the bank to see what was going on. He saw his pistol a few feet away, so he looked around and, seeing no one nearby, he quickly got it and reloaded the empty chambers. He looked farther around and saw no one. He put his head down and closed his eyes, trying to block out the pain from his shoulder and head. He was terribly exhausted and, once again, dehydrated.

When he looked up again, he saw a group of Confederate soldiers coming towards him. He raised his hands and identified himself quickly so that they would not mistake him for a Union soldier and shoot him or run him through with bayonets. They talked a few minutes of the confusion of the battle and uncertainty of where their own lines were. Things were such a mess. They all decided to head towards their last known lines to try to find their units and a hospital for Vlad. Before leaving, Vlad went over to his horse, which he had grown to love. He took a few items from a bag attached to the saddle, patted the dead animal gently, and quickly left with the others.

After a couple of hours of circling Union troops, they saw their own battle flag near dark and cautiously approached the group of men carrying it. From a safe distance, Vlad said, "Confederate soldier here, Lieutenant Vladimir Petrov, requesting permission to come in." Vlad was so excited that he forgot to use his American name "Harris." A guard shouted back, "Put your hands up and walk in slowly." Vlad did as he was told and the guard, satisfied that Vlad was a Confederate, said, "Okay, you can put your hands down, sir. We are preparing to fall back towards Maryland. We think the Union Army is planning to try to overrun us, so we plan to leave very soon."

Despite the excitement and his own pain, Vlad thought of how the grand plan to take the war into the North did not make it past a dozen miles into Pennsylvania. Talks of eating off the spoils of Yankee farms were merely pipe dreams. They would now be lucky to return to Virginia to the stalemate of two vast, disease-ridden armies 30 miles from Washington, D.C. The summers were brutally hot and filled with biting bugs, and the winters were cold, although not nearly as cold as Russian winters. The temperature extremes were hard to take, though, because the men were always outdoors, and tents provided little protection from the elements.

The group moved quickly to leave the area before the Union soldiers could rally and organize another attack to capture them. Given his rank, Vlad was offered a ride on a horse with a young lieutenant from Raleigh, North Carolina. The young officer was also wounded, having been shot in the side. He was slowly dying, but he did not want to die by being run though with a Union bayonet or neglected in a Union hospital. They rode for about twenty miles until they came upon a field where a large group of Confederates were camped. Vlad and the lieutenant went straight to the field hospital, where the lieutenant collapsed onto the ground. He had been riding with increasing pain and blood loss. Vlad got a doctor to see the lieutenant first, but the doctor confirmed that with a gut wound of that sort, it would be a slow and painful death. They placed the lieutenant on a cot, and Vlad helped him pen a letter to the young lieutenant's wife, promising to make sure she received it. The doctor then called for Vlad to come and be treated.

Before Vlad left, the lieutenant asked Vlad to pray with him. Vlad closed his eyes, and the lieutenant said the most poignant and meaningful prayer that Vlad had ever heard. The lieutenant not only prayed for his own soul and for the protection of his wife and small children, but also for Vlad's healing and care. Vlad shed a tear as he hugged the lieutenant through the immense pain of his broken collarbone. The doctor called Vlad again, and so he left the lieutenant, knowing that while a painful death awaited him, he would meet death with peace.

On the way to be treated, Vlad asked a soldier with minor wounds to sit with the lieutenant so he would not have to die without human companionship. The doctor looked at Vlad's shoulder and tried to touch it. Vlad reacted to the pain, so the doctor stopped. He told Vlad that he needed to probe it with his hands to assess the damage. The doctor pressed along the bone, and Vlad bit down on a lead bullet with the pain so sharp that his teeth deformed the bullet. The doctor pushed and pulled getting the bone back together. Finally, the doctor said that the break felt clean and was now fairly realigned. The doctor quickly dug out the bullet, causing Vlad to almost pass out from indescribable pain. He wrapped Vlad's shoulder in cloth bandages designed to immobilize it as best he could under the desperate circumstances, and sent Vlad on his way.

Vlad asked the doctor about his numerous cuts, and the doctor cussed at Vlad. The doctor added, "You should be thankful to have your collarbone put back right given the thousands of seriously wounded soldiers and the fact that I've haven't slept for three days! I'm going to be a prisoner soon because I can't leave several of my patients who have a chance to recover, but are too injured to move. I only saw you because of a gap in the flow of wounded coming into the field hospital. You'd better go quickly with the group of soldiers forming up about 100 yards away to travel south to keep from being captured. Now, get out!" Vlad felt guilty for even asking about the otherwise painful shoulder, collarbone, and cuts.

Vlad thanked the doctor, who had already turned to treat another soldier who had just come into the hospital. The doctor did not acknowledge Vlad anymore, but was hard at work trying to treat the new patient. Vlad left and went to meet the men. He was allowed to ride with one, who said he planned to move fast. Vlad told him that was fine, although Vlad knew that a fast trip was going to be painful for his broken collarbone and injured shoulder muscles. Still, riding beat walking, and it sure beat capture by some very angry Yankees.

True to his word, the soldier rode fast and hard. The pounding hooves caused excruciating pain to Vlad's collarbone and shoulder. He could hardly stand it when, finally, they all stopped for the night. They built no fires, so as not to betray their location. The heat and humidity on this July night and the lack of any food to cook made a fire unnecessary, anyway. Vlad moved away from the group and hid himself in the bushes in case of a surprise attack. He knew not to sleep out in the open among a group of men in that kind of situation. After about an hour, his pain diminished to a throb, his increasing fatigue overtook his pain, and he fell asleep.

He awoke at first light to the sounds of the men getting ready to leave. He was in such a deep sleep that he had briefly incorporated the noises he heard into his dream. He found his ride and climbed aboard just as the solder was departing. The soldier snapped at Vlad, telling Vlad that he had not seen him and was getting ready to leave him thinking that he had gone on ahead. In a brash, arrogant tone, the soldier warned Vlad not to be late again or else he would leave him without a second thought. Vlad did not say a word, but thought of the young lieutenant and wished that these two men could change places. The South would be better off with the young lieutenant and without this arrogant man.

Vlad felt his vest pocket to make certain that the letter to the young lieutenant's wife was still there. It was, and so Vlad thought of how and when he could mail it. He hoped to be sent to Richmond or maybe home with Rachel to recover. Of course, after a monumental defeat like the South had just suffered, he was concerned whether all soldiers would be needed at the front or whether the war would even be over now. He quickly dismissed the thought of the war being over. The Union had been beaten badly in battle, twice at Manassas, once at Fredericksburg, and elsewhere. Even in victory, the Union had lost tens of thousands of soldiers. Still, it kept pouring in its sons to fight and die. He figured that the Confederate Army would send more of its young men – almost children – to win or die. Vlad would soon learn that the Confederate Government ordered its Army to retreat to a point where the Union Army dared not follow, and things would be at a stalemate again until some general thought of a new way to kill 25,000 men.

Chapter 42
Richmond Hospital

After many days of painful travel, Vlad reached a large military hospital in Richmond. He was placed on a cot, and one nurse attended to him and about one hundred other soldiers. She was not well-trained in medicine, but then again, there was not really a lot a doctor could do for wounds. Amputation was often the remedy for arm or leg wounds, followed by cauterizing the remaining arm or leg stump. All of this was done without anesthesia, and whiskey, while sometimes available, did little to kill the pain. The pain was so severe that it reached through the drunken effects and tortured the patient.

Lying on his cot, Vlad heard the unearthly screams all the way from the operating room. He smelled gangrene in the faint hot breeze that passed through the hospital. It was the smell of death, and he thought that he would die if he stayed in such place, just as surely as he would die if he stayed too long in battle. He fought the urge to slip out and walk away, back home to Rachel. He was not a coward. Rather, this was just a clear realization of the truth of the situation in which he found himself. He had been through life and death struggles before, but now he had a wife and a home. He could not desert; he might never see Rachel again. He decided that he was not about to run out and make himself a criminal who would never make it home or, if he did, would be hunted until the end of the war or beyond. He had to stay where he was told to stay and fight to survive there. He had run from the Russians, but he had everything to gain by doing so. He could not run now; he had too much to lose.

Vlad slowly sat up and looked around the hospital. Some of the men had only nasty looking superficial wounds which required no medical attention to heal, other than to avoid infection. In fact, the filthy, disease-ridden hospital was probably worse than a chicken coop for risk of infection. There were also men there who were slowly and painfully dying of their internal wounds. Some had been gut-shot only slightly, but the infection was a time-bomb that worked its course to death with agonizing delay.

Unless infection got him, Vlad would probably live, but he did not know that. He laid in bed listening to the cries of young men, some teenage boys, as they contemplated their fate. Preachers ministered to the young men, which gave many of them mental comfort even though their bodies were dying. He thought about the young lieutenant, who must be dead by now. He hoped that the man had been properly buried by the Yankees, but he doubted it. They had probably thrown him in a pit with countless others or burned his body in a mangled pile of dead men.

Vlad also thought about the fact that he had no horse and no real chance to get one, which meant no cavalry position. He doubted he could get home to get another one of his own, even if any were left. If he went back into combat, he likely would be thrown into the infantry. He was in a Richmond hospital, hundreds of miles from the last known spot where his unit was all together. He thought that they all must have been captured or killed, but then he told himself that certainly some of them escaped and possibly reformed the company or merged into another one. He hoped that they were together defending a new front line in Maryland. His daydream changed completely to one where they were riding through the streets of Washington, D.C. burning everything as they went. He hoped that the Union Army that met them at Gettysburg had left the Capital undefended and that some units of Southern forces had taken advantage of it, but he knew that was too much to hope for.

He thought with the benefit of hindsight that, had he been in charge, he would never have attacked the Union Army at Gettysburg. There was no advanced plan, and the terrain favored the Union Army. Rather, he thought like a cavalryman. After discovering the large Union Army, he would have left a harassing force of mobile cavalry men and others to build a large number of campfires and construct fake wooden cannons. He would have led the others on a hasty flight across Maryland to Washington, where he would have attacked the city, burned it, and shot or, better yet, captured the leaders. Then, his men could have gone south or southwest towards Fredericksburg or Manassas and reestablished their lines in friendly areas. Such a move, if successful, would have rocked the North, which was starting to grow tired of war. It would have put the South on terms from which a negotiated peace could be made, especially if important Union leaders were captured and held hostage by the South.

While Vlad did not care for a new government or country, he daydreamed that such a move would have ended the war and stopped the painful loss of life. Then, the thought dawned on him that, had things been different, he just as easily would have fought for the Union and could have been in a similar hospital bed in Philadelphia or Baltimore dreaming of leading a war-ending assault on Richmond. His mind replayed for the twelfth time the newspaper advertisement that Rachel had read while in Philadelphia. Had it offered inexpensive land in Pennsylvania instead of Virginia, he would have been in blue, rather than gray. Still, he was on the gray side, and he had fought for it with all his being.

A scream from a dying man on the next cot brought Vlad back to reality. He then despaired over the knowledge that his chance of rejoining his unit was virtually nonexistent. He was certain that he would be reassigned to defend some point in northern Virginia. If he did get a horse, he would possibly be sent back to Warrenton, Virginia, where he would serve with Mosby. There, he would fight desperate ambush battles and probably die.

In a few days, Vlad received word that he was being shipped by rail to Kittrell, North Carolina to recover and make room in the Richmond hospital for more wounded. It was on a rail line in the interior of north central North Carolina, away from the coast and the mountains where the union had either troops or sympathizers. It was about 45 miles north of Raleigh. He had never heard of it, but he was told it was not far – a little over 20 miles – from Warrenton, North Carolina. General Lee's family was hiding on a farm near Shocco Springs, just south of Warrenton. General Lee would secretly go there to see his family and vacation from the war. General Lee would sometimes dress like a farmer while he stayed at the farm and traveled around the community without being recognized. He would still receive briefings and advise on tactics, but he was in the safety of the rural countryside where both his body and mind could rest. However, for the average soldier, the dangers and mental anguish of war never took a vacation. Such soldiers received few breaks from the disease, poor food, and squalid living conditions of the war.

Like most people, Vlad knew nothing about the General's retreat near there. Instead, he thought about Rachel and how far he would be from her. He saw a map on the wall about 30 feet away. He managed to get up and, with a great deal of pain, walk over to it. Looking it over, he said to himself, "Kittrell is a little over 20 miles from Warrenton, and Warrenton is the county seat of Warren County, a county that borders Virginia. Warren County also borders Northampton County, North Carolina, which, in turn, borders my own home county of Greensville, Virginia. Hmmm, the rail line to Kittrell splits at Petersburg, and that other route goes near home on its way to Weldon. That's the line I told Aaron to take north a few years ago."

Vlad desperately wanted to see Rachel, but he knew he would not be allowed to travel to her. Unless she traveled in a well-protected group or took a train through a safe route, it would be too dangerous for her to come to him. Still, he figured that they would only be about 50 miles from each other, more or less. Before he left Richmond, he hoped he could send word of his condition and the plan to go to Kittrell. He penned a quick letter to her about where he was going and wrote that he would contact her with a plan for them to see each other once he arrived. He asked a nurse's aide to post both it and the letter from the dying Lieutenant. The aide had been around the hospital since Vlad arrived, and they had become friends. The aide had fought in the war with Mexico and had his foot amputated in a canon accident. As a fellow soldier, Vlad hoped he could trust the aide.

The aide's eyes welled up with tears when Vlad told him of the dying young lieutenant. He took the letters and said, "I promise I will post them; both of them. I'll tell you as soon as they are mailed." Vlad said, "Thank you. I very much appreciate your kindness." Before the aide could tell Vlad that he had posted the letters, the army shipped Vlad and about 20 others off to the railroad station for transportation to Kittrell. Vlad rode in a wagon to the station and then waited there overnight for a train going south towards Kittrell. One of the men died while waiting at the station. The man was thought to be in better condition, such that he was well enough to travel. However, the bumpy wagon ride to the station re-opened an internal wound, and he bled to death. Vlad thought that the man at least was no longer suffering in this misery.

Chapter 43
Kittrell, North Carolina

The men were placed in box cars with straw. The nurses and aides tried to make them as comfortable as possible. Even some Army officers at the station tried to help. They all wished that they could do more for these men, but everything was in short supply due to the capture or blockade of the Southern harbors. What supplies did get through were brought north on the trains, and wounded troops were sent south on the return trip. When the train finally left the station, Vlad was lying comfortably in a soft bed of straw. The door was open and a cooling morning breeze filled the car. The train passed over the James River and rolled towards Petersburg. Vlad looked to his right at the cool flowing water as it rushed through the rapids at the edge of the Piedmont of Virginia. These were the last set of rapids before the river turned into a large water highway leading to the sea. He could see the Yankee soldiers held as prisoners of war on an island in the James. There was a large burme surrounding them with Confederate soldiers ready to shoot any who crossed it.

Vlad turned to the left and looked downstream with the sun in his eyes. He thought about how this was the first time he had been truly safe in a long time. The only Yankee troops nearby were prisoners. The train routes to northern North Carolina were heavily protected from raiding cavalry. This line from Richmond to Petersburg, and the line that split at Petersburg and headed towards

Weldon was the life-blood of the Confederacy. This train would take the western fork at Petersburg towards Henderson and Kittrell, North Carolina, which was even more secure than the Weldon line. The line connecting Weldon went on to Wilmington, which was the major port supplying the Army of Northern Virginia. The port received supplies from the blockade runners that made it through to the protection of Fort Fisher at the mouth of the Cape Fear River leading to Wilmington. The Union Army had captured New Bern, another port city, and much of the north and central coast of North Carolina during April of 1862, which was fairly early in the war. However, the Confederacy had held the line to the west of New Bern and kept the rail line open from Wilmington to Weldon, and on to Petersburg and Richmond.

Vlad realized that the train was about to complete its crossing of the James, so he moved a bit to see the part of the city situated on a large hill along the northern bank of the river. The long row of warehouses and another hill that was becoming a large cemetery quickly went out of sight, blocked by trees after the train completed its crossing of the river and steamed south. He looked at the trees and sunny sky as he shifted his body again to become more comfortable. He turned his head slightly more to the left to nestle into the soft straw.

After a brief stop in Petersburg, the train moved through the fields and woods as it headed towards North Carolina. The smell of freshly cut hay was so sweet. Vlad closed his eyes and thought of his own farm. He dreamed he was there doing chores before lunch with Rachel. He imagined that he was bathing with her in a nearby creek, as they used to do, and holding her white porcelain skin against his. She made him feel thoroughly loved, and he could tell by her kiss that she still loved him as much as she had when they were first together. Those were great times, and they seemed so close and yet so distant. The growing warmth of the day, the cool breeze, and the sweet country smells were comforting to Vlad. The soft hay made the rocking of the train relaxing, and Vlad was soon in a deep sleep.

Late that afternoon, the train rolled into the station at Kittrell. Vlad woke up and tried to get up, but his shoulder was on fire from his sleeping position. He pressed his right hand against his collar bone to see if that would help. It did not. Despite intense pain, Vlad had been able to keep his collarbone together so that the broken ends joined reasonably well. He knew from watching Russian doctors that if the ends were joined together, they might grow back better. If not, then a man could lose effective use of the adjoining arm.

Vlad waited for over an hour for the more seriously wounded men to be taken to beds in a local hotel, which had been converted into a hospital. Finally, a sergeant, who had to be over 60, asked him if he could walk. Vlad nodded, so the sergeant told him to get out and walk towards the hospital. The sergeant was considered too old to fight and, therefore, was posted to this duty. Vlad thought how lucky the sergeant was to be so far away from the fighting. Vlad was one of the last to get off the train, so the sergeant walked with him, and the two talked as they went. As the sergeant spoke, they walked by dozens of fresh graves. The sergeant thought nothing of them as he talked, but Vlad was shaken by the magnitude of death everywhere. The sergeant was from a small settlement along the same rail line. It was about 7 miles west of Raleigh. Even though the trains left Kittrell and went to Raleigh and even stopped at the settlement, he had only once received leave to be able to go home, and then only for a couple of days at Christmas. Still, it was far better than what most soldiers could do, and the sergeant knew it.

The sergeant asked Vlad, "Are you able to help me get the others settled in?" Vlad said, "I can do it," although he was in pain. The men assisted two doctors and a group of nurses with the most seriously wounded men. They then helped the lesser wounded ones with sheets and pillows. At about 10 p.m., the Sergeant told Vlad, "We should get some sleep." Vlad nodded his head, and turned to walk towards a barn. The Sergeant stopped him by saying, "There's an extra bedroom in the house I'm staying in. Why don't you stay there?" Even though he had been billeted in other homes, Vlad replied, "I feel strange about invading the house. I'll only stay if the owner doesn't mind." When he met the owner, she was an elderly widow, Mrs. Mollie Edna Minton, who convincingly said she did not mind having Vlad stay. She told Vlad how the sergeant had ploughed and planted her garden, brought fresh water from the well, and generally did things that she was no longer as able to do. Vlad understood that she intended him to be equally helpful, and that is why she did not mind.

Mrs. Minton showed Vlad to a small upstairs room which used to belong to her youngest child, a son now in his late twenties. He had been taken prisoner in 1862 at New Bern. He had a wife and twin sons in Tarboro. She kept hoping that he would be exchanged for some Yankee soldier, but she had not heard any news in a few months. "My son's worth a million Yankees," she proclaimed. "I don't know why they don't exchange him!" She added, "I pray for him and all my children several times every day. I know that God is watching over him. Also, I have a daughter in Wilmington, whose husband is in the Confederate Navy, and another daughter, who lives in Baltimore. Her husband was conscripted, forced into the Yankee Army, and I haven't heard from her in over two years. I believe she must be safe since there has been no fighting around Baltimore."

Mrs. Minton shed a tear, as she talked about the last time they had all been together. It was Christmas of 1859, and her late husband was alive then. He died the following autumn. They all had such a wonderful time for a solid week during that last Christmas together. The house was full of grown children, young grandchildren, and the smells of the abundant food of a time of peace. It always amazed her how different the house seemed without her loved ones. It was a place of fond memories, but it was also cold and barren without them.

She wiped her eyes and apologized. Vlad and the sergeant told her there was no need to apologize. They each fought back their own tears and thought of their own families. Turning to go, she asked, "Is there anything you need?" He softly answered, "Nothing, no thank you." She excused herself and went to bed. Vlad and the Sergeant then looked at each other not knowing what to say and then each went to their own rooms. Vlad laid down in bed. For the next fifteen minutes, he heard the faint sound of crying from her room below him. He thought of going to check on her, but decided that would embarrass her. He laid there, thought of Rachel, and could not help but to cry a bit himself.

Over the coming days, Vlad helped Mrs. Minton by cutting a little firewood with his right arm, although that caused excruciating pain to his left collarbone. He stopped because if an officer saw him doing that, he may be immediately placed on a northbound train to go back into the line. After all, if he was well enough to chop wood, he was well enough to hold a rifle. Vlad then fed the chickens, a cow, and some goats. Before supper, he repaired some loose boards on the staircase and did some other jobs around the house. That night, his left shoulder hurt so badly that he could not get to sleep for a few hours.

He spent two weeks there convalescing, doing odd jobs around the house, and helping with more seriously wounded men at the hospital. Vlad knew that his days of relaxation were numbered, even though he did his best to wear his sling whenever he was around other soldiers or medical personnel. He was not a coward, but he knew that his shoulder was not healed and that he was not yet ready for battle. He couldn't stay inactive, though, and every time he used his left arm in physical labor, he ached for hours afterwards.

Chapter 44
Franklin County, North Carolina

As Vlad healed, he was ordered to stand guard and do limited work. He wanted to do what he could to help around the hospital, but he did not want to be sent back to the front. About two dozen other men were in the same condition, and most acted more injured than they really were. The hospital commander, who was an older doctor, received word that Governor Zebulon Vance of North Carolina had thrown up breast works around the Capital City of Raleigh to protect against federal raids. The rumor floating around was that a band of Yankee cavalry troops had come from Elizabeth City, had gotten around the strong troops guarding the Wilmington-Weldon railroad line, and was raiding north central North Carolina towns and farms. The area commander asked the medical commander to send all able troops to Northern Franklin County to be stationed along a major road to protect the northern approaches to Louisburg and, ultimately, Raleigh. They were also supposed to protect the southwestern approach to Warrenton and Warren County in case of a flanking move by the Union troops to hit Warrenton. Vlad's group would be the first line of defense and basically serve as an alarm system.

In reality, they were ordered there primarily to serve as guards and lookouts to protect some of General Lee's family members, who were living just north of there in Warren County on a farm near Shocco Springs. As the war raged, the South grew fearful that the Union would try to capture family members of important Confederates to ransom for surrender. Annie Lee, a young daughter of General Lee had died from an illness in Warren County in 1862, and she was buried just a few miles or so north of where Vlad's group would be stationed. There was even an unfounded fear among some Confederate leaders that a Union patrol might try to dig her up and hold her body as ransom. Had such a thought crossed a Union leader's mind, the knowledge that such act would have had embittered and motivated the entire Confederacy, and disgusted the citizens of the Union causing a possible loss of their support, would have quickly stopped it from becoming a reality.

Vlad and the other two dozen or so able men were sent over to guard the southern bank of Buffalo Creek, near a bridge crossing where the swamp and creek narrowed that would be useful to any troops approaching Southwestern Warren County from the south. They guarded the Warrenton-Louisburg Highway. This assignment was most disturbing to the men involved because the Yankees would have to come through an area thought to be safe. Out of the total of twenty eight men, ten were officers, with the highest being a major. Normally, a lieutenant would lead such a group with a sergeant, one or two corporals, and the remainder being privates, but these were a collection of available mobile patients rather than a normal squad of men. The men varied in age; many were teenagers.

Instead of camping in the low area at the swampy creek where they could not see far, the men set up camp in a field on the northwest side of the intersection of Tollie Weldon Road and Warrenton Road. The field was beside the crest of a hill, which rose a long way to the south from Buffalo Creek. The creek was almost a mile to the north. Camping just below the highest point allowed them to position their camp so that it could not be seen from the opposite ridge across the Buffalo Creek valley to the north. Nearby woods to the south hid their camp from the Buffalo Creek valley and the other ridge to the south. They had a lookout tower constructed by the men from felled trees located at the crest of the hill nestled between some trees for concealment. A few men were posted at the bridge, and they could see up and down the swampy creek. The positions allowed them to guard the bridge and the southern approaches to the bridge on Warrenton Road. Being positioned off the major road further concealed them and prevented the main group from being ambushed by raiders riding very fast along the major road.

Beavers had dammed Buffalo Creek in stair-step dams for miles up and downstream. The creek had a deep channel and waist-deep swamps sometimes 200 yards wide, making large sections of those creeks all but impassable except at the bridges with raised roadbeds leading to them. Henderson was about 10 miles away to the northwest. A number of troops were stationed there, so it was thought to be secure. The creek, and others paralleling it, flowed to the southeast, so troops would have to cross the bridges or come from the southeast to attack them.

Vlad's group posted sentries and built their own breastworks as a make-shift fort around the field. They would be outmatched by any large contingent of soldiers. However, they might be able to withstand a hit and run attack by a cavalry raiding party. If they were attacked, they had orders to light a large prepared signal fire, which would alert men on hilltop towers to the north, south, east, and west to the presence of Yankee troops. In turn, they would warn the troops to the north protecting the Lee family, as well as the cities of Warrenton, Henderson, Louisburg, and even Raleigh. They would also alert the Confederate cavalry to engage and destroy the raiders.

Before he left for Tollie Weldon Road, Vlad told Mrs. Minton of his desire to have Rachel join him. She told him of an inn at Warrenton where she used to stay when traveling to Tarboro to see relatives. Warrenton was located north of Louisburg, and Vlad was about 15 miles from there. Vlad posted a letter to Rachel asking her to go to Warrenton, if she believed she could do so safely, by way of Rocky Mount, North Carolina and Raleigh, and check into an inn at Warrenton in the hopes that he could go there. He told her that he might be unable to join her, but that he would try to the point of temporary desertion. He emphasized that she should only attempt this if she was certain that she could get there safely. He hesitated to ask her to come with the threat of Union cavalry, but he thought she would be safe if she followed the route he suggested.

While discussing plans for their camp, Vlad's commander told Vlad, "We're supposed to get supplies from Warrenton. We'll need some men to go get them every week." Vlad planned to volunteer to get the supplies, which would allow him to ride to Warrenton. Once he arrived at Tollie Weldon Road, he immediately volunteered to ride to Warrenton to get supplies. His commander allowed him to do that along with two other men. Vlad stopped at the inn and paid the innkeeper to let him know when Rachel arrived by way of a messenger. The prospect of seeing Rachel lifted his spirits.

The inn was located just outside of town on the major highway that Vlad was guarding. It was set on a hillside that overlooked a beautiful rocky waterfall and stream. The land was fairly flat at the front of the inn, but it dropped off quickly to reach the creek. There were huge oak trees near the creek, a patch of woods, and hayfields beyond the creek and woods.

After about ten days of camping in the field on Tollie Weldon Road, Vlad received word one evening through an errand boy from the inn that Rachel was there. She had received his first letter written from the hospital in Richmond and cried with joy that he was alive. She had heard of the horrific losses from the battles in Maryland and Pennsylvania. Given the number of Confederate dead, she was so afraid that Vlad was among them. When she received the last letter about a possible meeting in Warrenton, she looked at the only map she had. Warrenton was considered a large and prosperous town in North Carolina.

Rachel immediately made arrangements with Aaron and the other workers to care for the farm while she was gone. She placed Aaron in charge. She then packed and, early the next morning, had Aaron take her by wagon to Emporia to catch the train to Rocky Mount, N.C. From there, she took another train to Raleigh. From Raleigh, she took a train to Henderson, and a horse-drawn coach to Warrenton. She then caught a ride to the little inn about which Vlad had written her. Once she checked into the inn and told the innkeeper who she was, the innkeeper immediately sent word to Vlad.

Chapter 45
Warrenton, North Carolina

Vlad was nervous about asking his commander for permission because he didn't know what to do if it was denied. Time was wasting, so Vlad went directly to his commander and plainly told him, "Sir, my wife is nearby, and I haven't seen her in almost two years. I request permission to travel alone to Warrenton for supplies and to spend four days getting them, sir!" His commander realized that absolutely nothing was going on in the way of contact with the Yankees. He had heard from his superior that roaming Confederate cavalry squads assigned to find and destroy the Yankee cavalry had seen nothing. One group of Confederate cavalry soldiers stationed near Weldon had ridden up and down the rail line for tens of miles. They had seen no evidence of Yankee cavalry sabotaging the tracks, which the Yankees would have done, or of trying to come westward. The commander responded, "Vlad, I'll give you orders to go get supplies and for general travel to and from Warrenton for three days. What is not on the written orders will be that you shall bring back to me two gallons of any type of liquor or wine you can find up there. Don't come back without some form of drinkable alcohol. Do you understand me?" Vlad said, "Yes, sir!" The commander then wrote the orders Vlad needed.

Vlad was elated. He took a horse and wagon and left immediately. When he arrived at the inn, he found Rachel, and the two embraced and cried for joy. He was so thankful that she was safe and there with him. The two went to the room she had rented, which overlooked the stream and trees. They sat together in a rocking chair with her on his lap. They spent hours talking, kissing, and getting reacquainted. As the sun set, Rachel closed the curtains and slipped out of her dress. The two held each other all night and slept until close to noon the following day. He brought her breakfast in bed, along with some freshly cut flowers for sale by the inn.

The next two days went by quickly. They took long walks around Warrenton and spent hours talking to each other while sitting on the top of a bluff overlooking the creek. Although it was mid-October, the high temperatures were in the lower 80's. The blue North Carolina sky and the early fall colors created a beautiful and memorable setting. The smell of fall flowers and cut hay were sweet fragrances to their reunion. They bathed together in a secluded portion of a deeper stream a few hundred yards away from the inn. They ate wonderful home-cooked meals prepared by the innkeeper's wife. They spent a great deal of time sitting on a quilt talking in a nearby hayfield that had not yet been cut. The surrounding hay gave them an intimate privacy in the middle of an open field bathed with sunshine. They reached a level of deep emotional intimacy and understood each other more completely.

Near noon on the third day, Rachel and Vlad got the supplies, and Vlad took Rachel to meet a horse-drawn coach leaving for Henderson. From there, she would take a train to Raleigh. They said long and tearful goodbyes, knowing that this might be the last time they saw one another. When they last said goodbye nearly two years ago, the South was full of hope. Both now knew the fear of war that they had previously dreaded. The deadly cost of each major battle was even greater than they had feared in 1861. Vlad had lived through a few of the deadliest days in United States history. He was an active participant. He saw death in Poland, Russia, and Alaska, but not on this scale, where tens of thousands of men could die on single day in frontal attacks of exposed infantryman walking into a hail storm of bullets and cannon fire.

When Vlad's and Rachel's lips parted for the last time, Vlad softly told her one more, "I love you," and she hugged him tightly, not wanting to let go. Interrupting the moment, the coachman said, "Ma'am, We have to leave to make Henderson in time for the train." Rachel then boarded the coach. It quickly left, turned a corner, and Vlad was alone. After standing there a full minute, Vlad walked toward the supply wagon and began the lonely trip back to his fellow troops and the uncertainty of the war.

Rachel arrived in Raleigh after midnight. She waited inside the station for a few hours before boarding an early morning train to Rocky Mount, Weldon, and finally Emporia. Since Aaron did not know when she would return so he could meet her, Rachel paid a local merchant to have his delivery boy take her home. She arrived at the quiet farmhouse that afternoon. Aaron lit a small fire in her bedroom fireplace to keep away the evening chill and poured freshly drawn well water into a wash basin for her.

Returning to the sitting room where Rachel stood looking at a photograph of herself and Vlad in New York, Aaron asked her, "Ms. Rachel, Can I get you anything, fix some supper for you, perhaps?" She quietly answered, "No thank you, Aaron. I'm very sleepy from staying awake all last night and getting bounced around by a coach and the trains. I think I will go to bed. We'll talk about farm operations tomorrow, OK?" Aaron said, "Yes, of course. Everything went well, just so you know." She nodded with a small smile of appreciation, turned, and went straight to her bedroom, hoping that sleep would cure her loneliness and exhaustion from traveling. As she laid her head against the pillow, she thought of Vlad. As she had done every night and countless times during the day, she prayed for his safety.

Back at the Tollie Weldon Road camp, Vlad helped unload the supplies while in a daze, feeling numb from the depression of missing Rachel. He thanked the commander and gave him a jar of honey that Rachel had brought Vlad and also three gallons of strong homemade wine that he had purchased from the innkeeper. Vlad told the commander, "I will never forget your kindness in allowing me to have that short leave." The commander told him, "My own wife and three children are in Southern Georgia. Don't tell the other men this, 'cause I don't want them thinking it's OK to desert, but if I could get away with it, I would drop everything to travel there just to spend a few minutes with them."

Uncomfortable with his confession, the commander then stood taller and, in a deeper tone, told Vlad, "We will probably receive orders to go back to Kittrell in a day or two, since it's been largely confirmed that the rumors of Yankee cavalry are false. Since the men have done so well, we will likely not remain at the hospital any longer, even though many of us are still in need of time to finish healing. We'll then get new orders and assignments, which will probably mean being thrown into the line somewhere to get shot or stabbed again."

Chapter 46
Vlad is Shipped Out

Soon after returning to Kittrell from the outpost at Tollie Weldon Road, Vlad was ordered to Petersburg to defend the line. The Union could not capture Richmond by a direct assault from the north. It had been soundly beaten at Fredericksburg and otherwise north of the Confederate Capital of Richmond, and it faced a stalemate approaching from the north. Instead, the Union Army came up one of the peninsulas formed by various rivers flowing southeast to the coast. Since it held an overwhelming advantage in ships in its navy, it seized the coastal ports and could deliver troops and supplies by ship down the Chesapeake Bay from Baltimore and by sea from New York and Boston for the Union Army to fight its way up the peninsula to Richmond. However, to get to Richmond, the Union Army first needed to take Petersburg, a major supply line for the troops protecting the Confederate Capital.

Vlad spent a fairly comfortable spring of 1864. He was held in reserve to counter the Union attack against Richmond or Petersburg. He even got to spend a few weeks quartered in a house. However, beginning in June, General Grant began Siege of Petersburg. Vlad's light duty in mild weather turned very dangerous just as the summer heat intensified. Vlad was placed right on the front line. He was a cavalry soldier, but without a horse or squad, he became an infantry soldier. He lived in the squalid conditions wrought by thousands of men living outdoors in trenches. Vlad preferred the cavalry because they moved from place to place. They camped in a new location practically every night when they were riding on patrol and could find fresh water.

Vlad swatted horse flies constantly. Their stinging bites tore into him, and his stinking wool clothes were hot and scratchy. He was drenched with sweat most of the day. He pulled small and large ticks off of himself, and he was surprised at their ability to crawl on him undetected. He ate stale bread and salted pork, which was mostly fat. He drank stagnant water, and had dysentery frequently. The only way to pass the time was to tell stories. Vlad befriended his commander, and they told story after story. Vlad even discussed his prior service in the cavalry of both the Russian and Confederate Armies, which fascinated his commander.

Finally, Vlad and his unit were rushed to defend the Weldon-Petersburg rail line from a Union cavalry attack. Based on Vlad's past cavalry experience, Vlad's commander sought Vlad's advice on setting up proper defenses against a cavalry attack near a vital bridge. The commanding Confederate generals thought that the bridge might be subject to destruction by the Union cavalry in a hit-and-run raid. Torn tracks could be repaired quickly, but a severely damaged railroad bridge presented a more time-consuming and costly problem.

Vlad advised on the locations and building of proper defenses with what they could scrounge up. On the main approaches by road, the men dug pits and covered them with branches and soil to hide the gaping holes. They marked trees to show the various distances away from their positions. The trees were marked so that anyone at or closer than them was within range of the men's single shot smooth-bore rifles. This prevented them from firing too soon, thus missing their targets and giving away their positions to an enemy who could then charge ahead and fire upon them while they were reloading.

At Vlad's encouragement, the men then spent their days planning and practicing. They watched each other approach and pass the signs. They developed patience so that if the real thing occurred, they would be ready. They divided up how the squad would shoot if presented with multiple riders. To prevent them from all shooting the first target, they developed zones in the road: left, center, and right. They planned stagger-firing and calculated reloading time, so that the group would not all be reloading at once. They had a few extra rifles for use by some while others reloaded. They all acted confident in their ability to follow the plan and remain patient.

A few nights later, the Union cavalry approached. They came up the road as expected. The men waited; it was all they could do to not fire. Before they fired, two of the cavalry's horses fell into the pits and threw their riders. Those men laid on the ground injured. Before the others could stop, two of the cavalrymen crossed the markers. Fear and the urge to fire were eating the Confederates alive. During the approach, Vlad's memory flashed back to his days being ambushed on the Polish border. His heart quickened. He thought of escaping from the Russians in Alaska and their dogged pursuit. All of his experiences blended together in one wave of sudden panic and fear. Vlad was the first to fire by a split second. All of the men unleashed a deadly volley of lead within a half-second of each other. No stagger-firing, just a wall of lead and burning powder, fear and confusion.

They shot the two cavalrymen who crossed the markers right off their horses. Stray bullets brought two other men off of their horses, too. Vlad and his fellow soldiers should have allowed more men to get within the markers, but they simply could not wait. By firing all at once, they left themselves vulnerable while they reloaded even with the few extra loaded weapons. Vlad knew they would fire as soon as someone crossed the markers, if not before, so he made the markers about 10 yards closer than the maximum effective range. This allowed them to hit the first two, plus the two behind and slightly to the side of them. The firing in unison and the surprise of it caused the Union cavalry to believe that there were even more Confederates guarding the bridge than there actually were. The surviving cavalry unit panicked and retreated. The Confederates held the bridge that night.

Vlad's commander had a pistol and ran to cover the injured cavalrymen. Vlad quickly reloaded and joined him. The rest of the squad followed as they completed reloading. The two injured men were mostly shaken, although one had a sprained or broken wrist. Of the four men who were shot, the two who were in the lead were dead with at least three bullets in each of them. Of the other two men, one was quickly dying from a nasty chest wound. The fourth man had been hit by two bullets, but one had lodged in a heavy pouch he had over his chest. The impact of that hit had knocked him off of his horse, and the other bullet had torn a small hole in the top of his shoulder. It was not a fatal wound, and Vlad's group had three prisoners.

Vlad's commander ordered his men back to their positions and to prepare for another attack. He sent two men forward to scout out the road and high-tail it back if they saw the cavalry returning. He also ordered two of his men to take the three prisoners back to his position, where he patched the wounded man and stopped the bleeding. At dawn, a patrol of Confederate cavalry approached from the north down the tracks. They said that they had been dispatched because word had spread of a skirmish from men stationed about a mile away who had heard the gunfire during the night. Vlad's commander asked them to take the prisoners to Petersburg because his men could not be spared to march them there. They protested because they wanted to patrol further down the line to try to catch the Union cavalry possibly trying to sabotage the track. However, the Confederate cavalrymen were outranked and agreed to take the prisoners. They turned around and marched the prisoners ahead of them up the tracks.

About five minutes later, Vlad was nodding off to sleep in the warm sunshine, dead tired from the excitement of the night before. All of a sudden, he heard the sounds of several gunshots from the north up the railroad tracks, which was the direction the Confederate cavalry had gone. There were no other shots after the first round. Vlad's commander was furious. He said, "Those cavalrymen just shot the Union prisoners. They shot unarmed prisoners because they were too lazy to follow my order and escort the prisoners back to Petersburg. Heaven help us if the Union Army finds out that we're executing prisoners."

Although the sound of the shots startled Vlad and the murders disgusted him, nothing truly surprised him anymore. Vlad looked over at the soldier nearest to him, who was a boy of about 17. Vlad thought that, under right circumstances, that boy would kill Vlad in cold blood.

Overall, Vlad's squad disapproved of the killing of the three prisoners. True, they had killed men last night, but they fired in an act of war with a group of armed enemy soldiers approaching the bridge that they had been ordered to guard. The shooting of the three unarmed prisoners was an act of brutality, not of necessity, and not within the accepted rules of war. Vlad's commander again remarked that if the Union learned of the killings, it would likely shoot Confederate prisoners. He emphasized, "With the war going badly for the South, none of you should ever repeat what we believe happened to those prisoners, or else we might be shot in retaliation if we're captured."

The commander then ordered that his men bury the three dead Union soldiers who lay in front of them. They dug three graves out of sight of the bridge and buried the men next to one another. The commander did not want the graves in sight of the bridge because if they were captured by Union cavalry, especially by cavalry that could not easily take prisoners, he did not want them to justify shooting him and his men based on seeing the fresh graves of Union cavalrymen. He found the names of the dead men from documents they had with them, and he wrote their names on boards to place on the graves. Vlad and two other men then fashioned crosses with wood and string. They also wrote the date of death below the names.

Vlad and the two other men wrote down names and addresses of the dead men's loved ones from letters they had on them. Vlad and several other men said the Lord's Prayer over the graves and asked God's forgiveness for taking human life. They promised one another that, should any of them survive this war, they would contact the relatives of the dead men and tell them where their sons and husbands were buried. While the men felt varying degrees of guilt for having taken human life, they all saw a glimpse into their own possible fate: to be gunned down at any given moment without any warning. They then quietly walked back to rejoin others keeping watch. They all had a solemn sense of death and many made silent promises to live better should they survive this war.

After a couple of weeks with no further action, the unit was ordered to return to their lines. Unfortunately, on their way back, they encountered a Union cavalry group, which came upon them quickly and without warning. The men were out of position and many fled. Vlad and some others tried to hold fast, but the cavalrymen had the advantage. The cavalrymen were trying to capture prisoners for questioning, and they ordered the Confederates to surrender. Seeing that they had no choice, the remaining five men, including Vlad and his commander, surrendered. Most of the ones who fled managed to escape, since the cavalrymen had five prisoners to take back to their lines. That was excellent work for which they would be commended.

Vlad was captured and taken by horse quickly to the Union lines. The prisoners had to ride with Union soldiers while others covered them. They were told the old threat, "If any man tries to escape, the whole group will be shot." None tried to escape. They were too worn out, anyway. When they reached the lines, they were questioned at length. The interrogators quickly learned that Vlad knew a lot about horseflies, ticks and general tactics, but nothing about the overall planning for the defense of Petersburg and Richmond. He had become a simple infantryman who followed orders and had no real idea of what was going on beyond the latest distorted rumor floating around. In fact, he learned more from the information contained in the interrogator's questions than they did from his answers.

Vlad was sent further to the rear and then marched to Yorktown where he was placed on a ship returning to Philadelphia for supplies. From there, he would go to a prison camp. If he was lucky, he would be fed regularly. Unfortunately, the Union was pouring its resources into crushing the heart of the Confederacy by trying to capture Richmond through Petersburg. Its available supplies in the region, including most of the available food, were sent to the Grant's Army near Petersburg. The Union would sacrifice tens of thousands of its own men, so treatment of its Southern prisoners of war was not a priority. It also wanted to retaliate for the South's horrid treatment of Union prisoners of war.

Chapter 47
The Yankees come through Purdy

Rachel managed the farm with the help of Aaron and two free black farm hands, both of whom she had hired after Vlad had left. The last one hired was married, and his wife also helped Rachel by preparing meals for everyone. Rachel made payroll and kept schedules for planting, harvest, slaughtering, and other tasks necessary to maximize profits throughout the year. She was gifted at running a business and turned a nice profit. While so many men were away, a great deal of women ran their family farms during the war. Just like men, some were successes and some were failures. Many who failed simply did not have the proper aptitude, education, or training. Rachel's success was the result of natural aptitude, learning from her late father, and a need to survive. She had no family within reach to run to should her farm fail.

She and Vlad had kept a bit of their wealth in the local bank owned by the Hawleys. However, on the eve of war, they had withdrawn their funds and bought gold with it. Most of the remainder of their wealth had already been in gold and silver, anyway. They both knew that precious metals were the only medium of wealth with lasting value. After all, paper money could lose all its value with a simple change in government. Rachel had kept the gold and silver in a wall cavity of their bedroom. However, once the threat of Yankee patrols and invasion became real, she dug a hole near the secluded banks of the creek in which she and Vlad had bathed. She wrapped the gold and silver in oilcloth and buried them. She was careful to leave no trace of what she had done. The nearby trees and the depression in the elevation of the terrain hid the area well. When she saw Vlad in Warrenton, she told him of the location in case something happened to her, but she told no one else.

As 1863 turned into 1864 and much of that year passed, the threat of Yankee cavalry raids increased. The Peninsula campaign in Tidewater, Virginia had brought the Union many gains. The community around Purdy feared that the Union Army could come at any moment from that direction or from Coastal North Carolina, which had been occupied since 1862. Finally, Rachel learned from an employee of the Hawleys that the government in Richmond had warned banks in their area to hide the bulk of their assets and to leave only enough to cover small transactions each day. Based on this information, Rachel devised a plan.

She readied an old flat wagon to ride at short notice and planned a route to the depressed creek bed that would minimize travel through soft soil, which would leave a trail. She gathered the rest of her valuables and food she had canned in glass jars. She got together dried beans and seeds needed for future planting and placed them in barrels, then had the farm helpers load them. They thought she was going into town to sell them. She then parked the wagon in the barn.

About a month later, the panicked cry came that Union cavalry was heading their way to try to raid Weldon, the northern terminus of the railroad from Wilmington. Wilmington was now the only port remaining open to the South. Rachel immediately went out, hitched the wagon, and drove it to the hidden creek bed. She had Aaron help her erase the tracks as she left the barn, but the rest of her route was over harder ground covered with leaves, so it did not give away her trail. She parked the wagon next to the tall bank and unhitched the horses. She covered the wagon with old quilts and oilcloth, and then dumped dirt down from the bank above. It was hot and dirty work. It took her about an hour to get the wagon reasonably hidden with dirt and branches she had left there from earlier preparations.

Rachel then stripped her dirty clothes, washed the dirt and mud off of her skin in the cold creek, and put on clean clothes she had brought. They were the ugliest clothes she had because she wanted to look unappealing to the enemy soldiers. She then rode one of the horses and led the other to a nearby pasture that was almost completely surrounded by trees. Months earlier, she had the farm hands build a wooden rail fenced enclosure around the hidden pasture to keep the horses from returning to the barn. She then left the horses secured by the enclosure and returned to the house. She told the workers, "Your very survival depends upon the Yankees believing that we are a poor and worn out farm. They will take everything we have, and you will starve if they find our hidden stores of food."

Rachel then had the workers take three-fourths of the farm animals to the hidden pasture, leaving enough to look as though they were on a poorer farm. If the enemy stole animals, then at least they would not get all of them.

About eight hours later, near 10 p.m., she heard the thundering sound of many horses. The Yankees did come through, and they stopped outside of her home. She quickly dressed in the unpleasant clothes and went out with a lantern, along with the wife of one of her workers. She had told Aaron and the two men to come out of their quarters without any guns, and they did. They all assembled in the yard, and the commander, a major, greeted her. "Hello, Miss. Would you please tell us, where is the nearest town?"

Rachel told him precisely. He was testing her. He then asked for directions to the town, and she again answered truthfully. He asked, "Where is your husband?" She said, "He's in the Union Army in Tennessee, the last I heard." Rachel then asked, "We don't have much, but would you and your men like some cornbread? We baked it this afternoon." He answered, "Why, yes. Yes, we would. In fact, we need your chickens and all your cornmeal, flour, and sugar, too." She begged him not to take them, as they were a poor farm and had several mouths to feed. Not quite believing that her husband was in the Union Army, but not wanting to harm her in case he was, he said he would take pity on her and take only half of the chickens and the other items. However, he did order three of his men to search the house.

He turned to the three men and one woman, all black, and said for the men to come over to him. All three men hurried to him, and he told them to gather up half of the chickens, wring their necks and give them to his men to carry. He then spit on one of them and told them that Lincoln had freed them, but they were not free until they finished doing that. The men, all free men, anyway, obliged him out of fear of his brutality.

The men searching the house found hidden only a few minor items of value, which Rachel had left to fool the men into thinking they had gotten all of her wealth. To make a convincing show and to act sufficiently harmed and contrite so that they would not torch the farm, she cried and pleaded with them not to take the items, but they stole them anyway. She thought to herself that the Union was nothing but a bunch of thieves for stealing minor valuables. Food was one thing. Even the Confederate soldiers were known to come by a farm and take food. Also, she knew that the cavalry had to eat and could not carry all the food they required. However, taking valuables from a farmhouse served no military purpose.

The Major and one of his lieutenants discussed camping there. One of the lieutenants had his eye on Rachel. The

Major, however, wanted to raid Purdy and go on towards Emporia. He reasoned, "The longer we stop, the better chance the Confederates have to organize enough troops to engage and attack us. Plus, we took too much time at those other, richer farms earlier today. If we want to rest in safety, we need to get moving."

The Major then facetiously thanked Rachel, and she looked at him with tearful eyes. They then rode away with their minor spoils.

Once they were out of sight, Rachel said, "Aaron, go get my horse from the hidden field while I go inside to change." "Yes, Ma'am," he said, figuring what she planned to do. She went inside to put on warmer clothes for riding at night. When he returned with the horse, she took it and rode towards Jarrett, Virginia, a town to the east of the farm. Since the Union cavalry had approach her farm down the road directly from the north and they rode off towards Purdy to the southeast, she figured that they had made a loop around Jarrett, missing it by a few miles. They had probably torn up track on the rail line and sabotaged the telegraph lines north of that town, but the telegraph lines between there and Emporia should still be intact. Since it was on the railroad line, she knew that Jarrett had a telegraph office. She could not warn Purdy in time, but she could get word to Emporia, provided that the telegraph lines were still intact.

When Aaron arrived with the horse, Rachel took off and rode as quickly as she could. Rachel rode hard for a couple of hours and arrived in Jarrett anxious to deliver the warning. She awoke the town with the news and found the local sheriff. The sheriff took her to the telegraph operator's room, who was sitting up, groggy from having been awoken from a deep sleep by all the yelling. He knew that the lines were down to the north, but he figured that it was just another malfunction, and he used the opportunity to sleep on the job. Rachel dictated the information directly to the telegraph operator, who dispatched it right away down the line to Emporia, where the operator confirmed its receipt. She then spent the night in the sheriff's home, and his wife allowed her to sleep as a special guest in their late son's room. He had been killed fighting in Northern Virginia only three months before at the age of 17. Rachel then returned home the following morning.

The Union cavalry burned much of Purdy. They shot three of the townsmen who were too old to fight in the army, but who tried to protect their families and homes. They had fired outdated flintlock rifles at the cavalry. The three men were all in their seventies. While some of the cavalrymen were raiding a small store, another one of them broke into a house and started molesting the widow of a soldier who had been killed at first Manassas. He did that right in front of her young children. She had lived in that town all of her life in safety, but the army that was sent to restore the South to the laws of the Union violated those very laws. Thankfully, the Major ordered them to leave town to head towards Emporia or else her attacker would have raped her.

Just after sunrise and about a mile outside of Emporia, the Union cavalrymen were ambushed by Confederate soldiers who had been protecting the railroad. The Confederate soldiers were quickly assembled as a result of the telegraphed warning. Four of them were killed and eight were wounded during the fighting, which was a one-sided turkey shoot. Six of those wounded soldiers would later die from infection. The remaining cavalrymen surrendered. The Major was one of the wounded. He was shot in the stomach, and semi-digested cornbread spewed out of the large bullet hole along with blood. He was in agony until he died of that gut wound the following day. There was nothing that could be done to save him; not that the doctors in Emporia tried much after they heard what had occurred in Purdy. In fact, many of the town's people wanted to lynch the survivors, wounded and all. However, a young Confederate captain stopped them by lining up some of his men and threatened to shoot the first person to cross a line he designated. He then told the people that if they lynched these men, the Union would retaliate directly against them by burning their homes and killing them when they returned in force. Realizing that the war was going badly for the South, the mob backed down.

The attack on Purdy had occurred near midnight. The following evening, Rachel heard of the deaths and attempted rape in Purdy. She also learned that the

Union cavalry had been killed or captured and that the Major had been mortally wounded. She felt neither joy nor sadness over the deaths of the Union cavalrymen. She simply felt relief that she, her workers, and her farm had been largely spared. She then thought that this was the horror that Vlad faced daily. That made her cry. She thought of him and wished he was there to hold her. She wondered where he was. She had not heard from him in many months, and she wondered if he was still alive.

Chapter 48
Deplorable Conditions

During Vlad's imprisonment, he slowly lost a lot of weight that he did not need to lose. He would have died had the war continued for several more months. Strangely, he accepted the conditions as just the way things were. He ate rats and roaches to survive. He drank filthy water because it was all that was available except during heavy rains and snow when he shivered from the cold. He suffered dysentery routinely. He wore soiled and tattered clothes, but he survived.

While he was there, he saw his former commander, David Hawley Jr. Dave was in terrible shape. He had been a prisoner since Gettysburg, in July of 1863. Vlad gathered what food he could and even roasted some rats and fed them to Dave. "Dave, you must eat. Take these. I'll help you," Vlad said. Dave slowly responded to the protein. He actually gained a few pounds over two weeks. He thanked Vlad for saving him and said, "I will never forget your kindness to me." He knew Vlad could have kept the food to replenish his own depleting body.

While Vlad was a prisoner of war, he had a great deal of time just to think. He usually had time to think at night when he could not sleep because of the hunger pangs, the cold, or the noise from so many people around him. It was hard to concentrate at times without nourishing food and good water, but he thought of his life. He understood enough of American culture and of the world to appreciate the differences between his life in Russia and his life in America. He was no longer an outsider, even though he still had a slight Russian accent and his English vocabulary, while large, was not as broad as some native-born Americans.

During his confinement, Vlad realized that even his shortcomings and faults made him who he was today. He wanted to change or improve them, but they helped define him. He also understood that he was changing. If he ever got out of the camp and back to Rachel, he wanted to be the best husband to her and to raise a family with her. He also wanted to fulfill his and Rachel's dream of becoming successful farmers. He worried about Rachel constantly throughout the day and into the night.

Additionally, he wanted to master different, unrelated things, like medicine and trades like brick masonry and carpentry. He knew his interests would change as he mastered new areas and discovered new challenges. He wanted to be well-educated. He did not necessarily want to quit farming and work full-time in those other areas, but he wanted to learn new areas so he could fully enjoy the richness of life. However, he knew that presently he was starving to death in a prison camp. None of his dreams could be realized without first getting out of there and safely back home to Rachel. He thought again of Rachel, praying she was alive and well. He thought about the days in Warrenton and their time together. It was so long ago now, almost a year and a half.

During April of 1865, news came that President Lincoln had been murdered by a Southerner. The Union guards wanted to start shooting prisoners, but their officers thought that would lead to a stampede by the Confederates, who, though weak and unarmed, greatly outnumbered their guards. If fired upon, the prisoners would naturally charge. Even weak and unarmed, they would charge because they had no choice.

When Vlad heard of Lincoln's death, he thought of how Lincoln had died from a bullet, just like some of his men and men from the Union whom he had shot. He then thought of how the average soldiers on either side were just alike; both wanting to go home to their families and their lives. It seemed to Vlad that Lincoln and the Union generals would sacrifice them all just to keep a country less than ninety years old together, a country formed from independent states that had volunteered to come together, anyway.

Although Vlad was not generally a spiteful man, he thought of the hundreds of thousands of men who had died from bullets and disease during this long war. He was full of hate and momentarily glad that Lincoln was dead, but it was fleeting because he had learned long ago that hate hurt the person hating more than anyone else. Vlad then thought how far the Czar would have gone to win a Russian civil war. Vlad blamed the Southern leaders, too. His thoughts quickly changed when the stark nighttime cold and hunger, his lifelong companions, returned to remind him of his current bleak situation.

Not long after President Lincoln's death came news of the end of the war. When Vlad heard the news, he fell down on his knees, placed his hands over his eyes, and put his head on the ground. He could not celebrate, and he could not weep. Through all the fear and hate, and after all the killing, suffering, and misery, he had nothing left inside at that moment. After a few minutes, he was simply thankful that the war was over, and then he began to hope for release.   A few days later, the prisoners were told that they could be discharged if they signed a pledge to never again take up arms against the United States and to be loyal to it. Vlad would have signed just about anything at that point to be free. He and Dave signed their forms together without bothering to read them. They had to wait a few more days, and then they were released.

Chapter 49
The Long Road Home

Missionaries were at the gates to help the soldiers when they were released. Once again, these selfless men and women helped others without discrimination. Vlad thought of what the world would be like if these people were its leaders. Most of them were abolitionists who did not agree with the South's policies. Even so, they saw other humans – enemy soldiers – in need of assistance, and they provided it. One of them gave Vlad some nourishing broth and helped him to a make-shift camp a few hundred yards away from the prison until he could travel. Vlad was fed and given a fresh clean shirt and underclothes. She ministered to his body with food and to his soul with Bible passages. The passages reminded him of James Tedder teaching him English at Fort St. John.

Vlad stayed at the make-shift camp a few days and regained some of his strength. He was over six feet tall, but weighed less than 130 pounds. His cheek bones almost poked through his skin, and he could count his ribs as easily as his fingers. Where he once had the beginnings of a small gut, he now had a skin-tight pouch. He had been in much better physical shape when he had walked into Fort St. John after a long time in the wilderness. At least during that journey, he had eaten fish and meat, and the exercise built his muscles. His legs now looked bowed and far apart. He had lost much of his fat and muscle. He was weak and pitiful, but, through so many conflicts and dangers, he had survived. He didn't know why.

As a group of former prisoners was preparing to leave, Vlad asked Dave, "Are you able to join them?" Dave answered, "Yes, I guess so. I just want to go home, Vlad." Vlad replied, "Me, too, Dave." Both men's eyes began to well with tears, which were just as quickly gone when they realized they had better get moving or be left behind. The missionaries gave the group some food for the journey, and they all began walking south towards their homes. Traveling with other Confederate soldiers offered some protection, or at least a comforting false sense of protection. They wore white cloth provided by the missionaries to show they were non-combatants. The former Confederates were also able to scrounge up food as they went, but it was mainly what they foraged and begged.

As they walked, they passed legions of Union troops heading north. Plenty of the Northerners whom they passed would have just as soon killed them as looked at them. The North had lost hundreds of thousands of men, although most of them had died of disease and causes unrelated to battle. That did not matter to the Union soldiers who had lost sons, brothers, and fathers. While there were many other people and causes to blame, in the eyes of the Union soldiers they passed, Vlad's group of Confederate soldiers was an embodiment of all those who were to blame.

Vlad figured that the Union commanders embedded a sense of hatred towards the Confederates in the Union troops to motivate them to fight, and this could not simply be turned off by the end of the war. He thought that both sides had tried to fill their soldiers with propaganda and hatred or else risk the common man deserting to return home. Even so, he knew that the common man was smarter than the leaders. Desertion was a huge problem, and it was not simply based on cowardice. The death penalty for desertion did not completely stop it.

Vlad thought that the common man rarely, if ever, had a grievance with someone hundreds of miles away. Rather, the wealthy large business owners and politicians were ones who had motives for war. No matter what the excuse, money, power, or both was always at the core. Vlad realized that the Russians may have seemed more blood-thirsty, but, in reality, they were just more open and direct about it. The leaders during the Civil War, both Union and Confederate, were just as quick to send tens of thousands of common men to their deaths. As with most wars, these men were either fathers with a half-dozen children to feed on worn out farms or boys whose bodies had just grown into manhood. Vlad then snapped out of his deep, concentrated daydream, saddened that countries like Russia and the United States had different cultures, but war and death were common to them.

The Civil War soldiers were from North Carolina and Massachusetts, Georgia and New York, and similar places. These men simply wanted to raise their families and grow prosperous in their hard labor to make better lives for themselves and their families. About a million of them met with death through a variety of dreadful means. Countless tens of thousands more had their bodies shattered by bullets, or limbs quickly cut off by overworked surgeons hacking through meat and bone.

During every battle, there was always a flood of wounded, far too many for the doctors to handle properly with their primitive medicine. Instead of returning home to work after the war, some of these men became like children to their young families. Although some states like North Carolina made prosthetic limbs for them after the war, the men would never be the same. Other men, without a physical scratch, would suffer mentally for years with what later would be called post-traumatic stress disorder. In the mid-Nineteenth Century, there was no accurate diagnosis, let alone treatment, for such mental injuries. Soldiers with such problems suffered in quiet despair or risked public ridicule from people who simply did not understand the frailty of the human mind.

When Vlad, Dave, and many others walking with them reached Baltimore, they met a Union Army officer on the road. "You Confederate vermin are going south on trains. Get over to the platform, and if I catch any of you off it, I'm going to shoot the lot of you."

The officer recognized that it was not a good idea to have formerly hostile soldiers running loose in the North. He thought of the potential danger to the Northerners and not of the safety and well-being of the Confederate soldiers. He, too, had lost family members to the South, and he thought, "I ought to line up these Confederates and shoot them all for my brother Jeremiah's sake." Jeremiah had died at First Manassas. In fact, he talked with his commander that night about how he wished he had done just that. Fearing Army discipline and the potential rush of even unarmed soldiers overcoming him, he had kept going with the process of moving the Southerners southward.

As Vlad and Dave were pushed onto the train along with scores of others, Vlad's mind was empty. He did not think about the good times or the bad. He simply lived second-by-second. However, once the train started to roll and Vlad got comfortable, he thought of his sweet wife Rachel. He wondered if she was even alive and if she had fled somewhere. He wondered if he would ever see her again. He wondered if she had been murdered by the Union soldiers, some of whom had raped women in Georgia. He worried that she had been raped and beaten by the Union soldiers.

Vlad again wondered why it had been so important to "preserve the Union." The Northerners he had met sure did not seem to care anything about slavery. In fact, he had seen some of the guards mistreat the black Southern soldiers worse than they did the white soldiers. He thought that the war had not been fought over slavery, but over money and power.

As Vlad looked around the crowded train car, he saw a young black soldier sitting alone. The soldier was freshly injured. Vlad nudged Dave, and they went over to him and tried to tend to the wound, which turned out only to be a flesh wound in the leg. A sharp piece of iron had cut the soldier when a Northern soldier shoved him hard for taking too long to get on the train. Vlad took a handkerchief a missionary had given to him and placed it on the wound, applying pressure to stop the bleeding. From seeing dozens of wounds from his days in both the Russian and Confederate Armies, Vlad was good at treating such wounds. The man smiled and the three began talking. Three men, each from diverse social and economic backgrounds, sat and talked as equals, without any pretense or prejudice, because of the common thread of experiencing and surviving horrific battles. They were now all just trying to get to a comforting place that they could call home.

The man was named Jesse Syme and he was from Raleigh, North Carolina. When Vlad asked him where he was going, Jesse explained, "I was sent to fight in my master's place, but now I don't know what I'll return to. I don't want to be no slave, and I don't know if Mr. Saunders will hire me as a paid laborer. I don't know nowhere else to go. I ain't got no wife nor kids. My parents and me, we was separated at auction when our old master died in 1854. We had lived near Clinton, North Carolina, and was brought to the slave market in Fayetteville. I was bought first, by a Mr. Saunders who was traveling through. He didn't have enough money or need to buy my parents. I ain't got no idea where my parents are or even if they're still alive."

Vlad, Jesse, and Dave talked for hours as the train rolled south. As they talked, Vlad figured that if there was anything left of his farm, he was going to need a lot of help making it prosperous. As Jesse talked of the despair of not knowing where else to go or what to do, Vlad offered Jesse the opportunity to work for him, should there be anything left to do. He explained the uncertainty of the situation; however, it sounded wonderful to Jesse. Jesse knew that returning to a former master would mean returning to slavery, regardless of what any new laws said. Jesse saw something in Vlad that made him trust Vlad. He could trust Vlad because of the way he had cared for his leg and spoken to him as an equal, which no white person had ever done before. Had the others on the train not been so starved, sick, and defeated, they may have cursed Vlad for his actions. However, they all just wanted to go home and were scared at what they may find or not find there.

As the train rolled south, all of the men became slightly more anxious about what they would find. Since their capture, the men simply did not know what fate had befallen their loved ones. To harass the men throughout their imprisonment, the Union prison guards had made it sound as if Abraham Lincoln had sent General Sherman and an army of a million bloodthirsty men to kill every Southern man and rape every Southern woman. In some rare cases, they would learn of the deaths or injuries of wives, parents, or children at the hands of northern troops. For most of the men who lost family members, though, the cause was disease and deprivation, not bullets and knives. For others, the war had bypassed their little farms and hamlets altogether, except for inconvenient shortages of manufactured and imported goods, which they could seldom afford, anyway.

The train ride was long and slow. They finally arrived at Washington, D.C. and were told by a Union lieutenant, "You shall wait four hours before continuing onward. If you go beyond the area designated for you with ropes, you will be shot." Even with the war over, the Union soldiers at the train station were concerned with Southerners rebelling or attempting to assassinate members of Congress, judges, or even President Johnson. After John Wilkes Booth had so easily gotten to President Lincoln, they were not going to take any chances with trained soldiers of the enemy. The fact that the war had ended and these men only wanted to go home did not dissuade the Union soldiers from their vigilant watch. Plus, once again, plenty of them either had a score to settle or had not seen any action and wanted to go home bragging that they had killed a Rebel. Four years of war had caused meanness to prevail in the hearts and minds of these men and many of their countrymen, both Union and Confederate. It was truly a horrible time to be an American.

After finding some fairly fresh water and eating several stale biscuits, Vlad, Dave, and Jesse got back on the cramped train. About six hours after they had arrived, and two hours late, the train finally pulled out of the station. They rode through town and could see the dome of the Capitol, which brought back fond memories of when he and Rachel had taken this train ride to Fredericksburg on the way to Emporia to see the farmland for sale. They went a little farther and crossed the Potomac River. Soon, the train picked up speed and headed south toward Fredericksburg.

About two hours later, they arrived near Fredericksburg. They were told that the rails had not yet been repaired into Fredericksburg and down to Richmond. They were near the former battlefield where Vlad and Dave had celebrated a fleeting victory a few years earlier. They both thought how drastically things had changed. As they walked into Fredericksburg, they could see houses destroyed by cannon fire from the battle when the Union had attempted to bombard the Southern soldiers stationed there into submission.

Vlad thought of all the dead on both sides during that battle. Each young man that fell was a son, a brother, a husband, or a father. Each man lived in a home and had grown up around people who knew and cared for him. Each of them had a life's story. They had hopes and dreams. The average one could have lived well into the next century, raising families and building the nation.

Vlad had been elected sergeant, promoted to lieutenant and had, at times, run his group until they were devastated at Gettysburg. He had fought hard, was wounded, and had nearly died many times. Had he fought for the Union, he may have been nominated for a high medal. Maybe being a foreigner helped him to see the war more objectively. Whatever the case, he simply could not see the sense of this war. That was the one thing that had never changed throughout the war.

As Vlad, Jesse, and Dave walked through Fredericksburg, they wondered how they would survive the trip to Southern Virginia. If Virginia was roughly shaped like a triangle now that West Virginia had been carved from the Commonwealth and made a separate state, they had to walk from Fredericksburg, a hundred miles southeast of the top point of Virginia, all the way down the east-central side. Vlad's farm was in the northern part of a southeastern county that bordered North Carolina.

Instead of taking the road, the three men followed the railroad line south, figuring that it would be safer than encountering thousands of people along the road. Also, it would lead them through Richmond and Petersburg, and then home. It was a direct route, but still a long trip, with only the grace of God to protect them. Before leaving Fredericksburg, they searched for food. They found a farmhouse where the farmer had extra potatoes and agreed to let them work for a half day in exchange for a good meal and several pounds of potatoes to stuff in a sack. By all accounts, the farmer was being quite generous to them.

As the three reached Richmond, they saw how the Union invaders had devastated it with fire. The Union soldiers had destroyed a beautiful city. There was little food or hope on the streets of Richmond. Since they had arrived in the late afternoon, the three spent the night and then kept walking. The railroad bridge that Vlad had ridden across on the way to Kittrell was destroyed, but they were able to cross the river by a boat that the Union Army occupiers had set up to ferry people.

They passed through Petersburg and continued along the railroad tracks until they came upon the bridge that Vlad had defended. It was still standing. Vlad's men had been successful in defending it, but the Union had destroyed and captured the line elsewhere. Vlad told Dave and Jesse of the events, and he saw the graves of the three dead men. He saw the faded names and re-memorized them. He remembered other details and recommitted himself to write their families. No doubt, they would be considered missing and presumed dead. However, without knowing for certain of their deaths, their families would hold out hope for their return and would live out their lives with the pain of not knowing. Vlad would make sure they knew.

The men continued onward until they reached the road leading to Purdy near sunset. They had only several miles left, but they stopped because they were exhausted. They camped away from the intersection to avoid being robbed. Despite being extremely tired, it took hours for Vlad to fall asleep because his mind raced. He was now so close to Rachel.

At first light, they broke camp and walked down the road towards Purdy. They first came upon Dave's house, just outside of town. It looked weathered, but it had survived the war. The Union cavalry had come into Purdy and left it by other roads. His mother was there, and she cried and hugged Dave. She was so relieved that he was alive. She had spent almost two years not knowing if he was alive or dead. She then collected herself, sat him down in his father's chair in the living room where they had enjoyed time together for many years, and told her son that his father had been killed near Petersburg.

The older Mr. Hawley had been a United States and then a Confederate congressman. Seeing the end of the war approaching and wanting to fight for his new country, he walked out of his congressional office in Richmond, went to the War Department, and got a commission as a colonel right on the spot. He then went to defend Petersburg and died in July of 1864 when he was hit in the head by a bullet during an attack on his position defending the city. A survivor, whose life Colonel Hawley had saved, wrote an account, a copy of which the War Department sent to Mrs. Hawley, telling of how the

Colonel had stood his ground while ordering his men to fall back, emptying his pistol into two Union soldiers before a third shot him at almost point blank range. His bravery allowed most of his men to escape from that attack.

War certainly was both the crucible and spotlight of a person's real, and sometimes hidden, character. For all of Congressman Hawley's shady business dealings and questionable political maneuvers, newly minted Colonel Hawley was a brave and honorable man at heart. Dave and his brother would now help their mother as head of the household and of the considerable land holdings and businesses that she owned. Mrs. Hawley had hidden much of the family's portable wealth. Old money often finds a way to remain rich.

As Dave cried over the loss of his father, Vlad came into the room and put his hand on Dave's shoulder to offer condolence and support. Mrs. Hawley was so grateful to have her younger son home alive that she asked Vlad and Jesse to come into the formal dining room to eat, but Vlad explained, "Thank you, Mrs. Hawley, but I must get home to Rachel. It's been so long." Almost too afraid to ask, Vlad hesitantly inquired, "Do you know how she is?" She told Vlad, "Rachel is alive, healthy, and living at the farm. You'll see how well she's managed, but you and Jesse simply must take food to eat on your way; I insist!"

Despite Vlad's burning desire to see Rachel, they were both hungry and waited for a servant to prepare the food. His hunger was that strong, but his impatience and anxiety to get home grew with the passing loud ticks on the nearby grandfather clock.

Mrs. Hawley's elder son, Stuart, was shocked at her inviting a black man and a foreigner into their home, much less into their dining room. Stuart had avoided service in the Army for a couple of years by sending a slave in his place. Once finally pressed, he claimed a commissioned desk job as a supply officer. He had his dad get him posted to Richmond, which he promptly fled once Petersburg fell and news of the approaching Union Army was received in Richmond. Instead of going with the Confederate Army west to Appomattox or with the cabinet west and eventually south into North Carolina, he deserted, circled counterclockwise in South-Central Virginia, and went home. He hid in the attic until he heard that the war was officially over.

As Vlad prepared to leave, Mrs. Hawley had taken her "little boy" Dave upstairs to attend to him personally. She wept as she put her arm around his emaciated body as they climbed the stairs with no assistance from Stuart. With Mrs. Hawley gone, Vlad humbly thanked Stuart for their hospitality, but Stuart made it clear in an arrogant tone, "You can thank my mother. It was all mother's doing. In the future, kindly don't use the front door," and then he mumbled, "Or any door for that matter."

Vlad's demeanor changed, and he glared at Stuart. A thought of how to kill Stuart with a nearby table passed through Vlad's mind, before he caught himself. He then made a mental note of where he stood with Stuart for when the two had future encounters, and Vlad knew they would have future encounters. Vlad thought that it was that very elitism that was partially to blame for the war in the first place. He also remembered something that a missionary had said to him after he was freed from the prison camp, "Rich and poor have this in common: The Lord is the Maker of them all." When Stuart saw Vlad's stare, he felt nervous and left the room.

When the servant brought the food, Vlad and Jesse took it and left. They ate it as they walked towards Vlad's farm. The fresh healthy food was so good to them. As they passed through Purdy, Vlad was horrified to see the destruction, but the people were already rebuilding.

As they continued walking, Vlad told Jesse that once a new government was established, he would try to find Jesse's parents and reunite them. Jesse thanked Vlad repeatedly. Vlad explained that it might take years and they might not be successful. Still, it offered Jesse hope, and that was more than he had before.

The two men finally turned and walked down the long dirt road leading to Vlad's farm. Rachel was out in the garden weeding when she saw two men approach. She reached for a gun that she kept near her at all times. She wanted them to see that she was no one to mess with, and she was so good at using the gun that she didn't bother calling any of the workers for additional protection. When they got closer, she recognized Vlad despite his unshaven face, severe weight loss, and rough appearance. She dropped the gun and ran towards him, almost tackling his frail body as she ran into him to hug him. She was so excited that she hyperventilated. She kissed him repeated. Her mind raced with joy, but also with fear for Vlad's health over how thin he had become.

Vlad introduced her to Jesse, and she took them into the house and fixed them more food. She gathered the workers and assigned them tasks. Tonight they would roast a hog and have a feast. She sent some of the workers to slaughter and cook the hog and others to attend to other preparations. The workers quickly obeyed her. She assigned a worker to fix Jesse a place to sleep and to attend to him. She personally attended to Vlad by taking him to the stream and washing him with her loving hands. She could not believe how skinny he was. He was never fat, but he had lost so much weight. She knew that she could take care of that. She shaved his beard and cut his hair the way she liked it.

During the war, Rachel had changed a great deal. She was now an accomplished and experienced business woman with a proven track-record of running a farm during the worst of times. One thing had not changed, however: her love of Vlad. It had grown even deeper since their time together at Warrenton, which she would forever remember as a second honeymoon as good as the first. She was determined to make up for the lost years and to never again be away from Vlad.

Chapter 50
Rebuilding Their Lives

As the weeks passed, Vlad gained strength, and Vlad and Rachel spent just about all of their time together. As Vlad healed under Rachel's care, the crops grew. With each nourishing rain, the fields became lush. There was weeding to do and many other chores, so Vlad pushed himself to work despite Rachel's protests. Through healthy food and vigorous outdoor work, Vlad quickly gained strength, and his anxiety from the harshness of war slowly began to diminish. However, nightmares occasionally haunted him, as they would for the remainder of his life.

Vlad saw how well Rachel had managed and had grown the farming operation. He was very proud of her, and she beamed with delight when he frequently told her so. Rachel said, "My dear late father taught me well," but Vlad knew it was Rachel's own abilities. He said, "I know your father taught you well, but you had the good judgment to see what needed to be done and the courage to do so all by yourself."

Vlad and Rachel became concerned about what the Union would do to them. They feared losing their land to the conquering policies of the military or to Northerners who were moving down as carpetbaggers. Virginia was now considered occupied enemy territory, just on the opposite shore of the Potomac from the seat of a vengeful, powerful federal government. Virginia was no longer a sovereign commonwealth, as it had liked to call itself. The Union Army was in control, with orders coming from Washington.

Thankfully for Vlad and Rachel, some of Lincoln's final policies were of reunification and reconciliation with the South. Plus, the South was large and the farms around Purdy were out of the way. Vlad and Rachel kept their land and had the gratitude of a number of free blacks who had worked for them as free men and women earning wages whenever any mention of them was made among the few carpetbaggers who came to the area. Vlad and Rachel also had their gold to pay the taxes that were assessed. Many families were not so able.

Jesse also gained strength. He made money for the first time and began saving it to someday buy a plot of land upon which to build a house and farm. He dreamed that when he located his parents, they could live there with him. Rachel insisted that Jesse and all of the workers take time during their lunch breaks to learn to read using the Bible Henry had given Vlad. She said, "Reading will help you throughout your lives."

Because of the former laws against teaching slaves to read and the continued prejudices against blacks and people who assisted them, Rachel warned them, "Keep your learning a secret for now and don't tell anyone when you travel into town on errands." Living away from town helped them all to live free.

Thanks to Rachel, Vlad had returned to a prosperous farm. Also, because of its location, it had avoided the destruction of other farms in the northern part of Virginia, especially in the Shenandoah Valley area and around Warrenton and Culpepper. While Vlad and Rachel's farm had been raided once by Union troops, other farms in Greensville County had been raided for food by Confederate soldiers passing through a number of times. All soldiers had to eat.

In Rachel, Vlad truly had a partner in all aspects of their lives together. She was a natural business person, and she ran the farm frugally before, during, and now after the war. She saved money and had bought gold and silver with money made by selling excess crops. Her father had often used gold and furs as a means of exchange, always trusting tangible wealth over paper money. She believed the same way. She did not trust in Confederate money during the war. Whenever she received any, she quickly converted it into tangible wealth, even if it meant chickens or seeds, and she kept only a small amount on hand with which to trade. This practice was another reason that she and Vlad were now relatively well off.

With the gold and silver that Rachel had saved when selling crops during the war, she and Vlad were now able to purchase farms that were in distress. They competed fairly with other buyers, and their bidding helped to boost the price for the land that they purchased. Also, they knew of two war widows nearby who needed to sell their farms because they could not work them and could not pay the taxes owed. Both wanted to return to their families in other counties for assistance raising their children. By this time, most of the land was practically valueless. However, Rachel and Vlad offered them a fair price. It was large enough to cover the taxes owed and more than provide for the widows to return to their original homes in other counties and establish themselves with or near their parents. The prices paid were not huge, but they were much more than the widows otherwise would have gotten had Vlad and Rachel not been in the market. Both widows expressed their appreciation to Vlad and Rachel.

When bidding on other land at auction, Vlad and Rachel found that some of the other people competing for the property resented them. Rachel started staying at home under the protection of their farm workers when Vlad went to bid for fear of her being harmed by jealous rivals. However, Vlad's reputation from his fighting in the Civil War made most of the other bidders respect him, or at least avoid crossing him. Dave told many of them of Vlad's deeds on the battlefield, embellishing even the stories of events that needed no embellishment. Dave also helped protect Vlad and Rachel by telling the other bidders that Vlad had saved his life in the prison camp and that he would make certain that anyone harming them would not go unpunished. Dave was becoming a powerful man in the county, with Stuart cowering behind an office desk resenting his every move. Dave was still very personable, but the war had given him a tougher, more distrusting edge, and he had matured by a couple of decades.

One bidder for land, who did not hear Dave's message, was a rich land owner in a neighboring county. Tired of being outbid by Vlad and wanting to purchase land in Greensville County cheaply, he sent two men to beat and intimidate Vlad before an auction. The men surprised Vlad in town as he walked from his wagon and between two buildings to reach the auction site. A short time later, an unharmed Vlad outbid that rich land owner, who spent the entire auction wondering why his men had not beaten Vlad senseless.

After the auction, the owner found his men in the back of his empty wagon with the horses untied and freed. The horses were standing nearby and were unharmed, but they easily could have been stolen. The men had broken ribs and were only half-conscience. Vlad had beaten them until they begged for him to stop. To deter the land owner from future similar acts, Vlad made the beaten men give to the poor of the town the sacks of sugar and other supplies that the landowner had just purchased at a store before the auction. Vlad also told the men, "You tell the landowner that I will kill him if he ever tries anything else, and no one in the town will stop me. You tell him that someone will find his body in the Merriman River." When they told the man, Vlad's message resonated with him, as he had assisted years before in killing the free black man whose body had been mistaken for Aaron's after it had been dumped into the Merriman River.

Vlad and Rachel planned their land purchases carefully. They tried to purchase land adjoining or near theirs, so that they could manage it more efficiently. When they purchased land farther away, they planned to hold it for resell once property values had increased. Rachel became an expert in valuing land and decided the maximum purchase price. Vlad then went and bid according to her plan. Finally, after purchasing nine farms, they decided that they had purchased all they could afford and manage. They then began implementing their management plan. They recruited former slaves who had served as head slaves over crop production on large farms, and paid them base wages and a percentage of the profits from each farm. Vlad managed the overall operations, dealing directly with each farm's manager. Rachel handled planning and financial matters. Vlad and Rachel jointly decided which crops to plant, where to sell them, and all of the larger decisions that impacted profits.

Vlad and Rachel contemplated their growing wealth, although they tried not to dwell on it. Their land holdings alone would likely make them very wealthy once the South got back on its feet. Likewise, their cattle, sheep, and other animals would be highly valued in Richmond and in markets in the north. Once rebuilt, they planned to use the railroad between Weldon, North Carolina and Richmond to transport their animals to markets in Richmond and in the north. Dave had already spoken to Vlad and Rachel about them all investing their profits into building branch railroad lines, which would haul goods to the main line. Dave thought that branch lines would be quite lucrative since they would have monopolies in the areas that they served.

Although Vlad and Rachel worked hard and saved their assets to buy more land, they agreed that wealth was a means and not an end for them. At heart, Vlad and Rachel were not greedy. Some wealthy landowners would allow tenant farmers, especially blacks, onto their land and agree to pay them only when the crops were harvested. In the meantime, the landowners would sell the tenant farmers basic necessities on credit at outrageous prices, interest rates, or both. At the end of the season, the workers had nothing to show for their back-breaking work, and most were still in debt, thus obligating them to continue working for their *de facto* slave masters. Vlad and Rachel refused to do this. They paid base wages weekly and a small percentage of the profits to their basic laborers, which motivated the workers to be very productive. Vlad and Rachel also assisted Aaron in bidding on a farm with the money he had earned. He purchased close to 200 acres about five miles from them.

Although their business took up most of their time, Vlad and Rachel valued relationships, both with each other and with friends. Rachel was able to exchange letters with her sisters, Mary and Edna, and she learned that there was no suspicion concerning William's death. Rachel invited her sisters to join her, but they were busy with families and farms of their own. They all agreed to visit one another at some time in the future.

Vlad and Rachel promised never to allow their growing wealth to interfere with their love for each other. They had both seen poor families very happy and rich ones miserable. Vlad had grown up poor and lonely, especially after his father had died. While poverty limited options, loneliness was far worse. They spent at least an hour every day together and away from their business. They went to church together each Sunday and Wednesday night, and they became very active in it. They took romantic walks to remote corners of their farm, and they bathed and swam together in their secluded creek in warm weather.

Chapter 51
The New Beginning

After several months, Vlad came into the house and found Rachel vomiting. With her hair in her face, Rachel steadied herself between bouts of nausea and said, "Vlad, I think I'm pregnant. I've missed two periods and, well, now everything makes me sick!" She threw up again, while Vlad yelled in excitement. Realizing that Rachel was nauseated and that his celebration might seem uncompassionate to her current situation, he asked, "Can I get you something, perhaps some water?"

Over the next week, a local midwife and country doctor visited the couple separately and thought Rachel was pregnant, too. The couple was ecstatic. Vlad and Rachel wondered why they had not conceived before, but they were thankful now to bring new life into their home. They promised that they would work their hardest to make their child's life full of love and protect him or her from the troubles, pain, and death that they had experienced. Upon saying those things, Vlad and Rachel shared looks that each understood to mean a slight fear of the unknown and of their inability to fully protect their child, especially from war. Still, they would do their best. They said a prayer asking God to make things different for their child.

Several months later, as Vlad walked towards their house, he heard Rachel calling, "Vlad, Vlad!" He ran to the house, threw open the door, and saw her in the pains of childbirth. He thought it would take longer for her to be ready to deliver, but there she was. There was no time to call for the doctor or a mid-wife. He went to her and really did more watching than anything else.

As Rachel's body heaved in contractions, Vlad saw the top of a head beginning to come out. He reached down and then withdrew his hands. The blood and juices that began to come out with the baby were almost too much for him. This man, who had survived fights with Poles and Russians, attacks by large bears, and the horror of the Civil War, almost turned and ran in fear. He stayed there, though, and held the baby as Rachel expelled it from her body. He then wrapped a towel around the baby from the shoulders down. There was no noise coming from it, but Rachel, still racked with pain, knew what to do from talking with the mid-wife. Through her pain, she took the baby and held it upside down. She gave it a spank and the baby cried. Vlad then took the baby and placed it on the bed to begin cleaning it. He was so excited that he kept going back and forth between Rachel and the baby. It was the birth of his first child, and it was a glorious event for him.

The baby was a girl, and Rachel and Vlad had decided that if it was a girl, they would name her "Ann Rachel." The name "Ann" was the English form of "Anya," which was Vlad's mother's name. When Vlad calmed down a little, he picked her up slowly, and looked into her eyes. Ann Rachel was crying loudly. She was covered in fluids and wrinkled. Even so, Vlad was convinced that he had never seen anyone so beautiful. She brought out feelings of love deeper than he had ever felt. She was a gift from God. Right then, he recommitted himself to making sure that she never knew the poverty, loneliness, and other hardships that he had known for most of his life. However, he also felt a slight sadness in knowing that he would not be in her life forever and that he would not be able to protect her completely.

Vlad continued to gaze into Ann Rachel's little eyes and held up her small hand with his thumb and index finger. He cradled her and loved her. He then held her against his voice box, so that the top of her head filled up the curve of his neck. He wanted her to hear and feel the deep soothing tones from his spoken words of love. Even though she could not understand him, the gentle vibrations from his vocal cords and his closeness were comforting to her. Vlad and Ann Rachel immediately bonded. She would grow to love him for the rest of her life. Vlad was her precious daddy. For his part, Vlad wanted to be perfect in her eyes. He was a product of his experiences, and they had been most difficult, but he decided not to be ruled by the negative ones.

Vlad now realized that he had achieved the dream he had dreamt so long ago in Russia. He had paid a terrible price physically and mentally from the time that he had taken his first step to escape the Russians until his return home from the Civil War to see first-hand that Rachel was alive and unharmed. He had dreamed boldly to escape from the Russians, and he was forced to fight in the Civil War against the very country in which he had dreamed to live. He was master of events and mastered by events. He had set the direction of his life towards freedom, but circumstances beyond his control had often taken him on a course different from the one that he had planned.

Vlad looked at Rachel, wet with sweat and weak from the pain of delivery. She smiled at him in such a way that he knew she loved him completely and that she was completely happy. He looked again at Ann Rachel cradled in his arms, and he was overwhelmed with love for Rachel and Ann Rachel. Vlad then realized that he had more than achieved the goal of which he had first dreamt so long ago in Russia. It had taken years, but he had never given up. He had persevered and had achieved freedom and now, safety. Through adversity, he had found peace. Through hard work, he had found strength. Through faith, he had found hope, and through love, he had found himself.

• • • The End • • •